PRAISE FOR THESE
AWARD-WINNING AUTHORS

National bestselling author
SUSAN KING

"No one weaves the magic and mystery of Scotland
into passionate romance better than Susan King!"
—*New York Times* bestselling author Mary Jo Putney

"Susan King's talent is a gift from the gods."
—*New York Times* bestselling author Virginia Henley

"Susan King casts a spell like a sorcerer—
her books never fail to enchant!"
—*New York Times* bestselling author Patricia Gaffney

"King deftly spins a mystical Highland romance…
(she) is a consummate story teller with a keen ear
for dialogue and the ability to create multifaceted
characters who capture the reader's sympathy."
—*Publishers Weekly,* starred review
of *The Sword Maiden*

and bestselling author
MIRANDA JARRETT

"Miranda Jarrett writes beautiful romance."
—*New York Times* bestselling author Patricia Gaffney

"Miranda Jarrett continues to reign as
the queen of historical romance."
—*Romantic Times*

"A marvelous author…each word is a treasure,
each book a lasting memory."
—*The Literary Times*

"Miranda Jarrett is a sparkling talent!"
—*Romantic Times*

MERLINE LOVELACE

spent twenty-three years in the air force, pulling tours in Vietnam, at the Pentagon and at bases all over the world. When she hung up her uniform in 1991, she decided to try her hand at writing. She's since had more than fifty novels published, with over seven million copies of her works in print. She and her own handsome hero live in Oklahoma. They enjoy traveling and chasing little white balls around the fairways.

SUSAN KING

Former art history lecturer Susan King is the author of several acclaimed, award-winning historical romances set in Scotland. An enthusiastic researcher, Susan has handled hawks, shot longbows and caught arrows in her hand; she has interviewed a harper, a stonecarver, a swordsmith, a falconer, swordsmen, martial artists and Gypsies. She lives in Maryland with her husband, three sons and a Westie puppy. Her most recent release is *Kissing the Countess* from NAL Signet.

MIRANDA JARRETT

considers herself sublimely fortunate to have a career that combines history and happy endings, even if it's one that's also made her family far too regular patrons of the local pizzeria. Miranda is the author of twenty-eight historical romances, has won numerous awards for her writing and has been a three-time Romance Writers of America RITA® Award finalist for best short historical romance. She loves to hear from readers at P.O. Box 1102, Paoli, PA 19301-1145, or MJarrett21@aol.com. For the latest news, please visit her Web site at www.Mirandajarrett.com.

MERLINE LOVELACE
SUSAN KING
MIRANDA JARRETT

APRIL MOON

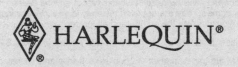

HARLEQUIN®

TORONTO • NEW YORK • LONDON
AMSTERDAM • PARIS • SYDNEY • HAMBURG
STOCKHOLM • ATHENS • TOKYO • MILAN • MADRID
PRAGUE • WARSAW • BUDAPEST • AUCKLAND

ISBN 0-373-83610-4

APRIL MOON

Copyright © 2004 by Harlequin Books S.A.

The publisher acknowledges the copyright holders of the individual works as follows:

SAILOR'S MOON
Copyright © 2004 by Merline Lovelace

WHITE FIRE
Copyright © 2004 by Susan King

THE DEVIL'S OWN MOON
Copyright © 2004 by Miranda Jarrett

This edition published by arrangement with Harlequin Books S.A.

® and TM are trademarks of the publisher. Trademarks indicated with ® are registered in the United States Patent and Trademark Office, the Canadian Trade Marks Office and in other countries.

Visit us at www.eHarlequin.com

Printed in U.S.A.

CONTENTS

Dear Reader,

I have two handsome nephews who are E.R. docs. They say they're always busiest on nights when the moon is full. The strangest things seem to happen—dogs howl, tempers rise and passions rule.

Passions certainly rule in these three novellas, which all take place on one fateful April night.

I hope you enjoy them!

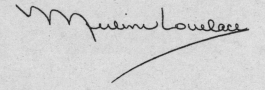

SAILOR'S MOON

Merline Lovelace

To Suze 1 & 2—
great friends, fun schmoozers and superb authors!

CHAPTER ONE

IN THE QUIET MOMENTS before the first shot boomed across the bow, Lady Sarah Stanton was in her cabin aboard the HMS *Linx,* preparing to take the evening meal in the officers' mess.

Stiff-spined, she stood before the fold-down writing desk that had doubled as her dressing table during the long voyage across the Atlantic. While her maid fussed with the laces of her corset, Sarah stared through the porthole at the low-hanging April moon.

The silvery orb, which had waned to a mere slice after the *Linx* sailed from Plymouth so many weeks ago, had since waxed full again. It now glowed fat and round above the indigo sea, signaling the imminent end of the long sea voyage...and of Sarah's reprieve.

Soon the *Linx* would drop anchor in the West Indies. Short days after that, Sarah would wed Captain Sir James Lowell, a battle-hardened veteran of the French War and master of this frigate.

A widower, James had wanted to say their vows

before they sailed from Plymouth, but Sarah had cited a desire to be married at her new home with his young daughter in attendance. She'd won that delay, but keeping him pacified during this damnable voyage had proved a good deal more difficult. She'd been forced to employ every coy, teasing skill she'd acquired during her five-year reign as The Notorious Lady S. to hold him off.

Sighing, she tugged on the curling auburn strand that fell across her bare shoulder.

The Notorious Lady S.

She was so very weary of that label! Not that she hadn't done everything in her power to earn it. As a girl, she'd been up for every dare and madcap scrape. As a young bride married to a doting, indulgent husband three times her age, she'd set London society on its ear. As a wealthy widow, she'd plunged into the desperate search for pleasure so characteristic of the generation that had come of age during a decade of war with Napoleon.

Looking back, Sarah could scarce believe only five years had passed since she'd wed Sir Cedric Stanton. Three since the dull but exceedingly rich Ceddie had died of an inflammation of the bowels. One since she, her father and brother had run through every penny of her widow's portion. How very long ago it all seemed now.

Yet the years ahead looked to be even longer.

And bleaker.

"There!" Maude gave the laces on the long corset a final tug. "Ye're all trussed up, right 'n tight. Will ye be wearin' the gold silk again to dinner?"

At the mention of the shimmering, topaz-colored gown, Sarah's stomach clenched. Early in the voyage James had declared a decided preference for that particular dress and requested she wear it repeatedly. Sarah had soon realized he cared little for the rich color or daring décolletage. Instead, he derived intense enjoyment from the lust that crept into his officers' faces when they feasted on the bare slopes of his intended's breasts.

The gown had opened her eyes to how cruel the captain could become when thwarted. A shudder rippled through her at the memory of that awful night she had declined to wear the topaz silk. The cabin boy serving in the captain's mess had smiled at her. Merely smiled. Yet James had declared him insolent, bent him across the table and whipped him viciously. The pleasure her husband-to-be had taken in the boy's cries still turned Sarah's stomach.

She had to force herself to remember this was the man who'd saved her father and brother from debtors' prison. The gallant sea captain who'd returned from war so rich with prize money he'd covered their staggering gambling debts *and* Sarah's own mountain of bills. James was handsome in his haughty way, charming when he wanted to be and drolly amused to have gained instant fame as the one who'd won the Notorious Lady S.

If the shaky peace negotiated only last year between Britain and France had not begun to unravel...

If James hadn't been ordered to take his 32-gun frigate back to the West Indies in preparation for the imminent resumption of hostilities...

If Sarah had spent more than a few hours in the man's company during their whirlwind courtship before accepting his suit...

If, if, if...

Angrily, she tossed her head. When had she become such a tiresome, wretched mope? She bored even herself.

"I'll wear the emerald silk," she declared defiantly to Maude. "And the Norwich shawl with the—"

She broke off, frowning as a dark shadow suddenly blocked out the moon. It came up swiftly, moving with deadly stealth, and swept past the windows. She caught a glimpse, only a glimpse, of what looked like a bowsprit silhouetted against the dark sea before a cannon belched fire and a monstrous roar shattered the April night.

Maude shrieked and threw herself down. Sarah cursed and did the same. Covering her maid's ample form with her own, she tried to gather her startled senses.

Where in God's name had this ghost ship sprung from? Why hadn't the watch spotted its lights and sounded the alarm? Was it manned by pirates? Or was it a French warship, signaling the end of the short-lived Peace of Amiens and outbreak of hostilities once again?

Her heart slamming against her corset stays, Sarah strained to sort through the burst of sounds coming through the louvers of her cabin door. Above the constant creak of a ship at sea and the noisy clatter of shot rolling in the wooden racks on the gun deck, she heard the thud of running feet. A confusion of shouts. A bellowed order to *man battle stations!* What felt like hours but was probably only moments dragged by before a deep voice bellowed across the open sea through a speaker's horn.

"Ahoy, *Linx*. This is the USS *Seahawk*. Set sails and heave to or the next shot goes through your rigging."

Sarah's immediate reaction was indignation. How *dare* an American ship send a shot across the bows of one of his majesty's frigates! All Europe knew the American navy was ragtag at best. Their untried crews and ships were no match for Lord Nelson's battle-tested veterans.

Pulse hammering, she waited for James to answer this incredible impertinence with a raking broadside. But when cannons roared again moments later, the fire came from the American ship. What sounded like a swarm of angry hornets buzzed through the *Linx*'s rigging. Spars cracked. Ropes snapped. Canvas ripped with long, screeching tears.

Sobbing, Maude buried her head under her arms. "We be dead, m'lady!"

"Not yet." Sarah scrambled to her feet. "Stay here. I must see why we're not returning fire."

"No!"

Frantic, Maude caught the chemise in a pudgy fist. She'd tended to Sarah since they were both mere chits, knew all too well how the mischievous, impulsive girl had matured into a headstrong woman.

"Remember what Sir James said when we first set sail! At the first sign of trouble, you're to hie to yer cabin and stay here."

Sarah started to argue, but the sudden rattle of musket fire on the deck above stopped the words in her throat. She waited, every nerve screaming, until a desperate rap sounded on the cabin door.

"Lady Stanton!"

Tearing her chemise from Maude's clammy grip, she threw on a figured silk wrapper, ducked under the low overhead beams, and rushed across the painted flooring. The paper-white face of a midshipman greeted her when she wrenched the door open.

"What's happening, Mr. Watkins?"

"A mutiny," the young officer got out breathlessly.

"Dear God!"

"Some of our men—we don't know how many yet—broke into the surgeon's stores and poured sleeping draughts into the soup pots. Half the men aboard ship, including the entire starboard watch, are lying about in a stupor."

"That's why the *Linx* didn't return fire?" Sarah gasped. "Our men are incapacitated?"

"Aye, m'lady. All, it seems, except the mutineers and the officers who were about to sit down to supper. Sir James sent me to tell you he has no choice but to set sails and heave to. You're to stay in your cabin until he settles this matter."

Stunned, Sarah retreated inside and addressed her still cowering maid.

"Come, Maude. You must help me dress. And quickly," she added over the shriek of creaking pulleys. The *Linx* had been cutting smartly through the moonlight sea. Within short moments, it merely rode the swells.

While Maude helped her scramble into the emerald silk, Sarah's mind raced. If what Mr. Watkins had imparted was true, a portion of the ship's company appeared to be in league with these American pirates. They weren't just mutineers. They were traitors!

Contempt burned hot in her breast. England had

been at war with France for almost a decade before a shaky peace was negotiated last year. Sarah had grown from girl to woman during the war years. Since earliest childhood, it seemed, she'd listened to her father bemoaning the embargo on French brandies. As a young debutante, she'd enthusiastically embraced fashions that called for slim skirts, tiny puff sleeves and abandonment of all but the sheerest of undergarments to save wools and linens for the armies. As a young bride, she'd pleaded with Ceddie to buy her brother a commission in the army. Unfortunately, David had taken the funds her amiable husband had supplied and wagered them at the faro table instead.

Only since setting sail from Plymouth had Sarah realized the war had influenced her choice of a second husband, as well. To her shame, she suspected she'd entered into her hasty engagement to James as much because of his exemplary war record and how well he carried himself in uniform as his willingness to pay her family's monstrous debts.

She had no sympathy—not one whit!—for scurrilous traitors. Although she deplored the enjoyment James seemed to derive from violence, she hoped he keelhauled the mutineers aboard the *Linx*!

SHE WAS STILL in the grip of righteous anger when the door to her cabin burst open some thirty minutes later. A tall, broad-shouldered figure ducked under the low lintel and entered, his naked sword dripping blood.

Maude gave a squeak of fear.

Sarah lifted her chin.

Two seamen crowded into the cabin behind him. "That's 'er," one of them said. "Sir James's intended."

Sarah flicked a glance at the speaker. He wore the white canvas pants and striped jersey of the Royal Navy. One of the mutineers, obviously. Her lip curling, she turned her haughty gaze back to the swordsman.

His eyes locked with hers. A clear, startling blue, they were framed by lashes as thick and black as his wind-tossed hair. Skin weathered by sun and wind to a deep mahogany proclaimed him a sailor. The gold epaulettes on his blue uniform jacket identified him as a lieutenant.

His manner, however, was anything but gentlemanly. Eyes glinting, he surveyed her from head to foot. His gaze lingered overlong on her breasts before lifting once again to her icily defiant face.

"Well, well," he drawled. "When I was told Lowell's intended was aboard, I expected to find a meek little mouse."

"Did you indeed?"

The frigid reply seemed to amuse him. His mouth curving, he issued instructions to the sailors crowding his back. "Give a hand to the boarding party. Make sure every gun is secure."

"Aye, aye, Cap'n."

The two seamen whirled and left, adding their voices to the medley of shouts that rang in the passageways. The one they'd called captain threw a glance at Maude. The timid, still sobbing woman gave a hiccup of fright.

"Maude is my maid," Sarah said swiftly to deflect his attention back to her. "She's harmless."

"Is she indeed?"

The mocking echo of her own words sent heat into Sarah's cheeks. Eyes flashing, she stood her ground as the American lowered his sword and strolled forward. Insolently, he curled a knuckle under her chin. His gaze roamed her features with lazy thoroughness, lingered on the fiery curls framing her face.

"Lowell will have his hands full with you, won't he, lass? Leastways until he beats you into submission."

It was said so casually, with such careless accuracy, that Sarah gasped. Jerking away from his touch, she took a step back. Her shoulder blades pressed against the bulkhead. Her fingernails dug into her damp palms.

"Who are you?"

He sketched a small, sardonic bow. "Lieutenant

Richard Blake, master of the USS *Seahawk,* at your service. And you?''

''I am Lady Sarah Stanton. You may refer to me as Lady Stanton.''

The glint in his eyes deepened. ''Well, you see, it's like this, lass. We don't hold with titles and such where I come from.''

Her teeth clenched. The man was deliberately provoking her. She longed to raise her arm and smack him soundly. With some effort, she refrained.

''How is it you know Sir James?''

The taunting smile left his eyes. In a single·beat of her heart, the planes and angles of his face took on a hard, merciless cast.

''Lowell stopped my ship on the high seas last year and impressed twelve of my crew.''

Sarah felt little sympathy for this man *or* his crew. England was an island nation. As such, she depended on the sea for her very survival. Although volunteers formed the backbone of the Royal Navy, not enough men cared to subject themselves to years of poor food, extreme conditions and harsh discipline to man all the ships at sea. As a result, the government resorted to press gangs to fill the empty berths.

Impressment was a way of life in England, had been for more than four hundred years. Press gangs were organized into districts and placed under the supervision of a naval captain. They roamed the slums and waterfront districts and snatched men right off the streets. Only those essential to the British maritime industry—sailmakers, shipwrights, riggers and such—were protected from being pressed, and they'd best not be caught out without their exemption papers or they, too, would find themselves at sea.

In the past decade the press gangs had been forced to double their efforts. The long years of war with Napoleon had cost many casualties and left naval vessels seriously undermanned. The only way to replace the dead or injured was to take them wherever they could be found. And to reclaim deserters who attempted to escape.

Unfortunately, desertion ran rampant in the Royal Navy. The same harsh conditions that made men fight to avoid sea duty also made them jump ship once pressed. American vessels, particularly, seemed to attract British sailors. Perhaps because the crews spoke the same language. Or because the American government dangled the inducement of higher wages to attract experienced sailors to its fledgling navy.

Whatever the reason, British ships regularly stopped American vessels at sea to reclaim deserters. Lately, officers from British ships docked at American ports had taken to going into houses and taverns and yanking suspected deserters right from their tables. Naturally, the Americans protested. The issue had become a matter of increasingly heated political debate between the two nations in recent years. Sarah cared little for politics, but was quick to defend her country's actions.

"If you Americans didn't lure away British sailors with the promise of higher wages," she said icily, "they wouldn't have to be reclaimed at gunpoint."

"If you British didn't feed your seamen raw hemp instead of ship's biscuit," Blake shot back, "perhaps they wouldn't jump ship at every opportunity."

She had no answer for that. This voyage had demonstrated beyond any doubt how frequently naval officers resorted to the lash to enforce discipline. Or rather, how frequently one particular naval officer resorted to it.

"And just to keep the log straight..."

Leaning forward, the American planted a hand on the bulkhead beside her head. Sarah's breath caught at his nearness. She could count the white squint lines at the corners of his eyes. See the bulge of muscle under the blue broadcloth of his coat.

"The men Sir James took off my ship were American citizens. They had the papers to prove it."

"Ha!" She refused to let his powerful presence intimidate her. "Such papers are simple enough to obtain. For a few pennies, a scribe will pen anything."

"Theses papers carried the seal of the Commonwealth of Virginia."

"Then your seamen should have lodged a complaint with the British Admiralty."

He gave snort of derision. "Do you know how many Americans have been pressed into service by you Britons in the past ten years?"

"No, and I—"

"More than eight thousand. Experienced, hard-working seamen all. Of those, not one has been returned to their families after lodging a complaint with the Admiralty."

"We've been at war those ten years and more. You must understand that."

"It was your war, not ours."

"So it was." Scorn dripped from every syllable. "You Americans tried so hard to remain neutral, did you not? Allowing ships of all nations to enter your ports. Supplying arms and cotton and foodstuffs to both Britain and France. It's a wonder Sir James merely stopped your ship on the high sea. I'm surprised he didn't sink it!"

"He tried."

The reply was blade-sharp. The look in the man's eyes just as deadly.

"Lowell hailed us on the open sea," Blake continued, his jaw taut. "When I refused to set sails and allow his men to come aboard to check my crew for deserters, the bastard ran up the gun-ports and fired in clear violation of the sovereignty of an American ship at sea.''

"He would not do such a thing!"

Even as she uttered the protest, Sarah suspected the man spoke the truth. If James had suffered losses to his crew, he'd take whatever measures necessary to replace them.

"Lowell impressed twelve of my men. He also left the *Seahawk* crippled and adrift against all the rules of the sea.''

His eyes blazed down at her. Sarah flattened her palms against the bulkhead, but held her head high. She would not cower before this man. She would *not!*

"It's taken me all this time to repair my ship and track the *Linx*." Satisfaction added a savage edge to his voice. "Now I have her. And her captain."

"What...?" Gulping, she swallowed the lump that insisted on forming in her throat. "What do you intend to do with them?''

"I was of a mind to hang Lowell from his own yardarm. But now..."

He stared down at her with an intensity that made Sarah's heart thump painfully against her ribs.

"Now," he murmured, dipping his head until their breath mingled, "I may have stumbled on a better way to exact vengeance."

She curled her fingers into claws and was fully prepared to rake them across his face when his mouth closed over hers.

Sarah had been kissed by a good number of men, both before and after her brief marriage. She'd had a reputation to live up to, after all.

A detached corner of her mind made note of the fact that the American was skilled. *Very* skilled! His hand was still planted against the bulkhead. His body still leaned over hers, not touching but close enough for Sarah to feel his heat. His mouth…

His mouth covered hers, promising dark, delicious delights she'd never experienced before. Sarah had never felt her blood race at the press of a man's lips, never felt her senses stir so swiftly.

Nor had the muscles low in her belly ever clenched with such sudden, shocking desire. For all her wild ways, Sarah had bedded only with Ceddie. Dear, fumbling Ceddie, who'd been so enamored of his beautiful young bride he'd spilled himself before he'd untied the laces of his drawers more often than not.

Sarah sensed this man wouldn't fumble. She longed to unclench her jaw and taste him fully, to abandon the restraints most of her acquaintances thought she'd left behind years ago.

Disgusted by the traitorous urge, she brought up her arms to shove him away. She'd just wedged her palms against his hard chest when Maude gathered her courage.

"Ye'll not maul my lady, ye scurvy sea dog!"

Snatching an unlit lantern from its overhead hook, she rushed across the cabin.

The American whirled and threw up an arm just in time to deflect her attack. The quick thrust loosened Maude's grip on the heavy brass lantern. Spraying oil in a wide arc, it flew threw the air and crashed against the bulkhead.

Her attack foiled, Maude's brief spurt of bravado died. She pressed both hands to her cheeks. Her eyes wide, she threw her mistress a look of sheer terror.

"Lordamercy!" she wailed. "We'll both walk the plank for sure."

"Don't be absurd." Quickly, Sarah placed herself between her maid and the American. "Not even Americans resort to such barbaric measures any longer."

Not nearly as confident as Sarah about the matter, Maude sought assurance from the lieutenant himself. "Be that true?" she asked fearfully.

Laughter rumbled deep in his broad chest. "You may rest easy, Mistress Maude. We rarely feed tender morsels like you to the sharks these days."

The laughter astounded Sarah as much as it did Maude. If anyone had dared to attack Sir James, he would have responded instantly with the whip or a primed pistol. This man, this American, seemed to consider such matters trivial. She stared at him, thrown completely off balance by the glint of white teeth in his tanned face and the blue lights dancing in his eyes.

"Besides," he added, turning to Sarah, "I have more important matters to attend to at the moment."

The laughter faded from his eyes. She felt the weight of his gaze on every inch of her, considering, calculating. Her heart began to pound again. Great, unsteady thumps that knocked painfully against her ribs.

"Ah, yes," she replied, fighting to keep her voice steady. "This vengeance you spoke of."

After the way he'd just kissed her, she had little doubt of his intentions. She squared her shoulders. Lifted her chin. And waited for him to order Maude from the cabin so he might take his revenge on James.

CHAPTER TWO

RICHARD WAS TEMPTED.

Christ's bones, he was tempted!

The flame-haired beauty stood with shoulders back, chin tipped, a martyr fully expecting to be sent into the arena for the lions to feast on.

And what a feast it would be. He'd had one taste of her, just one, and already he lusted for another. Her fiery hair, high cheekbones and green cat's eyes alone could set a man's blood racing. Add those creamy breasts and the curve of her hips under that thin emerald silk to the mix and it became explosive.

Yet he found himself admiring her proud spirit almost as much as her luscious curves. And wondering why the devil this glorious creature had agreed to marry a rancid bit of shark bait like Captain Sir James Lowell. Richard's brief encounter with the man had been sufficient to take a fix on his nature. Surely this woman had done the same. She must know Lowell would do his damndest to crush her spirit the first time she dared oppose his wishes.

Ah, well, it was no business of his.

With a shake of his head, he reminded himself why he'd chased after the *Linx*. Why he'd planned this boarding in precise detail, right down to the doxie he'd hired when the *Linx* stopped in Bermuda to take on fresh water. The woman had gone aboard with the rest of the whores who serviced sailors, carrying a message to his impressed crewmen. They were to break into the ship's store of medicines and drug the watch tonight, when the moon was at its fullest.

Since the *Seahawk* was a brig and mounted only sixteen guns against the frigate's thirty-two, such stealth had been necessary. And successful! Richard had bagged his prey and fully intended to make him squirm. Impatient now to attend to the *Linx* and Sir James, he wrapped a fist around the woman's smooth, bare arm.

"Come with me. You, as well," he said to the maid.

He'd intended to steer the lady toward the door. She declined to be steered. With a twitch of her elegant shoulders, she freed her arm and preceded him.

"Where, may I ask, do we go?"

"The captain's mess."

She gave a regal nod and ducked under the low

lintel. Her maid scrambled after her. Richard followed them through the door, his appreciative gaze on the maid's plump backside and the lady's willowy form.

The narrow passageway running the length of the gun deck was dimly lit with smoking lanterns and swarming with men. A good number of the Britons still lay below, snoring. Heavily armed Americans herded to the upper deck those of the crew who'd begun to shake off the sleeping draught's effects. The tall, rawboned third lieutenant from the *Seahawk* was in charge of the prisoner detail. Catching sight of his superior, McDougal stemmed the tide of groggy sailors and marines.

"Hold where you are, men, and let the lieutenant pass."

The sailors' glances darted past Richard and fixed on the American women with him. More than one jaw went slack as Lady Stanton and her maid navigated the dim passageway and paused at the door to the captain's quarters. Even the grizzled petty officer Richard had posted to guard the prisoner within goggled at the vision that appeared before him.

"Look sharp, Mr. North."

The drawled command brought the non-com jumping to attention. "Aye, sir!"

"Unlock the door."

The sailor fumbled the key into the lock and

Richard ushered the women into the officers' mess.
It was outfitted with the lavish attention to detail
found aboard all British ships of the line. Bolts secured a table of polished mahogany to the white-
painted floor. China plate embossed with HMS *Linx*
in gold lettering was racked in felt-lined cabinets.
Another rack contained a collection of brandy and
wine bottles, held in place by a padded wooden
yoke with holes cut for the necks. Brass lanterns
swung from hooks and added their glow to the
moonlight streaming through the skylight cut in the
poop deck above.

The mess had been thoroughly searched for
weapons before Richard had ordered the master of
the ship confined to it. Lowell now stood square-
shouldered against the far bulkhead, his face set in
tight lines of fury. At their entrance, his gaze skew-
ered Richard before whipping to his fiancée.

"Sarah! Are you all right?"

"Yes, quite."

The cool reply raised the lady another notch in
Richard's estimation. He'd expected her to voice
outrage at the kiss he'd stolen, had anticipated Lowell's reaction when she did. She must have guessed
as much. The haughty arch of her brow told Richard she refused to become a pawn in his game.

The maid was not as restrained as the mistress.
Scurrying across the mess, she poured out her indignation. "This bluidy pirate tried to 'ave 'is way

with m'lady. I misdoubt he would have ravished 'er on the spot if I hadn't laid into him with a lantern.''

Sir James balled his fists. A muscle jumped at the side of his jaw. His eyes hot with fury, he raked Richard with a scathing glance. "I would have supposed such conduct to be below that of an officer, even one wearing the uniform of such a sorry excuse for a navy."

"If we're to speak of conduct," Richard drawled, "perhaps we should discuss that of an officer who would leave a crippled ship adrift on the high seas."

The British captain stiffened. "My assessment was that you could bring your ship safely into port. Obviously, I was correct."

"Obviously," Richard echoed sardonically.

He was damned if he'd give this bastard the satisfaction of knowing the torment the *Seahawk*'s crew had endured during the days and nights they'd drifted. Short of water, low on supplies, they'd struggled to make repairs under a hot, unrelenting sun. More than one man had gone crazy with thirst and had to be forcibly restrained from guzzling down seawater before the *Seahawk* limped into port.

"We must hope the *Linx* is not too crippled to do the same," he said to Lowell. "Unlike you, however, I'll make sure of her condition before I abandon her. If you'll give me your parole, you may accompany me above decks to inspect her yourself.''

Lowell's lip curled. "A captain of the Royal Navy does not parole himself aboard his own ship.''

Richard had expected no less. He wouldn't voluntarily surrender himself or his vessel, either. Shrugging, he turned to the woman at his side. Sheer devilment had led him to toy with her before. She'd been so haughty, and he still fired with the thrill of having captured his prey.

His touch was more deliberate this time, intended solely to stoke the fury of the man watching from across the mess. She recognized his game. Scorn filled her eyes as Richard tipped her face to his.

Despite his every intent, he found he couldn't use her this way. His fight was with Lowell, not the lady. He contented himself with stroking his thumb along the line of her jaw.

"As much as I'd like to steal another kiss, I will forebear.''

"You cannot imagine how that relieves my mind.''

Chuckling at the icy reply, Richard made her a small bow and withdrew.

When the door thudded shut behind him, Sarah should have experienced nothing but relief. Instead, she felt the oddest sensation, as if a powerful force had swept out and left the cabin bereft of some vital energy. She had to summon all her resources to face the taut, angry man who stalked across the mess.

"Blake kissed you?"

"Yes."

"I did not think even the Notorious Lady S. would allow such liberties."

Sarah supposed she deserved that. She'd played her role to such perfection over the years.

"I did not 'allow' him anything," she replied coldly. "May I remind you the man is in a position of some power…as you, it appears, are not."

Spots of fury darkened James's cheeks. She knew she shouldn't taunt him with the fact he'd lost his sword and his ship to the American. The look in his eyes promised retribution for that later.

"Did you enjoy the kiss?" James asked with a sneer. "It's apparent he did."

"Really, this is hardly the time to dwell on something so trivial."

"The matter is hardly trivial, my dear. I saw how Blake looked at you. You stirred his lust, intentionally or otherwise. Now you must employ the same wiles you used to seduce me into marriage and—"

"*I?* Seduced *you?* As best I recall, you were the one who insisted on marriage. You knew you could not have me otherwise."

His mouth curved in a cruel smile. "Any man could have had you."

Sarah's breath left on a hiss. Without thinking,

she reacted to the vicious insult. Her hand flew up, palm open and aimed for his cheek. James whipped out an arm and caught her wrist in a brutal grip.

"Do you think me a fool? I'd heard tales of the Notorious Lady S. long before we met. Half the officers in the fleet claimed to have enjoyed your favors. I'd fully intended to add my name to the list, but decided there was more satisfaction to be had in a wedding than in a bedding. I rather liked the idea of being known as the one who brought you to heel."

"And to do that," she said in biting scorn, "you required legal control over me."

"Exactly."

His grip tightened. She knew she would wear a bracelet of bruises later, but refused to flinch.

"You were so very extravagant, m'dear. Practically wallowing in debt. As were your fool of a father and that irresponsible pup you call brother. I still hold so many of their notes I could send them both to debtors' prison were I to call them in."

She reeled in shock. He'd promised to tear up those notes and free her ramshackle father and brother from their obligations. She'd made that a condition of their engagement. Furiously, she reminded him of his pledge.

"You said you would release David and my father from those debts!"

"And so I shall. When we are married. Or when

you rid my ship of the vermin that have in-fested it.''

"How in God's name am I to do that?"

"Very simply. You'll seduce the American. Take him into your arms. Into your bed, for all I care. And when he's weak-kneed with pleasure, you'll snatch up his pistol and put a bullet through his heart.''

"You must be mad!'' she cried, stunned. "I cannot do such a thing. I will not!''

He gave her arm a vicious twist. "You will. I'll not let the bastard depart this ship alive. It's his life or the prison hulks for you and your family.''

Through a curtain of shock, Sarah recalled the American's words. He'd intended to hang James from his own yardarm...until he discovered the captain's betrothed was aboard the *Linx*. Blake had left no doubt in her mind he wouldn't object to making her the instrument of his revenge.

Apparently he and James were of the same mind. They both wanted to use her to their own ends.

Fury boiled up in her veins. At James. At the American. But mostly at herself. How in God's name had she allowed herself to come to such a pass? And what was she to do about it?

Could she seduce the American? Catch him at a weak moment? Put a bullet into him? She wet her lips, tried to find her voice, but couldn't force so much as a squeak through her tight throat. It was left to the faithful, fearful Maude to scurry forward with a frantic protest.

"Sir James! Lady Sarah can't shoot the American captain! His crew won't let 'er escape alive if she puts a bullet in 'im."

"Be quiet!"

The harsh command sent Maude back a pace. Gulping, she recovered and gamely tried again. "You must think on this, sir. If m'lady attempts such a deed, she'll—"

Keeping one hand clamped around his intended's wrist, the captain flung out the other and backhanded the maid. Maude stumbled to her knees, gasping at the pain, and Sarah yielded instantly.

"Enough! I'll do as you say."

"I thought you might."

With a final vicious twist, he released her and strode to the door.

"Guard! Attend to me."

The key turned. The whiskered petty officer allowed the door to swing open, but stood watchful and wary just beyond the threshold.

"I would speak with your captain," James said imperiously. "Immediately. You may take me to him."

"My orders are to see you remain in your cabin."

"Then send word above decks. I have a matter of some urgency to discuss with Blake."

The hardened veteran didn't move. The contempt

in his seamed face expressed more clearly than words what he thought of the captain who'd fired on his ship and impressed his fellow crewmen.

"Do you mean *Lieutenant* Blake, sir?"

James let out a long, slow hiss that raised shivers on Sarah's skin but didn't appear to unduly concern the American.

Dear Lord! Were they all as brash and daring as their captain?

"You'd best hope I don't regain command of this ship with you still aboard," James warned, his voice low and lethal.

"If you regain command with me still aboard, sir, I'll happily throw myself over the taffrail. Now who was it again you were wishing to speak with?"

"With *Lieutenant* Blake."

RICHARD KEPT BUSY above decks, assessing the damage to the *Linx.* There'd be hell to pay and then some if he allowed the British ship to scuttle.

The constant impressment of American sailors had already strained relations between the United States and England to near breaking point. President Jefferson had issued protest after protest to no avail. So volatile had the issue become the president had conquered his deeply ingrained reluctance to maintain a large standing army and increased the ranks of uniformed soldiers. He'd also grudgingly authorized the construction of a fleet of vessels and the birth of the American navy.

These precautions notwithstanding, Jefferson still hoped to avoid war. He'd not be best pleased with one of his captains for adding to the volatile situation. Richard knew he'd face a board of inquiry for firing on the *Linx*. If the frigate went down and took the fragile relations between the two nations with it, he'd no doubt spend the rest of his days in irons.

If that happened, it happened. The prospect hadn't stopped him from reclaiming his men. He'd handpicked every one of them and was damned if he'd leave them to the mercies of the British navy.

"Lieutenant!"

"What is it, Rogers?"

"Mr. North sends word that the captain of the *Linx* wishes to speak with you."

"About what?"

"Don't know, sir, but Mr. North indicated it was a matter of some urgency."

"All right. Tell him I'll come below in a moment."

Frowning, Richard skimmed another glance over the moon-washed deck. Rigging and broken spars lay in tangled heaps. The mizzenmast had sheared off and crashed to the deck, dragging its royal and topgallant with it. The tops'l had held, though, as had the spanker. The *Linx* had been injured, but not mortally wounded.

By the time the frigate's crew repaired the damage, the *Seahawk* would be well away. And if anyone tried to claim this was an act of aggression against the British Crown, Richard would offer the *Seahawk*'s log as evidence. In his view, he had merely returned the same salute Lowell had rendered last year. Satisfied, he went below and once again faced the captain of the *Linx*.

"You have something you wish to discuss with me?"

"I do."

"Unless it's your parole, I have no interest in anything you—"

He broke off, his eyes narrowing. Lady Stanton stood across the cabin, back straight, fists clenched. Her maid huddled in the corner with a corner of her kerchief pressed to her cheek. With a muttered curse, he strode across the room, caught Lady Stanton's elbow in careful grasp, and raised her arm.

"Did I do this?"

Sarah lifted a startled glance to his, as confused by his gentle touch as by the disgust in his eyes when he surveyed the marks on her wrist.

"No, you..."

She caught herself just in time. The role James had forced on her would play far better if she put the American at a disadvantage. Guilt could be as powerful a weapon as unrequited lust.

"You did not cause the marks," she finished

haughtily, knowing full well the disdain that accompanied the response would imply the opposite.

Richard swore again. He didn't remember grasping her by the wrist, but his blood had still been full up and singing with the easy boarding of the *Linx*.

"If I did, you have my most sincere apologies."

Bringing her wrist to his lips, he dropped a kiss on the reddened skin.

Sarah sucked in a sharp breath. She couldn't remember the last time anyone—father, brother, husband—had done more than laugh along with her when she acquired a new scrape or bruise. Hers wasn't the kind of meek, timid spirit to invite sympathy or gentleness. That this gruff American of all people would treat her with such tenderness both startled and confused her.

When she lifted her gaze from his bent head, dread chased away the brief confusion. James had observed Blake's kiss with a malevolent expression that boded ill for both Sarah and the American.

"That's the second time you've laid hands on my fiancée," he said icily when the American released her and stepped back. "Had I my sword, it would be the last."

"Is that so?" A feral light leaped into the captain's eyes. "That's easily enough remedied. I'd be more than happy to settle matters up on deck, with only naked blades between us."

James looked all too ready to take him up on the

offer. When he did not, Sarah understood that was her cue.

"No!"

She invested the sharp cry with all the emotion of a Cheltingham drama.

"I will not have your blood spilled, James."

Shoulders back, head high, she offered herself on the altar she'd built over the years with her foolish, foolish exploits and disregard for convention.

"You may not have heard of me, Mr. Blake. In London circles, I've gained something of a…a reputation." She swallowed, fought the nausea rising in her stomach, and forced herself to continue. "Sir James was good enough to rescue me from the debacle I'd made of my life. Now I will do the same for him and the *Linx*. If you're so set on revenge, I would ask you take it with me."

"What?"

"M'lady…"

"Sarah!"

The American was astounded. Maude distressed and teary-eyed. James coldly—seemingly—furious.

Ignoring her maid and her intended, Sarah stripped away the last of her pride.

"If you want me, I will bed with you. In return, you must promise to harm no one else aboard this ship."

CHAPTER THREE

RICHARD COULDN'T DECIDE whether he was more astonished, amused or offended. For the second time in less than an hour, this glorious creature expected him to pounce on her like a bilge rat would on a barrel of salt pork.

He was an officer in the United States Navy, for pity's sake! The son and grandson of deep water ship captains. He lived by the rules of the sea and held to a rigid code of honor.

He came within a breath of informing the lady of that fact. Rueful reflection held him back. His conduct in her cabin hardly qualified as that of a true gentleman. He'd given her little reason to think he would rebuff such an extraordinary offer. Still, it was one kettle of pea soup for a man to steal a kiss. Another pot of stew altogether to take a sacrificial virgin to bed.

Except...

She was a widow, not a virgin. And Richard was no fool. They'd hatched some plot between them, she and the captain of the *Linx*. Richard would bet every brass button on his uniform jacket Lady Stanton intended to bring him grief, not pleasure.

"Let me be sure I understand this," he drawled. "You'll bed with me and willingly. In turn, I'm not to line the crew of the *Linx* up at the waist-rail and shoot them."

She blanched. Rocked back a bit on her dainty heels. Steadied. "Nor will you hang the ship's captain from the yardarm."

Christ's toes! He'd forgotten all about that off-hand threat. He hadn't meant it, of course. In his own mind, he could justify firing on and boarding the *Linx* to reclaim the crewmen taken off his ship by force. He couldn't justify stretching her captain's neck. Unfortunately.

His glance went to the officer under discussion. "You agree to this, Lowell?"

"It's not his choice," the lady interjected. "It's mine and mine alone."

Richard's mouth curled. Whatever scheme they'd hatched, Lowell was certainly allowing his intended to carry the brunt of it. The man was a rosewater sailor of the worst sort!

He'd play the game through, Richard decided. See how far it would carry him...and the delectable Lady Stanton.

"I accept the terms and conditions."

Her eyes were huge pools in her pale face, as deep and green as the ocean and just as unfathomable. Swallowing, she swiped her tongue along her lower lip.

"Very well. Shall we retire to my cabin?"

"You may retire. I've matters to attend to yet above decks. I'll join you shortly."

Nodding, she moved to the door.

"Don't do this, m'lady!"

The wailing protest came from the plump little maid. She cast a fearful look at Lowell and would have said more if her mistress hadn't silenced her with an abrupt command.

"Come with me, Maude. I shall need your assistance."

The maid scurried to her side. Richard opened the door for them and instructed the petty officer standing guard to escort the women to their cabin. As the trio navigated the dim passageway, he rested a hand on his pistol butt and turned to Lowell a final time.

"It takes a rare breed of dog to let his mate crawl into a kennel with another."

The captain flicked the gold lace at his cuff. "You heard the lady, Blake. This was her choice, not mine. She and I will settle matters between us later."

Disgusted, Richard left the cabin and twisted the key in the lock. What the devil kind of hold did Lowell have over the woman that she would prostitute herself like this? Hell, you'd think she'd jump at the chance to be rid of such a lice-bag. Yet here she was, ready to sacrifice her honor to save him.

To all appearances, at least.

A quick, slashing grin cut across Richard's face. The next hour or so should prove interesting, at the very least. When North returned to resume his guard post, the captain climbed to the open deck.

"Mr. McDougal!"

At his call, his third lieutenant came running.

"What's the count on the crew of the *Linx*?"

"All two hundred seventy men at quarters and twenty-two boys accounted for. More than half are still snoring below decks. The rest are under close guard."

"How many dead or injured?"

"None dead, sir. Two wounded. A boatswain took a musket ball through the shoulder. A broken spar landed atop one of the master's mates and dented his pepperbox. He'll be seeing mermaids dancing jigs with sea dragons for a while yet."

"And our men?"

"Nary a scratch or a splinter among 'em."

"What about the twelve who were pressed?"

"All right and tight and ready to climb back aboard the *Seahawk*. So are another dozen or more who claim they, too, were shanghaied off American ships. I expect that number will rise when the others come awake," the lieutenant added dryly.

"I expect it will."

For the first time since dousing his ship's lights and laying on all sail to bear down on the *Linx,* Richard relaxed his taut muscles.

"Damned if we didn't pull it off, Mr. Mc-Dougal."

"That we did, sir."

The two men shared a grin until Richard shipped a quarterdeck face again.

The slang expression was more than appropriate, he thought. Officers might relax discipline among themselves or with the crew during a theatrical or musicale put on to relieve the boredom at sea. When a captain assumed a more deliberate demeanor, it prompted a return to strict observance of rank and protocol.

"Signal the *Seahawk* and advise that we've secured the *Linx* and her crew."

"Aye, aye, sir. Do you want me to ready the boarding party for departure?"

"Not yet. As you said, there may be more pressed Americans among those still in a stupor below decks. I mislike leaving them behind."

Not to mention leaving the lady awaiting him below. Richard's blood heated at the thought of taking another taste of her, but he was too experienced a captain to sail into an uncharted harbor without taking careful soundings.

"Where's Jenkins?"

Carpenter's Mate Jenkins was the senior of the

Americans taken off the *Seahawk* by Lowell's men. He'd spent the past five months aboard the *Linx*. If anyone knew the scuttlebutt concerning the British captain and his intended, it would be him.

"He's on the aft deck, sir, mounting guard over the officers."

Richard found the tall, spare North Carolinian easily enough. He stood silhouetted against the flare of the ship's lanterns, pistol cocked and finger itching for just one of the officers who'd made him dance under the lash these past months to make a misguided move.

They were a sullen lot. Richard supposed he would be, as well, if he served under a captain like Lowell. He'd addressed them earlier when he'd taken their parole, and spared them only a swift glance now.

"A word with you, Jenkins."

"Aye, sir."

Leaving the other guards at the ready, the carpenter's mate joined his captain in the dark shadow cast by the mainmast.

"What do you know of Lady Stanton?"

"She came aboard at Plymouth, sir. Word 'tween decks is she has a reputation that would put a waterfront whore to the blush."

She'd said something close to that, Richard remembered. Try as he would, though, he couldn't make the picture of a high-born doxie fit. She had a sensual air about her, to be sure, and her gown was cut low enough to set a man's juices to running. But Richard had bedded his share of obliging whores and saucy wenches. A few more than his share, if the truth be told. Sarah Stanton didn't kiss like a woman well used to being handled by men. The question was whether she would bed like one.

"According to the boy who serves the captain's table," Jenkins continued, "Lowell's been paradin' his lady half-naked before his officers. They're layin' bets as to which one he'll finally let have her."

"The devil you say!"

"It's true, I swear. He's the kind as gets more pleasure from makin' others dance to his tune than doin' the jig himself, or so they say. Has a tendency to put his eye to the peephole, too."

Well, that explained a great deal. Lowell wouldn't have his eye to a peephole this time, but Richard didn't doubt he would demand a full report of the night's activities from his intended.

"Come with me," he instructed Jenkins. "I've another sort of guard duty for you to perform."

The carpenter's mate trailing, Richard informed Lieutenant McDougal he'd be below.

"I've unfinished business to attend to with Lady Stanton. Send word when the rest of the frigate's crew begins to come to their senses."

SARAH STOOD at her dressing table once more and stared through the thick, wavy glass at the moon. It rode high in the night sky now, a round, gleaming ball that mocked her with its brightness.

How long since she'd last stood here? Two hours? Less? What a turn her life had taken in such a short time.

She knew now her marriage to James would be one long, unending series of humiliations. Had she only herself to consider, she'd book passage back to England the same day the *Linx* reached anchorage in the West Indies. She'd rather be hauled before a London magistrate and serve time in debtors' prison than tie herself to a man who would use her as James wanted to.

There was the rub, though. She couldn't consider only herself. James, damn him, still held the notes he'd collected on her father and brother. He'd promised to pay them off, but hadn't. For all her faults, Sarah loved her father and brother with the deep, uncritical affection of one who shared their reckless nature and hopeless irresponsibility when it came to financial matters.

Now she was well and truly snared in a trap of her own making. Try as she would, she saw no way out except to do as James had directed and seduce the American—despite the sick feeling the mere idea left in her stomach. Not to mention Maude's vociferous protests. The maid hadn't ceased haranguing Sarah since they'd returned to the cabin.

"You can't do it," she protested once again. "For all you loved to thumb yer nose at those London biddies what tried to tell you how to go on, you've not a treacherous bone in yer body."

"It's not treachery to assist in quelling a mutiny aboard one of his majesty's ship," Sarah returned, trying to convince herself as much as her maid.

"Ha! I'll wager Salome said something of the same sort when they talked her into luring John the Baptist into her bed. And that's another thing."

Planting her fists on her ample hips, the maid directed a fierce glare at the mistress.

"I've been tending to you since we was both in pinafores. I know you went to Sir Cedric a virgin and held true to yer marriage vows whilst he lived. I know, too, you've taken no man into yer bed since he died. It was just yer high spirits—and stubborn pride—that set tongues to wagging and rumors to flying about you the way they did."

"There's no need to list my many failings. I'm well aware of them."

"Then ye know you cannot do this!"

"I can and I must. No! No more arguments."

Sarah pressed the heel of her hand to her forehead in a futile attempt to relieve the pounding ache that had begun just above her brows. She had to think, had to prepare for...

A sudden rap on the cabin door stopped her breath in her lungs. She tried to speak, couldn't, finally forced out a husky command.

"Enter."

The moment Richard Blake ducked his head under the deck timbers and stood before her, Sarah experienced the same strange, unsettling phenomenon as when he'd left her such a short time ago. Then, his departure had seemed to take some vital aura from the cabin. Now his presence filled the room, as if infusing it with a vibrant life force.

Perhaps it was his size. He was so tall. So broad of shoulder. His white knit pants clung to muscular calves and thighs. His blue uniform jacket with its standing collar, white facings, and gold epaulets only emphasized his physique. Resisting the effort to swipe her damp palms down the sides of her skirts, Sarah tipped her chin and met his gaze head-on.

The glint in his blue eyes promised nothing.

And everything.

"Need I remind you of the terms and conditions of our agreement?" she asked coolly.

"I think I have them."

"Then... Then let us proceed."

His mouth quirked. "As you wish."

"Maude, you may leave us."

The plump maid threw a last, imploring look at

her mistress. "M'lady, I beg of you. Think on what you do here."

"You may leave us!"

The American stepped aside to reveal a tall, spare sailor waiting in the passageway. He looked vaguely familiar to Sarah, but Maude seemed to recognize him instantly.

"Mr. Jenkins! A bluidy mutineer, are you?"

"No, ma'am. As I told you that day we spoke at the rail, I'm an American seaman pressed into service aboard this ship against my will."

"Huh! A pirate, more like!"

"Perhaps you and Mr. Jenkins could continue this discussion topside," Blake suggested. "Jenkins, you'll stay with Mistress Maude and see to her safety."

"Aye, cap'n."

The contrast between the American's concern for her maid and Sir James's casually brutal treatment of Maude almost—*almost!*—undid Sarah. Her resolve weakened, and she came within a breath of telling Blake their bargain was off.

She might have done just that, if he hadn't bolted the door, strolled into the cabin and pulled his pistol from his belt. Her throat closing, she watched him casually deposit the weapon on the fold-down dressing table. It lay there amid her brushes and combs and pots of powder and paint. The silver scrollwork on its handle gleamed dully.

Just as casually, Blake removed his sword belt and hooked it over the back of the desk chair. Unarmed, he closed the distance between them.

"All right, lass. As you so eloquently phrased it, let us proceed."

He folded his arms. Stood with legs spread. Surveyed her with a look of polite anticipation.

Taken aback, Sarah realized he was waiting for her to initiate matters. She stared at him blankly for a moment, her mind whirling. The Notorious Lady S. would know how to proceed at this point. Sarah was somewhat at a loss.

Men had always pursued *her*. They'd whispered outrageous compliments into her ear. Held her closer than they should have in the waltz. Tried to steal a kiss on a darkened balcony. She was far more skilled at laughing and turning aside her more persistent admirers' advances than in initiating them.

Impatiently, she shook her head. She'd been married for three years, after all. Her infrequent beddings with Ceddie had been rather clumsy affairs at best, but she was no silly, untried virgin. She knew well enough what brought a man to passion.

Shutting her mind to everything but the pistol lying just out of reach, she stepped forward, slid her palms up the lapels of the American's uniform and wrapped her arms around his neck.

Still he stood impassive, unbending.

Slowly, the sick feeling in Sarah's stomach gave way to a simmering indignation. She was prepared to endure his kisses, to remain stoic while he undressed her. She was *not* prepared for him to stand like a lump of oven-baked clay while she seduced him.

"You'll have to bend your head if you wish me to kiss you," she ground out. "Unless, of course, you prefer to dispense with such boring preliminaries."

Richard couldn't help himself. He'd intended to play the game out, to discover what scheme the lady had hatched with Sir James, but the farce proved too much for him. Laughter rumbling in his chest, he wrapped an arm around her waist and tugged her hard against him.

"Oh, no, lass. Such preliminaries never bore me. You may kiss away."

Eyes dancing, he grinned down at her. He fully expected her to vent the temper that flared hot and quick in her eyes. He thought for sure she'd try to clout him on the side of the head or kick back a foot to whack him in the shins. To his intense disappointment, she attempted neither.

"This may be a matter of levity to you," she said, her voice quivering with fury. "It is not to me."

His grin took a crooked bent. "No, I can see it

is not. Rest easy, sweeting. I'm not about to let you sacrifice your honor for a fouled oyster like Sir James."

The high color in her cheeks leached away. "You swore… You promised…"

"I promised I wouldn't harm anyone aboard this ship. The thing is," he said apologetically, "I never intended to. Not if I could help it, leastways. Why do you think I had my men break into the surgeon's stores and drug the crew of the *Linx* if not to minimize the chance of injury to all aboard?"

"But—but…" She sputtered, almost incoherent. "You threatened to hang James from the yard-arm!"

"Yes, well, my blood was up. A man tends to let loose with a bit of bombast after boarding an enemy ship."

Her mouth opened, closed, opened again. "That's all the threat was?" she got out after a stunned moment. "A bit of bombast?"

"That's all it was."

The rueful admission left Sarah breathless with astonishment, with indignation, with fury. At that moment, she would have snatched up the man's pistol and put a bullet through his heart without the least qualm.

In the space of an hour or two, he'd sent her whirling through a maelstrom of emotion. First by scaring her near witless. Then by forcing James

to reveal his true nature and Sarah to recognize
her own.

Now...

Now he dared to keep her body pinned against
his! To smile down at her like some big, besotted
dolt! To make her wish, despite her anger, despite
her despair, that they could finish what they'd begun here.

It took her some moments to realize he felt the
same biting regret. Slowly, his grin faded. The
roguish laughter left his eyes.

"It must be the full moon," he said on a rueful
note. "It makes wild dogs howl and even the most
civilized men suspend rational thought. But I've
never fallen so completely under its spell until tonight."

She wanted to weep with the irony of it. Of all
the men and all the times to feel this wild, furious
racing of her blood! Swallowing the lump in her
throat, she admitted the humiliating truth.

"Nor have I."

"One kiss, lass. One kiss and we'll call this bargain done."

"One kiss," she agreed in a moment of breathless insanity.

CHAPTER FOUR

ONE KISS. That's all Richard intended to take. All he *would* have taken if the damned moon hadn't cast such a spell over him.

Or was it the delectable Lady Sarah?

She bedazzled him. Bewitched him. Stirred a fierce, unrelenting need with just the slow, soft glide of her lips over his. Hunger leaped inside him, instant and greedy, and he deepened the kiss.

Tongue met tongue. A searing heat danced along his skin. Hers, as well. Richard could feel it under the hand he curled around her nape. The smooth skin fired to his touch. With an inarticulate growl, he widened his stance, roped an arm around her waist and dragged her up against him.

Sarah had never felt the slightest patience with the fainting, die-away airs displayed by the more delicate of her sex. Yet the crush of Blake's body against hers made her senses reel. She felt breathless, dizzy, as though she tumbled head for heels, swept toward some distant shore on a rushing, crashing wave.

She knew she could end the kiss. For all his bone-squeezing hold, Blake wouldn't force her to give more than they'd agreed upon. She'd taken enough of his measure by now to know she could jerk her head back, push out of his arms and call the matter done.

She should do just that. A tenuous thread of common sense told her clinging to him like this was dangerous. Yet everything that was female in her gloried in the feel of him, the hardness of him.

His heart pounded beneath her palm. His muscles corded as taut as an anchor cable. His shaft rose to strain against her hip, thick and round and stiff as a ship's mast behind the flap of his trousers. In response, a liquid heat swirled low in Sarah's belly. She ached to let the fires burn out of control once, just this once.

And why should she not?

The question speared through the swirling mists and lanced into her heart. James had sent her to seduce this man. Why not take what pleasure she could, whilst she could? Why not give substance to the reputation she'd woven for herself over the years with her reckless daring and disdain for the conventions?

Why not taste passion, just this once?

Blake must have sensed something of her tumultuous thought. Slowly, inexorably, he did what

Sarah could not bring herself to. Raising his head, he broke the spell.

Or so she thought, until she looked into his eyes. They blazed down at her, lit with the same hunger that gripped her. In that one reckless moment, she committed herself to the flames.

"Don't speak," she whispered. "Please! Just… Just take what I offer."

Pinpoints of blue sparked in his eyes as anger crowded aside desire. "I've already told you," he snapped. "You aren't required to sacrifice yourself for Sir James."

It took every ounce of courage she possessed to admit the truth. "This would not be for James. It… It would be for me."

The whispered admission stunned Richard. Had Carpenter's Mate Jenkins spoken the truth? Were the shipboard rumors true? Was the lady indeed no better than a waterfront whore?

His instincts said no, that there were forces at work he didn't understand. Yet here she was, offering herself to him like a two-penny slut. Damned if he wouldn't show her how close he was to taking what she offered. Tightening his arm, he canted her hips and pressed her belly hard against his.

"You can feel how much I want you. If we start again, know that I won't stop at a kiss."

"Nor will I."

The husky promise dragged hard on the sea anchor Richard had tried to throw out. The naked need in her face snapped its cable right in half.

He didn't begin to understand the dark currents swirling between this glorious creature and Lowell. At this point, he didn't *want* to understand them. All he knew, all he cared about, was that the lady burned as hot for him as he did for her.

More than willing to accommodate her, Richard swooped down and captured her mouth with his once more. She arched against him, supple as a swan and every bit as sleek. Arms twined around his neck, body straining against his, she made no attempt to hide the hunger that mounted with every breath, every slide of breast against chest, belly against hip.

They were both panting when he dragged down her arms and turned her around. His body screamed at him to lift her skirts, unbutton his trousers and give them both the release they craved. They had not much time.

Still, he couldn't bring himself to simply bend her over the table and rut with her. Despite the doubts Jenkins had planted, despite the fact Richard was already sweating with the effort of holding back, he would take her with some attempt at finesse.

A few quick fumbles freed her hair from its pins. It spilled over her shoulders and down her back, a river of gold-tipped red. Brushing aside the silky mane, he bent to nuzzle the warm skin of her nape. All the while his busy fingers worked the buttons on the back of her dress.

Straining against his breeches, he dropped kisses on her bare shoulder. Her skin was as warm and sweet as a sun-ripe peach. He savored the taste of her as he finished with the last button and peeled the emerald silk down her arms. One glimpse of the lush, perfect breasts plumped up by her corset and covered only by the thin lawn of her shift was like a cannonball straight to his gut. He might have been some untried, pimple-faced midshipman, Richard thought in disgust, almost doubled over with the lust that gripped him.

The corset strings tangled under his clumsy fingers. The resulting knots would defeat the most patient sailor, and Richard didn't lay claim to that particular virtue at the best of times. With a muttered curse, he reached for the dirk strapped to his calf just below his boot top.

She glanced over her shoulder. Her eyes went wide when she caught sight of the gleaming blade.

"What are you doing?"

"Freeing you. Be still."

He dug the tip of the dirk under the first lace. A quick upward tug and the stiffened fabric fell away.

Sarah gulped at his ruthless efficiency. With one slice, the American had freed her from the same laces Maude had been struggling with when his ship had first swept across the stern of the *Linx*.

If only he could free her from the master of the *Linx* as easily.

No! She wouldn't think of James now. Nor of her father or her brother or even Maude. This moment was hers. Hers alone. To savor. To smile privately over at some distant date, in some distant place.

A dank prison cell, most likely.

So be it! Whatever came, she would have the memory of his calloused hands raising shivers on her skin as they nudged down the straps of her shift. Of those same hands cupping her bared breasts. Kneading the tender flesh. Teasing her nipples into stiff, aching points. With a low moan, Sarah let her head drop back against his shoulder. He pushed her shift down until it puddled around her waist. The straps caught at her elbows, harnessing them.

Blake had no such restraints to impede his movement. His hands continued their torment. One caressed her breast. The other dipped lower, skimming her belly, tugging up the hem of her shift, parting her legs to find the slit in her drawers. All the while he put his lips and teeth and tongue to wicked use.

She was wet and gushing into his palm when he let go of her long enough to yank off his uniform jacket and toss it to the floor. Freed of its constriction, he swept her into his arms and carried her across the cabin. The bed was little more than a cupboard cut into the bulkhead. Sarah could barely stretch out in the cramped space. She couldn't imagine how a man as tall and well-muscled as Blake would fit in with her.

He made no attempt to do so. Instead, he dropped into a sitting position on the bed and settled her so she straddled his lap. Her knees folded back on the edge of the bunk, allowing her just enough leverage to lift up when he went to free himself from his trousers.

She expected him to flex his thighs and drive into her. To plant his hands on her hips and hold her so she would take his thrust. What she didn't expect— almost couldn't *bear*—was the gruff tenderness in his voice when she tensed at the first probe.

"Easy, lass. We'll take this slow and easy. I'll not hurt you."

The taut angles of his cheeks and chin told Sarah what it cost him to make that promise. Grateful for his restraint and embarrassed that he would sense her inexperience in such matters, she linked her arms around his neck and forced her muscles to relax.

He pushed in gently, letting her get the feel of him, the size of him. The first moves were slow, as he'd promised, easy. Then deeper. Surer. Faster.

Sarah caught the rhythm, almost lost it again

when he dipped his head and fastened his mouth over hers. He pushed his a hand through her hair, held her steady, and pleasure curled low and tight in her belly.

Moments later, he slid his other hand between their bellies and added the unbearable pressure of his thumb. Sarah felt a fleeting dart of wonder that she could experience such exquisite sensations. Another dart, this one of disgust. How could she have established such a scandalous reputation and never, *ever* dreamed such wild delight could come with it.

Suddenly, she froze. Her eyes widened in startled surprise. A moment later her head went back, a groan ripped from her throat and her entire body convulsed.

The small corner of Richard's brain still capable of rational thought took note of that look of utter astonishment. No whore, highborn or low, could have feigned such stunned surprise. Or the shudders that wracked her body as her pleasure took hold.

Gritting his teeth, he let her ride the waves to their crest before he flexed his thighs and drove up into her hot, slick depths.

DAZED, SARAH EMERGED from what felt like a near stupor to find herself cradled against a broad chest. One of her legs was still folded under her. The other lay hooked over the American's thighs. Stiff and awkward and more than a little embarrassed now at the wantonness of her behavior, she struggled to right herself.

He lifted her easily, allowing her to straighten her bent leg. She scrambled off his lap and dragged up the straps of her shift. For some absurd reason, Sarah couldn't bear to face this man until she'd covered herself again. Even then, she had to summon all her courage to turn and meet his gaze.

It was lazy. Smiling. The look of a man well satisfied with the night's work.

As he should be, she thought. The *Linx* had surrendered to him without so much as a token resistance. So had the Notorious Lady S.

And in doing so, she'd been awakened to a pleasure she'd often heard alluded to when married women gathered in gossipy little circles, but had never before experienced. How odd! How very, very odd. And so exceedingly ironic. After three years of marriage and several more playing the role of merry widow, at last she understood the magic that was supposed to take place in the bedchamber.

Forcing her limp limbs to move, she went to gather her gown. Blake rolled to his feet, righted his clothing and followed.

"Turn around and I'll do the buttons."

Dragging her tangled hair over one shoulder, Sarah dipped her head to allow him access to the loops and cloth-covered buttons. The brush of his fingers against her back raised tiny tremors, just as before.

What *was* it about this man's touch that stirred her so?

The knowledge she would never feel it again raised another shiver, this one of despair. Her brief interlude of insanity was over. This moment out of time had ended. Sarah could no longer ignore her past or the future that awaited her when she and the American left this cabin.

Blake finished with the last button and rested his hands on her shoulders. "Are you all right?"

The concern in his voice was too close to pity for her pride to bear. Her back stiffened. Her chin came up. She'd made her bed, in the most literal sense of the word. She would now have to lie in it. Drawing in a deep breath, she turned to face him.

"Yes," she answered coolly. "I'm fine."

He searched her face, his own troubled. "What happened in this cabin is known only to us. No one else need be privy to it. You can tell Lowell—"

"Tell him what?" she interjected scornfully. "That I employed all my wiles and failed to seduce you?"

"Well, you see, lass, it's like this. The truth of the matter is you *didn't* seduce me. That implies a certain measure of gullibility on my part. I knew exactly what I was doing...and what I wanted."

"It doesn't matter how we dress the matter, or

whether we dress it at all. James will believe what he wishes to. He thinks me a whore, you see. As I have just proved myself to be.''

''If you've proved anything,'' Blake said sharply, ''it's that you're much a woman. With far more heart to you than Lowell deserves.''

That this man should hold her in more esteem than the one who wanted to wed her almost proved Sarah's undoing. Tears stinging her eyes, she turned away.

''If you're quite finished with me,'' she said through tight lips, ''I should like you to send Maude to me. I worry for her safety.''

''She's in good hands with Jenkins. He'll see she takes no hurt.''

Richard wished he could offer the same assurances to the woman standing with her back to him. He suspected she'd not fare well at Lowell's hands come the dawn. The thought of leaving the lady to her fate stuck in his craw like a sharp-ended fishbone.

He took a step toward her, only to stop short at the rap of knuckles on the cabin door. Frowning, he strode to the louvered panel and yanked it open. ''Yes?''

His third lieutenant stood in the passageway. McDougal raised a brow at finding his captain out of uniform. His glance darted past Richard to the other occupant of the cabin, swept quickly back again.

"You wanted to know when the rest of the *Linx*'s crew came 'round, sir. All but one or two are awake."

"Thank you, Mr. McDougal. Line them up midship. I'll be above deck shortly."

"Aye, aye, sir."

With the door closed once more, Richard scooped up his uniform coat.

"All right, m'lady," he said briskly, shrugging into the blue jacket. A roll of his shoulders straightened the facings and gold epaulet. "We don't have much time. Tell me exactly what Lowell intended you to accomplish while you had me alone in your cabin."

Sarah blinked at him in surprise. She'd thought the game played out. "What does it matter now?"

"A great deal. To me, if not to you."

She hesitated a moment before deciding she had little to lose by admitting the truth at this point.

"Sir James intended me to save his life, which apparently was already saved."

Blake's keen blue eyes bored into hers. "And?"

"And to save his ship."

"All that by enticing me into your bed?"

Shame coiled in her stomach. Pride wouldn't let her look away from his steady gaze.

"Actually," she said coolly, "I was instructed to

get you weak-limbed with pleasure, snatch up your pistol and put a bullet through your heart.''

''I thought as much.''

The facade Sarah had just assumed came apart. She stared at the man blankly, unsure she'd heard him aright. ''What do you mean, you thought as much?''

''I knew there had to be more to the scheme than your noble offer to sacrifice yourself.''

''Is that why you left your pistol lying within easy reach on the table?'' she demanded incredulously. ''To see if I would use it on you?''

''To see if you would try,'' he replied with one of his quick, slashing grins.

The realization burst on Sarah with shattering clarity. Blake had been toying with her! All the time, he'd been toying with her! And here she'd thought... She'd imagined... For those insane moments in his arms, she'd let herself believe...

What a *fool* she was!

Struggling to contain her fury and her hurt, she drew herself up. ''How disappointing for both of us that I did not attempt to shoot you. It would certainly have added more spice to the game.''

''That it would,'' he agreed with a cheerfulness that curled her hands into claws.

Seething, she watched him stroll across the cabin to retrieve his weaponry. He buckled on his sword with a swift efficiency that bespoke long practice.

When he hefted the pistol, its silver scrollwork gleamed. And when he aimed the barrel at Sarah's heart, she thought for a stunned second he intended to pull the trigger.

Just as quickly, she dismissed the absurd notion. Nevertheless, her pulse hammered wildly as he closed the small distance between them.

"The game's not done yet," he said. "Tell me why you agreed to Lowell's plan. I would guess it wasn't just to save his leathery hide."

"My reasons are my own."

"Tell me, lass. Perhaps I can help."

She couldn't imagine how, but the overwhelming need to confide in someone—anyone!—overcame her reluctance to discuss her family's financial failings.

"Sir James holds a number of my father's notes. A rather staggering number, if you must know. He holds almost as many of my brother's. He said he'd pay them off when we became engaged, but held back. Now he's promised to settle them if I... I..."

"Bring me down?"

"Yes."

He didn't hesitate. Reversing the pistol, he held it butt-forward.

"Take it."

"What?"

"Take it. You struck a bargain with Lowell. He won't honor his end if you don't honor yours. You'll have to shoot me."

CHAPTER FIVE

"YOU'RE MAD!" Sarah gasped, the weight of the pistol heavy in her hand. "I can't shoot you!"

"Of course you can." He caught her sagging arm and steadied it. "All you have to do is wrap your finger around the trigger, like this, and squeeze."

"Sir! Lieutenant Blake! You cannot expect me to…"

"Richard."

Stupidly, she gaped at him.

"Richard," he repeated, a smile in his blue eyes. "My name is Richard. I should like to hear it on your lips before you pull the trigger."

"I have no intention of pulling anything!"

He was mad, Sarah decided. He had to be to stand with legs wide braced, laughing down at her while she held a loaded pistol mere inches from his gullet.

"Say it. Just once. Richard."

"Richard! There. I've said it. Now do, for pity's sake, take this thing."

Desperately, she shoved the butt against his

chest. He refused to accept it. Instead, he wrapped his big hand over hers, pointed the barrel at an awkward angle, and pressed his fingers on hers.

The pistol belched fire.

Smoke blossomed.

Richard flinched.

Sarah shrieked as the bullet grazed his upper arm and plowed into the bulkhead behind him. The acrid stink of powder stung her nostrils and burned her eyes. She could barely hear above the ringing in her ears, had to struggle to catch Blake's offhand comment.

"There," he said with a nonchalance that stunned her. "It's done."

It certainly was. Blinking away the burning tears, Sarah stared in horror at the red stain darkening his uniform sleeve. He grinned at her obvious dismay and dragged a handkerchief from his coat pocket.

"It's just a scratch, lass. I've nicked myself worse with my razor of a morning."

Still rooted in shock, she made no move to assist him as he tied the white linen around his arm one-handed and used his teeth to tug the knot tight.

"Now you may tell Lowell the truth," he told her when the makeshift bandage was in place. "You took aim and fired, but the shot went wide of its mark and you merely winged me. He can't fault you for not attempting to hold to your end of the bargain. Or hurt you,'' he added under his breath, flicking a glance at her bruised wrist.

She could hardly believe what she was hearing. Or what he'd just done. He was an American. A mere colonial. As near to a pirate as made no difference. Yet he'd *shot* himself! Put a bullet through his own flesh to aid a woman he scarcely knew.

Tears stung her eyes again. In the few short hours Sarah had known this man, he'd shown more concern and consideration for her than any of the other males in her life, her father, brother and betrothed included.

Not only concern, she thought with a sharp ache just under her ribs. He'd also given her a taste of a woman's pleasure, dark and rich and all compelling. The memory of it shimmered inside her, only to shatter at the thud of pounding boots. She didn't doubt they heralded the precipitous arrival of several members of his crew, come to investigate the shot.

''Lieutenant! Sir!''

''You'd best let them in,'' Blake instructed, busy reloading the discharged pistol.

Sarah had no sooner pulled the bolt than the door burst open. A grim-faced officer rushed in, primed pistol in hand. The tall, cadaverous seaman—Jenkins—came hard on his heels. Maude pushed past them both, her eyes wide and frightened.

''M'lady!'' Her face paled as she spotted the red-stained handkerchief tied around the captain's arm. "Oh, no! Did ye do that?"

"I—I..."

The lie stuck in Sarah's throat. It was left to Blake to answer cheerfully.

"She did, indeed."

With a wailing cry, Maude rushed across the cabin, flung herself to her knees, and wrapped her plump arms around his boot tops. He stumbled back, almost knocked off his feet.

"Don't hurt her, sir! It weren't her fault. Sir James forced her to this desperate act."

Sarah shook herself and tried to stem the hysterical tide. "Calm yourself, Maude. There's no call for this unseemly display."

The maid ignored her. Determined to plead her mistress's case, she clung to Blake's knees.

"She's good and kind and generous of heart, sir. She tended to Sir Cedric night 'n day all those weeks he lay a-dying, his bowels putrefying. Niver once retched or showed him a disgusted face, as did them so-called nurses what couldn't take the stench. And after her papa and brother ran through every penny Sir Cedric left her, she always managed to scrape together the servants' wages one way or t'other."

"Maude, do be still!"

Too wrought up to stop, the maid rattled on. "Why, she even sold her gold locket to pay the bonesetter when Cook fell and broke her leg. It was the one trinket of her mama's her papa hadn't yet pawned to pay his gambling debts.''

Sarah felt heat flame in her cheeks. She could only hope Maude ran out of breath before she spilled every sordid family secret. She couldn't meet Blake's gaze as he bent to help the maid to rise.

''Here. Let's get you off your knees.''

Still Maude wasn't done. Once on her feet, she clutched at his coat sleeves. ''You must believe me, sir! M'lady wouldn't so much as step on a spider were she not forced to it. She didn't want to shoot you.''

Laughter danced in Blake's eyes at being classed with an insect, but he kept it from his voice.

''I believe you.''

The solemn assurance acted like a spur on the distraught serving woman. She burst into noisy, sobbing tears and threw herself against Richard's chest. If Sarah hadn't been so agitated herself, she might have laughed at the look of comical dismay that crossed the captain's face.

''Mr. Jenkins,'' he said in a strangled voice. ''Escort Mistress Maude above deck.''

''Aye, aye, sir.''

The seaman peeled the sobbing woman off his captain's chest and led her away. Heaving a hearty sigh of relief, Richard addressed his lieutenant.

"Mr. McDougal, you'll see that the boarding party is standing ready to return to the *Seahawk.* Lady Stanton, Sir James and I will join you in a few moments."

With a nod, the officer left. Nothing was left to Sarah but to offer a stiff apology.

"Please excuse Maude's hysterics. She's been with me a long while and tends to…to forget herself at times."

"From the sound of it," he said drily, "she forgets nothing."

Rolling his shoulders, the American settled his uniform across his shoulders and ran a quick eye over Sarah.

"You'd best retie your garters before we go to fetch Lowell."

She lifted the hem of her skirt an inch or two and saw her right silk stocking was bagged around her ankle. It must have come down during their wild coupling. She hadn't noticed, her attention being rather taken up afterward with such minor matters as firing off a pistol.

Turning her back, she lifted her skirt. The lacy garter was twisted as well, but she managed to untie it and straighten the sagging silk. Her heart was thumping when she dropped her skirts and faced the American again.

His eyes held no trace of a smile now. "Are you prepared to face Sir James?"

No.

Not yet.

Not ever.

"Yes."

She started for the door. A gentle tug on her arm stayed her.

"I'll be taking the *Seahawk* back to Virginia so the men we've reclaimed can see their families. If you wish, I'll take you and Mistress Maude, as well."

Sarah's heart knocked against her ribs. Once. Twice. In that infinitesimal bite of time, she actually considered his offer.

She could sail away with him. Leave Sir James behind.

Leave, as well, her father. Her brother. Her heritage, such as it was.

Leave everything and become the woman she'd let so many people believe she already was—a highborn wanton who lived only for the pleasure of the moment. Regret bitter in her throat, she shook her head.

"I can't go with you."

"Surely you don't intend to marry Lowell after the way he's used you?"

"No, I don't."

"What will you do, then?"

"Return to England," she said with a small shrug. "My family is there. My home."

What was left of it, anyway. Ceddie's ancestral holdings had been entailed on a distant nephew and the elegant town house he'd purchased for Sarah had gone under the auctioneer's hammer last year. She could always join her father at his ramshackle estate in Devonshire, she supposed. *If* James held to his promise to tear up the notes he held on her papa and brother, that is. If he did not, her entire family might soon take up residence in Newgate prison.

Sighing, she smoothed the wrinkles out of her gown as best she could and preceded the American from the cabin.

THE WHISKERED petty officer was still at his post outside the captain's door. While Richard exchanged a few words with him, Sarah tried to prepare herself for the ugly scene she knew would follow.

James would have heard the shot. The slap of running feet. The shouts. She didn't doubt he was all astew to learn what had happened and would be bitterly disappointed to discover she'd only wounded Blake. Dragging in a deep breath, Sarah entered his cabin for the second time that fateful night. Blake followed.

James swept her with a single cutting glance before turning his gaze on the American. The blood-stained handkerchief sent as clear a signal as any flag flown from the yardarm.

"May I assume my intended put that hole in you, Blake?"

"You may."

"How unfortunate her aim was off."

"Yes, wasn't it?" He made no attempt to conceal his disgust. "Perhaps next time you'll fight your own battles instead of allowing a woman to wage them for you."

Fury flared in James's face at the insult. "I told you I would meet you above decks, sword in hand. I'm still prepared to do so."

"You had your chance. It's too late now for swords. You may thank your lady, though, and be glad that I admire courage whenever and wherever I find it. Hers saved your ship and your own sniveling hide."

It was a lie. He'd sworn he hadn't intended to harm either the *Linx* or her captain. Yet he spoke so convincingly that Sarah had to clench her fists and stare straight ahead to keep from throwing him a look of gratitude. Maintaining her icy demeanor became even more difficult when he scraped a hand over his chin and smiled ruefully.

"I can only wish she'd followed through with her noble offer to give herself to me before pulling the trigger. Perhaps next time, lass?"

Sarah wanted to weep. Instead, she lifted her chin

and stared down her nose at him. "There will be no next time, Lieutenant."

He gave her a look of warm approval before turning to Sir James. Instantly, the warmth left his eyes.

"I'll have your parole, sir, or I swear I'll have you put in irons and parade you in front of your men like the shambling shim-shanks that you are."

The threat was so low and fierce that even Sarah believed it. She held her breath while James considered his choices, now narrowed down to two. He could surrender his ship or his pride.

His lips pressed tight. His cheeks reddened. With a churlish nod, he conceded. "You have my parole."

"Very well. Let's join our men topside."

THE MOON GLOWED bright and full when Sarah poked her head through the hatch. A brisk breeze tossed the ends of her hair. Holding her skirts up with one hand to keep from tripping over them, she climbed the last few stairs and stepped onto the deck.

The first thing she saw was the *Seahawk.* No longer a ghost ship, the American brig blazed from stem to stern with lanterns. Sleek and trim, she bobbed only a few dozen yards off the starboard side of the *Linx* and rode the waves with the grace of a gull. Her gunports, Sarah noted with a gulp, were all raised.

Gingerly she stepped over pieces of debris and made for the waist of the *Linx,* where the frigate's crew was lined up along the rail. The officers stood to the fore, grim-faced and stiff-shouldered. Having given their parole, many of them had been allowed to retain their weapons.

That wasn't the case with the seamen and marines. Evidently their word of honor wasn't sufficient surety of their conduct. They stood in ranks behind their officers, many still blurry-eyed and groggy from the sleeping draught they'd been administered. Those who'd fully awakened scowled at the Americans standing guard over them.

Sarah searched the assemblage anxiously. To her relief, she spotted Maude off to one side, still under the protection of Carpenter's Mate Jenkins. As she and James moved to stand with his officers, she saw that a number of British seamen had joined the ranks of Americans. Far more than the twelve James had reputedly taken off the *Seahawk.*

James spotted them, as well. His voice taut with anger, he promised retribution. "I'll see you men hung for desertion. Every last one of you."

One of the turncoats hacked up a gob of spit and launched it through the air. The mess landed on the captain's boot with a loud plop.

"I'd rather take me chances with the 'angman than with you," he said scornfully. "At least 'is rope does its work quick and clean."

"We ought to give *him* a taste of the cat," the sailor beside him growled. "See how well he wears his stripes."

Others fell in with the idea and voiced a chorus of eager suggestions.

"Soak the whip in seawater first so it burns more, like he ordered done for us."

"Grab 'im, boys. Let's tie 'im to the grate."

"I want first cut!"

Several started for their former captain, only to be stopped in their tracks by a stern command.

"Hold where you are!"

Richard strode forward and put himself between the angry deserters and the captain of the *Linx*.

"Sir James has given his parole, as have his officers. We honor such pledges in the American navy. If you're to sail with me, you will honor them, too."

Only one of the deserters dared challenge that flat ultimatum. "You don't know what he done to poor little Billy, the lad what waited on his table last voyage," the burly seaman protested. "We buried the boy at sea."

"I repeat," Richard said, his voice steely, "the captain has given his parole. If you wish to sail with me, you'll haul yourself to the rail and climb down into the one of the *Seahawk*'s boats. Now!"

The hulking seaman threw a last, loathing glance

at James before spinning on his heel and marching to the far rail. The rest of the deserters followed.

Over the painful pounding of her heart, Sarah watched them grasp the ropes and disappear. She heard a series of thumps. A muttered curse or two. The splash of oars as a boat pulled away.

In the silence that followed, the two captains faced each other. The moon's bright glow bathed them both, and the brisk breeze tossed the fringe of their gold epaulets. Aside from those visible symbols of their rank, they had little in common. One was thin, elegant, tight-lipped with anger and burning with the desire to avenge this insult to him and to his ship. The other stood tall, broad-shouldered, his hair as black as midnight, his eyes a cold, silvery blue.

Until he turned to Sarah.

His harsh expression softened. Something close to pity flickered across his face.

"It's not too late to change your mind."

That fleeting look spurred her pride. Her spine stiffened. Her chin tilted.

"Yes, it is. Far too late."

He looked as though he wanted to argue the matter, but refrained. With a smooth grace that belied his size, he made an elegant bow. "Farewell, Lady Stanton. I wish you a fair wind and a safe harbor at the end of your journey."

She couldn't speak over the lump in her throat. A mere dip of her head had to serve as her answer.

"All right, Mr. McDougal. Get the boarding crew into the boats."

Bound by their oath of parole, the officers and men of the *Linx* could only watch with clenched fists while the Americans departed their ship. One after another dropped over the side and scrambled down into the waiting boats. Blake was among the last to leave.

With a mocking smile for the captain of the *Linx*, he turned and made for the rail.

"Bastard," James growled.

Snarling, he spun to the officer next to him and snatched the pistol from the man's waist. When he leveled it at Blake's back, Sarah didn't stop to think.

"James! No!"

She flung herself at him in a desperate attempt to throw off his aim. For the second time that night, a pistol belched fire just inches away from her. The deafening report was still hammering against her eardrums when the night seemed to explode around her.

CHAPTER SIX

RICHARD HEARD Sarah's desperate cry a mere heartbeat before a pistol barked and a bullet whizzed past his left ear. In an instinctive move honed by his years in uniform, he ducked, whirled and came up with his own weapon in hand.

A single glance at the smoking pistol in Lowell's hand told the story. The bastard had violated his parole. And Sarah had without doubt saved Richard's life by throwing off Lowell's aim.

Richard's jaw clenched as the British captain whipped his arm free of her clinging grasp and sent her crashing to the deck. Stunned by his actions, his officers had yet to draw their weapons and violate their own sworn oath, but the shot had galvanized their seamen. Those not still affected by the sleeping draught were scrambling toward their stacked swords and muskets.

The American marines Richard had ordered high up in the *Seahawk*'s rigging to provide cover for the boarding party saw what was happening. Wild shouts carried across the water as they let loose with a volley designed to keep the British seaman away from their weapons. When bullets sliced through the rigging above Richard's head and splintered the deck some yards away, his heart jumped into his throat.

"Sarah!" he bellowed to the figure still prone on the planks. "Stay down!"

Sincerely hoping the moon's bright glow would allow his marines to distinguish between his uniform and that of the British officers, Richard charged back across the deck. Those few of his men still aboard the *Linx* pulled their cutlasses and prepared to follow him.

"To the boats!" he bellowed, knowing he had to get them off the British frigate before they lost the advantage of the marines' covering fire. "Jenkins, take Mistress Maude to safety!"

He had one chance, only one, to get to Sarah. Using the confused melee to his own advantage, he charged straight for her and scooped her up right under Lowell's nose. The British officer roared in outrage.

"Damn you!"

Whirling, Lowell lunged for his first officer and snatched at his sword. Thrown off balance by his superior, the lieutenant stumbled back into the ranks of men behind him. Both officers went down and took a number of the seamen with them.

Richard gave a fervent prayer of thanks for the lieutenant's clumsiness. As much as he ached to put his own sword into Lowell's gullet, his main concern now was Sarah. Snatching her up, he crushed her to his chest and ran back through the rain of covering fire. Once at the rail, he shifted her upward, tossed her over his shoulder, and swung a leg over the side.

"Dear God!"

Sarah's piercing shriek carried even over the rattle of musket fire. Upended and dangling high above the *Seahawk*'s bobbing boat, she snatched at Richard's coattails and hung on for dear life. Once in the boat, he dumped her in the gunwales. She pushed to her hands and knees, scuttled crablike toward the sobbing woman Jenkins had carried down to the boat, and shielded her maid's body with her own.

In that instant, Richard knew he'd done right by following his instincts and snatching the lady out from under Lowell's nose. Her heart was as wide as the sea and as true as a compass. If she went to any man's bed, he'd do his damndest to see it was his.

First, though, he had to get her aboard the *Seahawk* alive and unriddled by musket fire.

Thankfully, his marines kept the British away from their weapons. Firing in alternating waves, they maintained a steady volley while Richard and his men pulled at the oars of their boat. Long, muscle-wrenching moments later, the boat bumped against the *Seahawk*'s keel.

"Come on, lass. Let's get you and Mistress Maude aboard."

"I can climb the ladder."

"We've no time for you to attempt it on your own, I'm afraid. I'll take you up."

Tossing Sarah over his shoulder once again, Richard went up the rope ladder with the agility of long practice. Jenkins came right behind him with a wailing Maude.

Once on deck, Richard made for the aft hatch. He didn't set his burden on her feet until he got her below decks and away from the musket fire now being returned by the marines aboard the *Linx*. Jenkins followed hard on his heels and deposited Maude in the narrow passageway as well.

"You *are* mad!" Sarah exclaimed, shoving back her tumbled hair. "I thought as much when you put a bullet through your own arm. I'm sure of it now."

"Not mad. Just willing to fight for what I want."

"And fight you will." Her face grim, she wrapped an arm around Maude's heaving shoulders. "James will blow your ship out of the water."

"Do you think so?"

His cheerful unconcern had Sarah gritting her teeth. She knew little about sea battles, but even the most ignorant landlubber understood that a frigate carried twice the firepower as a brig. Before she could point out that basic fact, the American preempted her.

"I'd best get up on deck. The officers' mess is

straight ahead. Take your ease, lass, and don't worry.''

Since he punctuated that bit of absurd advice with a long, hard kiss, Sarah had no breath left to refute it. All she could do was stare at his back as he disappeared up the stairs. A long, keening cry from Maude snapped her attention to the distraught maid.

''We'll be kilt along with him and all his crew!''

''I suspect you have the right of it. Come, let's find the wardroom and take what shelter we may.''

The *Seahawk*'s officers' mess was half the size of the *Linx*'s but very well fitted. Wood shone. Brass gleamed. Benches were bolted to the floor on either side of a long rectangular table. The center of off-duty life for the ship's officers, the wardroom cabinets displayed the usual assortment of pewter crockery, books, musical instruments, board games and well-worn decks of playing cards.

Maude collapsed onto one of the sturdy benches, shaken to her shoes by the extraordinary events of the past few hours, quivering with fear over what was yet to come. Almost as distraught as her maid but trying desperately not to show it, Sarah paced the mess. It was located in the center of the ship and had no windows, no view of the sea or the ship riding the waves just yards away.

If Sarah couldn't see the *Linx,* she could well imagine it. The gunports drawn up. The cannons run out. The matches lighted. Powder boys running from the ship's magazine with cartridges tucked under their jackets to keep them from catching a spark and exploding. Officers issuing cutlasses and pikes to the sailors and marines who would board the *Seahawk* once it struck its colors.

Her heart in her throat, Sarah waited for the cannons to boom and braced for the shriek of torn sails and falling timbers. Instead, the only sounds that came to her and Maude were continuing bursts of rifle fire and a shouted command to raise all sails.

The deck above her came alive with the slap of running feet, followed shortly by the shriek of pulleys. Mere moments later it seemed, the *Seahawk*'s sails caught the breeze and she lunged forward. The pewter crockery rattled. Maude gasped and clutched the table's edge. Sarah put out a hand to steady herself and waited in agonizing dread for an explosion of fire and death.

Seconds crawled by. Minutes.

The rattle of rifle fire died. Canvas snapped. Masts creaked. The ship picked up speed.

It took a while for both women to grasp the fact that they were away. Well and truly away. Without a cannon being fired on either ship!

Maude ceased quivering with fright and turned a confused face to Sarah. "Why did Sir James not fire?"

"I have no idea."

Not out of concern for his intended or her maid, of that she was sure.

"What...? What do we do now, m'lady?"

For the first time, Sarah considered her abrupt change in circumstances. She was on an American ship, bound for God knew where, with only the clothes on her back.

She should have been awash with worry about her family, her fate, her future. Yet all she felt was the most ridiculous sense of relief. And excitement. And adventure.

"What can we do," she said to Maude, "except go wherever the ship sails."

She was free! The realization rushed through her veins. By tossing her over his shoulder, Richard Blake had taken all choice out of her hands. For however long it took the *Seahawk* to make port, she was free of both her worries and her past. The heady wonder of it still filled her when the captain and his officers crowded into the wardroom.

"Lady Stanton," he said with a punctilious formality belied by his broad grin.

"Lieutenant Blake."

She dipped her head in a regal nod, but Richard caught the gleam of suppressed excitement in her green eyes.

"I hope you and Mistress Maude will excuse the rather clumsy way you were brought aboard the *Seahawk*."

She arched an auburn brow. "Have we a choice in the matter?"

"None," he admitted, his grin widening.

What an incredible woman she was! Snatched from a ship, carried off amid a hail of bullets, and as cool as a north-water pike.

"May I present my officers?" he asked with the same formal courtesy.

"You may."

They filled the wardroom, their faces jubilant. Those seeing her for the first time gaped in open admiration at the tumble of fiery curls and swell of snowy bosom above her gown's square-cut neckline. Those who'd been with the boarding party showed somewhat more restraint, yet Richard could see them falling under her spell as she acknowledged each introduction.

"And this is Mistress Maude," he said with a smile for the plump maid who'd wedged herself into a corner.

The woman blushed furiously as the officers acknowledged her and looked to her mistress in an agony of embarrassment.

"Perhaps you'll explain why there was no exchange of cannon fire," Sarah said, drawing their attention back to her.

"Well, it's like this," Richard admitted, his eyes alight. "My previous encounter with Sir James did not inspire me with confidence that he would hold to his parole."

"So we spiked the cannons," his first officer put in with a grin.

"All of them?" she asked incredulously.

"All of them."

"The *Linx* will be a long time in port being re-fitted before she goes on the prowl again," the *Sea-hawk*'s surgeon added gleefully.

And Sir James would face a court martial to explain how his guns came to be rendered inoperative, Sarah didn't doubt. She could only hope that would keep him distracted long enough for her to find some way to raise the funds to pay off the notes he held on her father and brother. Maybe, just maybe, she could keep her family from being hauled off to Newgate, after all.

Her head whirling, Sarah stood beside Richard as his officers broke out what they claimed was the ship's best cognac. Golden liquid splashed into pewter mugs in liberal portions. The third lieutenant, Mr. McDougal, offered a mug to both Maude and Sarah before proposing the first toast.

"To Lady Stanton, who saved our captain's hide."

She blinked in surprise. Red rushed into her cheeks as the rest of the officers echoed the charge.

"To Lady Stanton!"

"To the lady!"

Richard grinned down at her and offered his own toast. "To the beautiful Lady S., who I intend to woo and hope most sincerely to win."

Sarah choked. The overfull mug shook in her hand. Cognac slopped over her wrist as the mess room rang with a raucous chorus.

"Hear, hear!"

Heads went back. The cognac was tossed down. Mugs were refilled.

"Most men would wait to announce their intentions in private," Sarah commented amid the general jubilation. "Do you *never* do as expected?"

Laughter danced in his blue eyes. "Never, sweeting. You'd best remember that if you take me to husband."

"I'm far more likely to take a belaying pin to you!"

The tart reply generated a round of hearty laughter from his men and another toast from Mr. McDougal.

"To the captain, who hopes to spike Lowell's guns in more ways than one!"

"Hear, hear!"

Additional toasts followed, each more raucous than the last. Sarah joined in the one honoring all ships at sea, another celebrating unfouled anchors, a third to the wives and mothers of sailors—surely the most sainted, patient, hardy women on earth.

Maude joined in the toasts, as well. The maid was giggling like a schoolgirl when Richard sent for Carpenter's Mate Jenkins and issued a stern order for the seaman to see to her comfort. A grin creased the man's weathered cheeks.

"Aye, aye, sir."

"You may escort her to the purser's cabin and

see it's cleared out for her use. I'll take Lady Stanton to my cabin and do the same.''

Offering the furiously blushing maid his arm, Jenkins led her away. Richard did the same for Sarah. He needed to get her alone, to make sure she understood he was entirely serious in his intentions.

There was only one way to accomplish that, he decided. Kicking the door shut behind him, he gathered the lady into his arms and covered her lips with his. She stood stiff and unbending for a moment or two, then her arms came up to lock around his neck and her mouth opened under his.

Richard's entire body was tight with desire when he raised his head. He swept his palms over her cheeks and buried his hands in her tangled hair. With everything in him, he ached to tumble this glorious creature to his bed.

She wouldn't resist him. He had only to look down to see the same heat that raced through his body warming her cheeks. Her breath came as hard and fast as his. Her neck was taut under his touch.

He wanted more than a quick tumble this time, though. He wanted her. Smiling down at her, he pleaded his case.

"Will you consider my suit, lass?"

The light went out of her eyes. Pulling away, she crossed her arms over her chest and looked away from him.

"I cannot."

Curling a knuckle under her chin, he tipped her

face to his. "I haven't forgotten those notes Lowell holds. Don't let them trouble you. I have a bit set back. More than a bit, if the truth be told."

"You cannot have that much set back."

"How much is 'that' much?"

"Almost ten thousand pounds."

"Ten thousand, is it? Well, such an amount will cut into the bride's gift I plan to give you, but I suppose it can't be helped."

Her jaw sagged. "You have ten thousand pounds?"

"That and more."

He couldn't help but grin as she stared at him in speechless astonishment.

"My grandfather was something of a pirate in his day," he admitted ruefully. "My father took to merchanting instead of piracy and built a fleet of ships. The *Seahawk* came out of our family yards. She was one of the first ships to be commissioned in our navy, you know."

"How... How could I?"

"I'll be going back into to the family business when I finish my naval service. I'll have my own ship and will most likely try my hand at the China trade. Have you ever been to Cathay, lass?"

"No, I—I..."

Taking pity on her near incoherence, he brushed her mouth with his, gentler this time, and infinitely tender.

"I'll make you a good husband, or try my

damndest to. I admit I've not had any experience at marriage.''

She recovered a bit at that. "Well, I have. All of London will tell you I would make you a most wretched wife.''

''All of London would be wrong.''

''You haven't heard the tales they tell of me,'' she said with a touch of desperation, determined he should know the truth. "Whispers buzz like a storm of hornets when I enter a salon or a ballroom.''

''I've heard what Maude has to say about you, and seen your courage under fire.''

''You've also seen me at my most wanton,'' she reminded him, red flags staining her cheeks. "You cannot wish to marry a woman who bedded with you less than an hour after you met her.''

His laughter rang out, rich and strong. "Oh, sweeting! That above all else is exactly why I wish to marry you. I've never felt such hunger or burned with such desire. Nor, I'll wager my best pair of boots, have you.''

The red in her cheeks deepened. "How can you possibly know that?''

His eyes danced. He wasn't about to admit his considerable expertise outside the marriage bed, for all he lacked any in it.

''Suffice to say I saw the wonder in your eyes. The same wonder filled me.''

Then *and* now, although at the moment the lust Richard felt was more painful than wondrous.

"Say you'll marry me, my lady, and sail to the far corners of the earth with me."

Sarah looked into his blue eyes and knew her answer. He called to the wildness in her spirit, seduced her with his impossible gallantry, and fired her blood with his touch. How could she *not* sail away with him?

"Yes," she answered with a heady recklessness that matched his, "to both propositions."

"Good. We'll scare up a vicar in the first port we come to. In the meantime…"

His mouth brushed hers, once, twice. Rising up on tiptoe, she wound her arms around his neck.

"In the meantime," she echoed, the words a warm whisper against his lips, "I *do* have a reputation to live up to."

With a wicked grin, he swept her up and carried her to his bed. Sarah caught a last glimpse of the full moon glowing outside the window before she opened her arms and welcomed him joyfully into her heart.

Dear Reader,

The same gorgeous moon that shines on England one April night in 1803 pours its romantic light over Scotland, too. As Jenny Colvin races desperately over the moorland intent on saving her father from the hangman's noose, she meets Sir Simon Lockhart—again. This time Simon is far more than the handsome rogue she kissed years before, the man whose smuggling deeds were legendary, the man who stole her heart as well as her father's treasure, and then disappeared. Now he's back, and even more dangerous—and he is the last man Jenny wants to meet that night.

Simon has returned with one secret and heartfelt purpose in mind—but an unexpected meeting with Jenny Colvin throws his careful plans to the winds. She is impetuous, lovely and even more desirable than he remembers, and soon Simon must decide what means more to him—a pledge of honor or a promise of the heart.

Follow Simon and Jenny through the moonlight as they hunt for treasure, encounter a legend and discover the power of love under the magic of a full Scottish moon.

Susan King

WHITE FIRE

Susan King

For the marvelous Murs, Merline and Miranda,
and for Cathy Maxwell, too.

PROLOGUE

THE HARD RHYTHM of his boot heels matched the measure of his thundering heart. Walking the length of the Tolbooth's stone corridor with a sure stride, black Hessians gleaming in the torchlight, Sir Simon Lockhart passed a row of small, dank cells. He noted but did not acknowledge the curious glances of a few prisoners as he continued toward the last, shadowed door.

Keep away from my daughter.

In four years, Simon had not forgotten the words that Jock Colvin had uttered to him, nor had he let go of the pain he had felt on hearing them. *Jenny Colvin will never marry a free-trading rogue. Keep away.*

Well, the free-trading rogue had returned a changed man, Simon thought. He was now a baronet and Writer to the Signet, and he had lately accepted a post for one year in the region where he had grown to manhood. The smuggler was a respectable man now, and intended to woo Jenny Colvin properly, as she deserved.

Improved suitor or not, he had arrived too late. The High Sheriff of Whithorn had informed him that Jock Colvin was in residence at the Tolbooth, and sentenced to hang the next day.

Though he had given no sign of it, Simon had felt his hopes slip away, wrecked like a ship on a reef. Jock Colvin had been Simon's mentor and friend, and Simon had looked forward to restoring that. Nor would he regain Jenny's regard, now that her father was about to be executed by king's men—and Simon was one of them. He knew her too well to expect forgiveness for that.

Damn fool, he told himself, to let his own steely vein of pride keep him away so long. He should have come back earlier, should have let them know that he was well, that he dreamed of them, that he loved them despite all.

Pausing at the last door in the passageway, he peered through the iron grate that pierced the thick wood, seeing only shadows beyond. Through a tiny window across the cell, Simon glimpsed the pale glow of a full moon against a twilight sky.

Inside the cell, a tall, lanky man moved in the shadows. The torchlight in the passageway illumined his gaunt features, his eyes blue and rheumy above crinkled cheeks and a limp grayish beard. He looked old and spent, but for the spark in those eyes.

"Jock Colvin," Simon said quietly.

Jock stared at his visitor. "Well," he said slowly. "It's the Laird o' Lockhart, back from the dead."

"Back from Edinburgh, actually," Simon said mildly.

Jock grunted. "Four years gone, with nae farewell to those who tutored you and trusted you. At first, we thought you dead. But I see you've become a fine gentleman."

"So it would seem. I'm glad to see you, Jock."

"Another few days, you'd have missed me altogether." Colvin came closer and poked a grimy finger through the iron bars to flick the snowy cravat that spilled over Simon's shirt and the front of his dark blue, neatly fitted vest and jacket. "Huh. That's good cloth—Flemish weave, I'd say. And gold buttons, too, by the de'il." He leaned closer. "What gives you such means? Free trade along the coast somewhere? French brandy and costly laces? Nae the whisky trade, or I'd have heard about it."

"I practice the law now," Simon answered.

"Nahhh," Jock growled, disbelieving.

"You knew I had a university education, on my father's wishes. I'm a Writer to the Signet in Edinburgh. Or was, for two years. Lately I've accepted a new post."

"Have you come to argue my case and set me free?"

"Your case has been argued and decided, Jock."

"What're you doing here, then? You didna come to chat."

Simon paused. "I've just been appointed a preventive officer along the Solway coast—to this very region, actually."

Jock laughed, a harsh explosion. "An excise man? A gauger? That's a bitter stab indeed! The cleverest free trader I ever knew, gone like a fox down a hole for four years—now ready to hunt those who gave him board and bread when he was a lad."

"Jock, it's not that way—" He stopped, unable to explain how it really was. Not here. Not now.

"Do they know, Simon Lockhart? Do they know they've set a wolf to watch after their sheep?" Jock hissed.

"They know," Simon said curtly.

Jock narrowed his eyes. "Then you made a devil's bargain, to escape a hanging or prison."

"Something like that."

"Something like a traitor. Go away, then," Jock growled.

"I signed a commission to patrol for illicit distillers and any who avoid paying judicious fees to the Crown for traded goods. I'm authorized to find horse thieves, too." Simon stared hard at him.

"I ne'er took that horse," Jock said, "but they'll hang me for it. They'd hang me on smuggling charges if they could prove them, too." He huffed.

"I'm told you boldly took a Connemara gray mare from the magistrate's own stable, and sold it on a ship bound for France, and were seen doing so by witnesses."

"Aye...'twas Angus MacSorley's old cousin who saw me...that half-blind rapscallion. I wasna out that night at all, even if he could see past his nose. So I'm innocent. There. Now open the door, lad." He gestured through the grille.

"I cannot do that. But when I learned of your situation, I came straightaway, though I knew you might not want to see me. Is there anything you need?"

"Aye. The key," Jock said pragmatically.

Simon huffed a reluctant laugh. "The sheriff would not trust me with it, so soon in my new position. He knows I once ran with rogues. It's why they were so eager to have me take this post. I know all the secrets, Jock," he added.

"Huh. So you might. Why did you come back? To watch me hang?" He leaned close. "Or to break my daughter's heart again?"

Simon lifted his chin and flared his nostrils in silence.

"I'm glad Jenny left before you came," Jock said.

"She was here?" Simon asked quickly.

"Aye, and went away in tears to see me in here.

My heart broke, too, for Jenny is a fiery lass and a brave one. I havena seen her cry…since you left.''

Simon frowned. ''I came back hoping to make amends.''

''Too late for amends. She'll never forgive you what you did. Nor will I.'' Jock took hold of the bars. ''Laird o' Lockhart, you listen close to me. For all the ill between us, I must ask two things of you now.''

''Aye.'' Simon waited.

''Since you're the new gauger, find the vipers that put me in here. I'm a free trader, aye, I dinna deny it. But excise men often look away when a man smuggles only to maintain his household. I've been a weaver most of my life, and I make scarce more than a croft hand at that, though I be an artist at the loom, and I can read and write some. I canna pay the king's duties on my own private still. What choice but free trading in whisky and other goods?''

''It's not whisky smuggling that put you here, Jock.''

''Nor horse thievery, either. Find who blamed me for their own crime, and I…well, I might forgive you what you did.'' Jock lifted one brow.

Simon smiled faintly. ''That's a devil's bargain. What is the second thing you want of me?''

Jock leaned close. ''Keep away from my daughter.''

"Ah." His heart slammed hard. "So your forgiveness does not extend to that matter."

"Nor ever will. I willna forget that I found you both in a loft, and you loving her like a rascal. And I willna forget that you asked me for her hand, and I said nay."

"I remember it very well," Simon murmured.

"Jenny was brought up educated and refined, like her mother. She isna for a rogue like you, Lockhart, nor ever was."

"I'm no longer in the free trade, Jock."

"You're still a rogue in blood and bone."

"So are you," Simon pointed out.

"And I wasna good enough for my sweetheart, either, though she loved me for my sins. Now, thanks to you, Jenny willna wed anyone ever, so she says. She thought to be a help to her da…until this. But I know my kinsmen will look after my lass, though they be a band o' rogues themselves." Jock sighed, and glanced through the tiny window. "Full moon, Lockhart. No rogues will be about on such a bright night as this."

"I will be out there," Simon murmured. "If you do have false accusers, Jock, I will find them." Still, he knew very well that Colvin might be guilty. Little could be done to save Jock now, but Simon would try his utmost for his old friend—no matter what the man thought of him. "You have my word."

"You gave me your word years back."

Simon frowned. "I will guarantee you one thing more, Jock Colvin. I promise you that Jenny will always be safe and happy. Always," he added in a growl.

"Good," Jock said. "Then she willna be wi' ye."

CHAPTER ONE

April 17, 1803
Scotland, the Solway Coast

THE RIDER PURSUED HER, moving swiftly over the moor through moonlight and shadows. Jenny glanced anxiously over her shoulder, gripping the reins tightly as her horse and cart hurtled onward. The man was gaining ground behind her—now she saw his dark silhouette clearly in the purple twilight, and realized that there were three others riding behind him.

The leader was a tall man, broad-shouldered and long-legged. His greatcoat and boots were as black as his horse, and his hair was that black, too, thick and whipping in the wind, hatless, for she had set him a mad pace. He rode with ease and seemed so close to catching her that she leaned forward to urge the bay faster.

"Halt!" the man called. "Stop, you! Preventive officer!"

She felt a sudden spike of fear. Excise officers

would not only keep her from her task, but they often delighted in searching women on suspicion of smuggling. Her father never allowed her out alone on the moors or near the coast after dark.

But tonight she had no choice, nor was Jock Colvin there to prevent his daughter from this errand. In fact, he had sent her in his place, for he sat in a cell in the Tolbooth, accused of horse thievery, and awaiting a sentence of hanging.

She had but one more chance to prove his innocence, but she could not risk delay. If the excise men caught her and realized that she was Jock Colvin's lass, they would not be inclined to let her go.

Snapping the reins, she sensed the bay mare surge as the cart hurtled over the moorland. In the distance, Jenny glimpsed the glittering sweep of the Solway Firth. Like a pearl riding on lavender velvet, the moon rose in the twilight sky.

A full moon revealed too much, and smugglers stayed home on such nights, she knew. But Jenny had no choice but to see to this task tonight. If she did not, her father's imminent death by hanging would weigh heavily on her heart and in her soul.

Her father had sent her out to find a cache of goods stolen from him, and she needed secrecy for that mission. Darkness had eluded her in the full moon, and now she was being followed.

Over the rattle of the cart and the thud of the bay's hooves, she heard the relentless drumming of other hoofbeats. Looking back, she saw that the lead rider was even closer. She sensed the steel of his determination. Behind him the others—including two dragoons, for she glimpsed their white gaiters in the darkness—pursued her steadily, as well.

"Halt!" shouted the rider in black once again.

Jenny slapped the reins, and the bay gave a burst of effort. The little cart rumbled over the turf, wooden crates sliding about in the cartbed, tin lantern jangling on its hook.

Was the new excise officer chasing her? Her kinsmen had learned that the new man would be nothing like the complacent, sly fellow who had accepted smuggler's bribes for years. The new preventive man would cut through the net of Solway smugglers like a hot blade through butter, or so her kinsmen had heard it said in the town.

As yet, no one knew his name or had seen him yet—he was that freshly arrived from Edinburgh— but word had spread throughout villages, crofts and hills. Everyone with a cellar or a cupboard full of hidden, untaxed goods, every man with a whisky still tucked away in the forest or on some remote hill, would stay wary until the measure of this fellow had been taken.

Had these men watched her father's house at Glendarroch, in the hills north of the moor, waiting for suspicious activity among Jock Colvin's kin? Had they seen her take the cart and head for the coast? The new man must have begun his patrol before the dust of Edinburgh was even wiped from his boots.

Another rapid glance showed her that the rider in black was within reach of her cart now. Frantically Jenny whipped the reins, bending forward with the increased pace.

Her pursuer shouted again, then drew alongside her, sending her a dark and furious glare, but she did not slow. Streaming past her, the man leaned over and snatched the bay's bridle, then rose in his saddle as if to leap onto the horse.

Jenny pulled hard on the hand brake, and both horses and cart pounded to a halt. The rider turned to glower at her over the wide shoulder of his caped greatcoat. Black brows furrowed over blue eyes that were brilliant with anger.

"What the devil are you about, driving a cart like that?" he demanded.

Jenny stared, stunned. His face was so familiar— and so totally unexpected—that she felt the impact like a pistol shot.

Simon Lockhart.

Moonlight revealed the handsome, all-too-familiar planes of his face, now drawn down in anger. She should have recognized his tall, strong silhouette, the limber grace of his horsemanship. She should have known. Her heart slammed as she gazed at the man who had disappeared from her life four years earlier, taking her hopes with him.

"I might ask what the devil you've been up to," she said crisply, "for four years."

"Still swearing like a rogue, Jenny Colvin," he growled, as he let go of the bay's bridle.

"I'm a rogue's child," she snapped.

She was not sure of his reaction, or even the moment when he had recognized her in turn. He had always been like that, keeping his secrets and his thoughts close. Now he stroked the horse's neck and muzzle, murmuring calmly to the bay, which soothed readily beneath his leather-gloved hand.

Frowning, Jenny irrationally wished that the horse could resent the man, too.

"Hey, Sweetheart," he told the horse. "I see at least you recall me kindly."

"Sweetheart remembers you for the carrots you gave her," Jenny said. "It will take far more than carrots for the rest of us to remember you kindly."

He folded his hands on his saddle pommel and regarded her. "Greetings to you, too, Miss Colvin. How nice to see you again."

"I canna say the same, Mr. Lockhart." She had dreamed of seeing him again, longed for it—but she was not such a fool as to admit it.

"Actually, it's 'Sir Simon' now. I was knighted recently."

"How nice," she said coldly.

He inclined his head with a faint smile, cocking an eyebrow, and her heart gave a little flip. In the clear moonlight, she saw that he had grown even more handsome, filled out and strengthened by manhood and unknown adventures. Wherever he had gone, whatever he had done, her deepest heart still belonged to the rapscallion who watched her now. She lifted her chin proudly.

"Have you been here long? Seen your kin as yet?" She sounded like a dimwit, she thought, but she still felt flustered and stunned. His property, inherited from his father years ago, lay in the hills miles north of the firth. In his extended absence, the castle and lands had been rented out to tenants by his cousins, Jenny had heard.

"Not yet. I arrived in Whithorn only today, and I'm at the inn there until certain affairs are settled," he answered. He glanced over his shoulder at the approaching riders, then looked back at her. "Miss Colvin, I beg pardon for interrupting your evening jaunt, but I must ask you some questions."

"Oh? Perhaps you'd like to know how we've fared while you've been gone—dinna worry that I will try to get away," she added, when he reached out to tug the reins from her hands.

"Ah, but I do worry," he said, as he wrapped the reins around one gloved hand, "very much, about you, and your kin."

"So your absence proved," she snapped, striving

to hide the trembling that ransacked her limbs beneath her dress and cloak. "At first we thought you dead, or thought you had made off with my father's cargo that night. Then we heard you were in Edinburgh, even in prison for a bit. I thought a cell was just the place for you." She glared at him.

"And Miss Colvin apparently wishes I had stayed there," he drawled. "I did not expect much of a welcome upon my return. And I did not even know it was you I was chasing at first. Any cart traveling that fast over the moors at night and avoiding the hail of an excise officer must be stopped."

"Excise officer!" In the shock of seeing him again, she had forgotten that he had identified himself as a preventive man. She stared at him, uncomprehending. "You? How—"

"I lately accepted the commission as Chief Customs and excise officer for this part of the Solway coast."

She shook her head in disbelief, and glanced at the men about to join them. "And they are—"

"Another excise officer and a couple of dragoons. We were patrolling this evening, following a group of men and horses—too many for the four of us to stop, though I'd like to know their intentions. Likely they're smugglers," he said mildly. "Would you happen to know, Miss Colvin?"

"If you are asking if they are my kinsmen, I

canna say. Smugglers travel openly here—the larger the group, the better, for no one dares stop them. As you will recall, Sir Simon.''

"Aye. While we were out, we saw you racing for the coast. There's an odd sight, I said to myself—a lass alone on a moonlit night, with smugglers out and about.''

"And did you say to yourself, aha, here's my chance to make the apology I owe that lassie?'' she asked in a spicy tone.

"I'll save that for another time,'' he answered quietly.

She sat forward. "You asked after my kinsmen. Well, my father…is in the Tolbooth at Whithorn, and—'' Suddenly her throat tightened. "They mean to hang him for horse thievery.''

"I know, Jenny. I saw Jock earlier today.'' His voice, low and mellow and suddenly very kind, sent shivers through her.

She did not want to melt for this man, as she had done before. She wanted to be angry with him, though she fought against the impulse to throw her arms around him and feel his arms close secure and loving about her. Gazing at him for a moment, she allowed herself to be deeply glad that he was safe.

But she knew that he no longer loved her, although he had once persuaded her that he did. She had spent four years convincing herself that she did not love him.

Years ago, he had been her father's protégé, gradually becoming her friend and her hero—brave, daring, quick-witted and so charming and compelling that her heart had melted at his smile, at his slightest touch. When she had sneaked along on midnight smuggling ventures against her father's will, Simon ensured that she was safe, even let her take part. They had spent more and more time together, until he knew all her dreams and had shared his own. And when he had begun to learn her body, as well, and she had explored his, she had reveled in discovering passion with him. On that last evening, she had very nearly given herself to him completely.

Thank the Lord she had not. One night, after promising her that he loved her, he had disappeared, taking her father's cargo with him. His betrayal had hurt all of them deeply, and Jenny had thought she might never recover.

Now she could not allow him to undermine her hard-won strength. She lifted her chin. "I hope you made your peace with Da when you saw him. He has little time left."

"I tried, though he is…well, still perturbed with me. I think it will not be easy to make peace with you, either."

"We thought you lost, stolen or dead, Simon Lockhart! We endured a hell of worry for you. Then we heard you were living a fine life—and never a word to us.''

"I did send word.''

"Aye? The postal coach comes from Edinburgh every week,'' she pointed out.

"I—Jenny, we've no time for this now,'' he said abruptly, as the three other riders cantered toward them, reining in their horses. Jenny turned.

"What's this? Ah, Miss Colvin, good evening!'' The leader tipped his wide black hat politely. "Riding about, are you? We'll need to see what you have there, Miss.''

"Mr. Bryson,'' she said stiffly. Donald Bryson had been accepting bribes of whisky and other goods from Jock Colvin for years. Jock had always thought him unsavory and ineffectual, although not wholly bad, as some of his kind could be.

"What's in the cart, Miss?'' Bryson asked. He gestured toward the wooden crates.

"Empty boxes. You're welcome to look. We use them to pack whisky in flasks—legitimate whisky that we produce at Glendarroch from our licensed still,'' she added pointedly, glancing at Simon. "We make less than five hundred gallons, for the use of our own kinfolk.''

"Ah.'' Simon nodded. "Under five hundred—small enough that you need not pay duties on the whisky.''

She nodded. "So none of you have any business with me."

"Dinna believe her, Sir Simon," Bryson said. "Glendarroch whisky is the finest in southwestern Scotland—some say the whole of Scotland. Jock's got stills hidden everywhere in that glen."

"Does he?" Simon asked, managing to sound surprised. Jenny shot him a little glare. He knew well enough that her father had stills tucked away in the hillsides and forest groves near Glendarroch, where her family had lived for generations.

"Aye, we just canna find 'em. His spirits are in great demand in the south. He makes a pretty living smuggling it out. I'll wager this lassie knows more than she will let on."

"I see," Simon murmured. He looked bemused.

She leaned closer to him. "Does Bryson know about you?" she asked quietly.

"Aye, some of it. The customs office regards my background as an asset, now that I've...reformed," he answered.

"Jock Colvin is a rogue and a thief, and in prison for it. He'll hang, too," Bryson said. "Sir, she must be searched." He dismounted. "The women in this area are notoriously clever helpmates to their men-folk. They smuggle whisky in places, well, that are not proper for gentlemen to search. But excise of-ficers must sometimes see to it. Come down, lassie.'' Bryson reached toward her. Jenny stiffened, leaning away from him.

"Mr. Bryson,'' Simon barked, dismounting. "I'm the chief officer here. If Miss Colvin must be searched—''

"Oh, ho, you'll do it?'' Bryson grinned at him. "Not so green at this as I thought.'' He grinned at Jenny. "It's the law, lassie, that you must submit to a search if we think it necessary. Come down, my bonny, and show us what you've hidden under your skirts.'' He grabbed her around the waist.

"I said I would take care of this, sir.'' Simon clapped his hand hard on Bryson's shoulder and moved him aside abruptly. Reaching up to take Jenny by the waist, Simon swept her neatly to the ground before she could draw breath to protest. "My girl, if I don't search you,'' Simon murmured, "Mr. Bryson is eager to show me how it's done. And I would hate to have to pummel a king's man on my very first night as excise officer,'' he added blandly.

Heart pounding, she nodded, aware that Bryson stood watching, his mouth hanging open, eyes intent. The dragoons sat passively on their horses, but their eyes were alive as well.

Taking her by the shoulders, Simon turned her so that her back was to the other men. The yardage of her long hooded cloak, tied at the throat, shielded her from the men's leering glances.

But nothing would shield her from Simon Lockhart.

She stood motionless as he slipped his hands around her waist, skimming there, then tracing his fingers over her back, then her upper arms and gathered bodice. His touch was so featherlight that she scarcely felt it, yet tingles rushed through her, threatening to buckle her knees. Blushing, furious, she squeezed her eyes shut and stood in proud, motionless silence.

Far better that Simon Lockhart do this than Bryson, she thought. Although she had never been searched before, she knew women who had. Few had fared well in the officers' keeping.

Simon dropped to one knee and slipped his hands under her skirt. She felt his fingers close around her left ankle, then slide upward over her drawers. His touch was warm, gentle, scarcely there, yet her heart leaped as he neared the top of her thigh. Moving his hands to the other leg, he skimmed downward.

She kept her eyes closed, wishing he would stop—and remembering the pleasures she had once known under his hands. Feeling a sharp and poignant longing, she fisted her hands, and knew that her cheeks were hot and blazing.

"Jeannie Simpson was a Highland widow," Simon said, as he traced his palms over her hips, ruffling the fabric of her chemise, "who carried whisky in bladderskins strung under her skirt. She transported the stuff every day, totalling gallons each month, riding past the excise man and greeting him as she went. She made a handsome income and kept her family nicely.''

"I am not a widow with a family to support," she replied. "If I was, you can be sure I would have whisky bladders hanging under my skirt and flasks tucked in my bodice, and the de'il take the excise man."

"I do not doubt it," he murmured. His hands rounded over her behind, ran along the backs of her thighs. She took rapid little breaths. His touch still held magic for her, and she hated that fact. She wanted to shove him away as much as she wanted to feel his arms around her again, in another setting, in another mood. But that dream was not possible anymore.

He withdrew his hands, straightened her skirt hem and stood. She lifted a hand to slap him, but he caught it deftly in his and lowered it, concealing their joined hands in the folds of her cloak. "She's carrying nothing," he told Bryson. "She's free to go."

He guided her toward her cart and assisted her into the seat. All the while, her heart slammed, and she fought both her rising temper and the profound befuddlement brought on by his touch.

Simon looked up at her. ''I apologize for the search,'' he murmured.

''Sir, that is the least of your offenses with me,'' she said, and snapped the reins.

CHAPTER TWO

"HEY," BRYSON CALLED. "That lass is not headed home!"

"So I see," Simon answered, already setting his foot into the stirrup to vault into his saddle. Taking the reins, he turned the black stallion's head. "I'll correct her direction. I want her out of the area tonight—something is afoot this evening."

"Aye, those men we saw leading packhorses must be moving contraband somewhere. Bold rascals, to ignore a full moon. They dinna care if they're seen."

"We'll need more men if we're to do anything about it," Simon said. "Ride back to Whithorn and appeal to the sheriff—I believe he's still at the Tolbooth—for dragoons and rangers."

"We can summon no more than ten or a dozen," Bryson grumbled. "The shortage of revenue men is a problem here."

"Do what you can." Simon glanced toward the sky. "Those smugglers have something planned, and I mean to know what it is."

"Aye, then. We'll come back to the lookout point near the Kelpie's Cave. Do ye know it?"

"I do," Simon said, and turned the stallion's head to ride after Jenny, while Bryson and the dragoons headed northeast.

The girl proved easier to catch this time, for her cart was proceeding at a more sedate pace. When Simon pulled up alongside once again, she glanced at him in surprise, then scowled.

"Have you nothing better to do, Sir Simon?"

"Miss Colvin, Glendarroch is to the north. You're heading south," he said pleasantly.

"It's none of your concern where I'm going."

"If you're angry about the search, I don't blame you. But Bryson was twitching to see what you keep under your skirts."

"Then I suppose I should thank you for doing the gentlemanly thing," she snapped, looking ahead as she drove the cart.

"You're welcome. Now tell me where you're going and why."

"I'm going about my own business and you can go about yours."

"I *am* going about mine," he pointed out.

"Surely you have real brigands to catch. You needna prance after me all night."

"Ah, Miss Colvin. Even more full of charm than I remember." He reached out and took Sweetheart's bridle again, slowing the cart and horse.

While Jenny stared at him, he dismounted, tied his horse's lead to the back of the cart, and climbed inside to sit on the bench beside her. He took the reins from her hands.

"What is it you want?" she asked irritably.

"To escort you safely home. There are naughty men about in the night."

"And you're one of them. Hey, stop that—I willna go home," she protested, as he snapped the reins to turn the bay's head north for the hills that edged the Solway plains.

"I might be persuaded to escort you wherever you're going, if you'll tell me your business."

"I doubt it." She folded her arms.

"Trust me," he said, leaning a shoulder toward her.

She flashed him a fuming glance in silence.

"Aye, well. You have a right to be perturbed with me."

"I do. The way you left was…villainous." She lifted her chin and looked away.

Simon glanced at her. In the moon's pale glow, he saw deep hurt glimmer in her eyes, and he felt the blow of it in his own heart. Perhaps it was only what he deserved, but he could see that his intention of making amends would be a long road.

He watched her almost hungrily in the blue-gray light. God, how he had missed her, he thought. She took his breath with her simple yet uncommon beauty. Delicately balanced features, eyes of a keen and lovely blue, the gleaming sweep of dark brown hair spilling over her shoulder in a single loose braid matched the memories he had kept close. She had changed only a little, leaner in the face, her form lush perfection. His quick search of her body earlier had proven that—and had nearly undone him.

Being with her nearly undermined the restraint and reserve he strived to keep about himself. For years, he had loved her and dreamed of her, and now he saw that her beauty and spirit had blossomed. The earnestness and honest intelligence he loved in her, the verve and strength he had always admired were still there. Her pride and temper still sparked, too.

In the past, he had also known her compassion and gentleness, and he had the knack of making her laugh when she was overly serious. But he would be hard pressed to coax a smile or a kind word from her tonight, he knew.

All he wanted, suddenly, was to see her smile again. Aware of the hurt he had dealt her, and knowing she was heartbroken and distressed over her father's situation, he sighed.

"Jenny," he said. "I did not mean for it to happen quite as it did. I had my reasons, but I can't explain now, out here, with rascals about in the night."

"I dinna want your explanation. I want—" She tossed her hands as if she had not yet decided.

"I think you want to be angry with me."

"Aye, for now. And then I want to forget you."

"I have not forgotten you."

She was silent for a moment. "Why did you come back, Simon?"

"To gauge the whisky and count the copper coils in the hills, of course," he said lightly. "To patrol the hills and cliffs at night, and stop rogues and smugglers from making tracks through the laws of king and Crown." *And to find the friends and the winsome lass I lost,* he added to himself.

"You used to make tracks through the king's laws yourself, and gladly."

He shrugged. "I've reformed."

"So have I," she said. "I'm no longer a foolish wee lass eager to believe in bold, bonny Simon Lockhart."

"I cannot blame you for that."

"Then we agree on something." She looked away, her gaze scanning the hills, black silhouettes against the purpling sky, with the luminous moon shining above a veil of clouds.

"Will you be collecting the copper coils wherever you can find them, to disable the stills?" she asked.

"Aye, some," he said. "I will have rangers to assist me."

"I expect you'll offer to pay five pounds per coil, so that the locals will turn them in. Bryson and the other excise officer have done that here."

"Aye, the revenue board wants that. Though I suspect that every man with a worn-out coil turns his own in, collects the fee, buys a new coil with the money and moves his still for good measure." He lifted a brow.

"I have no idea," she said, while Simon chuckled.

"Jane Colvin," he said, using her christened name with mock sternness, "be honest, now. How many coils has Jock turned in?"

"Several every year from his own stills, which you will never find, for we willna cooperate with a gauger who is a traitor to us," she said. "Is that honest enough for you?"

"Painfully," he replied.

"Why did you leave without a word, without warning?"

"I thought you did not want to know why."

"I'm just curious."

"I'll tell you, but…not yet." *I left because I loved you that much, Jenny Colvin, and wanted to protect you,* he thought to himself. *And because I wanted to make a better life than smuggling for both of us.* But now he must make his way carefully into her heart again. Love had sent him away, and so had pride. Though the love had sustained him, he battled the pride still.

"Will you be there?" she asked softly.

"Be where?" He glanced at her.

"When my father—when they—the gallows are ready for tomorrow morning."

"I will be there," he said. "I owe Jock that much. And you."

She lowered her head in silence.

"I'm sorry, Jenny," he said softly. *Sorry for Jock and sorry for all my secrets.*

"'Tis wrong to hang a good man, even if he does a bit of free trading now and then. And he's no horse thief."

"Jock told me the same. The sheriff says differently. What the devil—" He pulled up on the reins, slowing the cart as he looked ahead.

A group of men rode toward them, ten or twelve in all, leading horses. Wondering if they were part of the group he had seen earlier, Simon put a hand beneath his coat to touch the polished wood-and-steel grip of his pistol.

"Those are my kinsmen," Jenny said.

"Ah, Jock Colvin's own. The Royal—what is it they call themselves?"

"The Royal Defiance Bladder Band," she said. "They were angry with the king's laws at the time they made that up."

"And fou," he drawled.

"Very fou," she agreed, and when he chuckled, she did, too. The sound warmed his heart. "They're rather fond of Glendarroch whisky," she went on. "After all, 'tis the best in Solway, and perhaps all Scotland."

"All four hundred ninety-nine gallons of it," he drawled.

"Tax-free," she agreed blithely. Simon rolled his eyes.

The man in the lead waved. "Jenny Colvin!"

"Uncle Felix!" she called. Simon halted the cart as the men came nearer.

"Jenny, what's this? Ye shouldna be about in the moonlight. And what are ye doing wi' my niece, sir?" Felix growled. He stepped forward, a large man with a craggy face and a dark beard.

Simon nodded. "Felix Colvin, greetings to you."

"Lockhart! You're back!" Felix grinned. "Alive, and returned to us! A miracle!" He turned to his kinsmen, cousins all, Simon knew, recognizing many of them. "Lockhart o' Lockhart has come back at last!" Two or three smiled and greeted him, while the others frowned, unwelcoming and suspicious.

"Hey, lads," Simon said, though the cool reception of some of his former comrades bothered him more than he cared to show. Well, he told himself, it was part of the price he must pay to come back to Glendarroch and the Solway shores again.

"Lass, take the cart home," Felix said. "Simon, ye'll come wi' us, and tell us where ye've been, and join us this evening—"

"Hush, Felix," Jenny warned.

"—we're off for a wee bit o' sport, as it were," Felix continued.

"A ship coming along the coast?" Simon asked.

"Hush it, Felix!" Jenny said, more loudly.

"Aye, a lugger from the Isle o' Man, keen to trade French goods for fine Scottish whisky—and we plan to—"

"He's an excise man!" Jenny blurted.

"Nahhh," Felix said. "Simon? Nah."

"Actually, I am," Simon agreed. "Chief Customs and excise officer, newly appointed to my commission."

"What?" Felix set his hand warily on a hidden dirk.

"He's not looking to arrest you," Jenny said. "But do not be quick to share secrets with him."

"Aye," Felix said grimly.

Simon frowned. "If there's a ship expected this evening, I'd like to know about it."

"Ship?" Felix asked. "Who said aught about a ship?"

"Then what fine sport are you lads up to?" Simon asked.

"We're off to visit wi' Jock," Felix said. "'Tis all."

"Bringing him a hot toddy and a word of comfort, are you?"

"Sure," Felix agreed. He glowered at Simon. "I want to know how ye became a gauger, when we tutored ye in the free trade. And I want to know what happened that night ye disappeared wi' Jock's cargo. That was a blow to all of us." He glanced at Jenny.

"Circumstances," Simon said. "One day I'll explain."

"I might want to hear it," Felix said, "or not. 'Twill depend on what sort o' gauger ye prove to be. Jenny—take the cart back to Glendarroch and stay there. Simon, if that's yer horse tied there, I recommend ye ride out. Sir," he added, resting a hand on his dirk.

"I'll see Miss Colvin back to Glendarroch," Simon answered.

"I can see myself home," Jenny said.

"There's rogues about," Felix said. "Ye'll go with Simon."

"But Felix," she murmured, "I have something else to do."

Felix nodded, and a spark of awareness seemed to pass between uncle and niece. Simon was unsurprised that neither of them offered to enlighten the preventive officer.

Simon lifted the reins of the cart, about to bid Felix farewell, when a lanky youth ran toward them, having dismounted while they spoke. Simon recognized him as Felix's youngest lad and Jenny's cousin, nearly grown to manhood. He approached the wagon, nodded shyly to Simon, and looked up at Jenny.

"Nicky, what is it?" she asked.

"Jenny, I wanted to tell you—" Nicky leaned toward her. "Walter and I saw the Beauty tonight! We came back and told Da, and he said none of us were to go near the cliffs tonight."

"The Beauty!" Jenny looked at her uncle. "What did you see?"

"It was pale as the moon, running along the cliffs near the beach, just as high tide was coming in," Nicky said. "I've never seen such a sight. A bonny horse, perfectly white—it near glowed with fairy magic. It reared up its forelegs, then galloped away and disappeared. Walter ran," Nicky added. "But I stayed to watch. It galloped behind some rocks, and I saw it no more."

"Nicky, that's amazing," Jenny said. "Are you sure?"

"Och, aye. A fine sight, but a bad omen."

"The Beauty?" Simon asked. "That old legend?"

Jenny turned to him. "Do you remember the tale of the Beauty? A kelpie sort of creature, a white horse that sometimes appears out of the sea on the night of a full moon."

"Aye, generally before some catastrophe strikes. But it's not seen often, as I recall."

"Not often," Felix agreed. "But it appears now and again along our part of the Solway coast, and has for centuries. I've never seen it myself. 'Tis a poor omen indeed." He glanced toward the full moon, nesting briefly in some high dark clouds. "Some poor soul will meet his fate this night. And it's ill timing, too, what with the—well." He stopped and glanced at Simon.

"I saw a large group of men traveling earlier this evening, north of here," Simon said. "About thirty men and twice as many horses, many of them sturdy pack animals with panniers on their backs. Free traders, certainly, to walk out so boldly at night. Were you lads with them?"

"Them? Och, nay." Felix shook his head. "That'll be Cap'n MacSorley's band. We worked beside them years back, when you were still wi' us, Simon Lockhart—Sir Simon."

"So I recall," Simon murmured. Angus MacSorley was of an age with Jock and Felix, and Simon had been part of many smuggling raids involving the three smugglers and their men.

"MacSorley and his lot are more pirates than free traders these days. Jock and me have naught to do wi' that band now." Felix fixed Simon with a dark stare. "Do ye wonder if MacSorley had a hand in Jock's plight? I'd say 'tis so."

"Have you proof?" Simon asked.

"Not a whit, but I feel it in my bones. If ye're the new preventive man here, then ye should follow that lot. They'll keep ye and yer rangers busy enough."

"Too busy to follow you?"

Felix grinned. "Could be. But I'm as sincere as my mother's heart about this. Ye follow the Cap'n, and ye'll find a man who hates Jock Colvin and wants the whisky trade to himself."

Simon nodded, considering. He glanced at Jenny. "If there's anything to this, I intend to find out," he said.

"Please," she said, her plaintive tone surprising him.

"Ye'll find them heading for the coast this night, I'd guess," Felix said. "Should ye and yer rangers and dragoons stop them before they make their trades tonight—some of us would appreciate it."

"Trading under a full moon?" Simon asked.

"Sometimes, though we dinna prefer it," Felix answered. "If 'twere us, we'd hope ye'd look the other way. But them...well."

Simon handed Jenny the reins. "Go back to Glendarroch, Miss Colvin. I'll see you there later. Nicky lad," he said, addressing the young man. "See that your cousin gets home." He climbed out of the cart, while Nicky clambered inside.

Untying his horse's lead, Simon leaped into the

saddle and turned the black stallion to head for the cliffs and the coast. But something made him glance over his shoulder.

Wide-eyed and lovely in the pale moonlight, Jenny watched him. She looked fragile somehow, vulnerable. He felt troubled, realizing that he was leaving her again without a word.

He leaned down. "I'll be back. I promise," he told her. While she watched him in silence, he rode off.

CHAPTER THREE

ONCE SHE HAD PULLED the cart into a clearing edged by gorse and hawthorn trees, Jenny unbuckled Sweetheart's harness. She tethered the mare to a thorn branch not far from a narrow, fast-running burn that cut through the moor. Taking the lantern from the iron hook on the cart, she turned the wick down to a glow and lowered the punched-tin shutter.

Having no intention of going home, she had asked Nicky to join his father's group again, which the boy was glad to do. Then she had reminded her uncle that Jock had given her a task that night. Aware of this, Felix had agreed, waving her on her way after promising to meet her by the cliffs later to assist her.

Glancing around, she saw no one else as she ran across an open expanse of turf. The moonlight was cool and eerie, and the sea surged loudly in and out of the estuary. Water foamed over the beach and the dark rocks that littered the sand, and gulls flocked overhead, crying out as Jenny neared the cliff edge.

All her life, she had avoided these particular cliffs and caves. Legend claimed that the honey-comb of caves extended for miles beneath the moorland, and that they were haunted by other-worldly creatures. She remembered stories from childhood of the beautiful but terrifying sea kelpies that took the form of horses, as well as tales of mischievous fairies and even the ghost of a lost piper.

Logic told Jenny that the caves were dangerous enough without supernatural help by virtue of the free traders who used them as smuggling caves. While Jock Colvin and his band did not stash their cargo in these caves—the fast-rising tides were too unpredictable—over the years many others had braved the tales and tides to leave smuggled goods in the Kelpie's Cave.

Remembering Nicky's report of seeing the Beauty, the legendary white horse of the Solway shores, Jenny felt anxious for a moment. But she dismissed it as fancy—even she had seen, now and again, the illusion of white horses in the high, foamy waves that sometimes rushed to shore.

The caves in these cliffs were her goal, and she would go forward despite trepidation. She had promised her father to look here for what had been taken from him.

Fifty casks of Glendarroch's finest whisky had been stolen out of Jock's own storage caves farther along the coast. The casks would be worth a fortune in the south, where Glendarroch whisky was in high demand. Suspecting MacSorley had taken them, Jock had entrusted his daughter to discover the truth.

MacSorley's band had long frequented the area near these caves, so Jenny had agreed to go inside to see if Glendarroch casks were stored in the sea caves. If she found them, she was to alert her kinsmen, who would retrieve them and exact revenge.

Her father had cautioned her to go into the caves before the tide got too high, and while MacSorley and his men were occupied elsewhere. Jenny had known that MacSorley and his smugglers were still out on the moor, but Simon Lockhart's arrival had been a shock—and had delayed her.

Whoever had taken Jock's store of whisky might have also accused him of stealing the magistrate's horse, thereby neatly eliminating Jock from the local free trade. Her father had sworn that if he must die, he could only go in peace if his veritable fortune in stockpiled whisky was recovered.

Approaching the cliff edge, Jenny glanced around, relieved to see no one else about. As she descended a rough incline toward the beach, she was grateful for the moon's clarity, which lit her way toward the dark cave mouth.

Underfoot, the rocks were wet and slippery, and she made her way carefully. Moonlight rippled on the sea, and lacy breakers rushed toward the shore as the tide swirled into the broad, low arch of the sea cave's entrance.

The water level was already too high for her to simply walk inside, so she made her way across the field of rocks and stones at the base of the cliff, and finally stepped into the cave mouth at the nearest edge of the entrance.

The sea roared as it filled the great, dark cavity of the cave, and moonlight gleamed on the swirling water. Overhead, the ceiling soared into a black expanse, and the curved rock walls glittered back in the moonlight.

A crescent-shaped rim provided a natural walkway, and she followed it deeper into the cave. Waves slopped over the shelf as she walked, and she held up the hems of her dress and cloak with one hand, while carrying the lantern in the other.

Tracing a hand along the damp, rough curvature of the rock, she moved cautiously. An explosion of sound and sudden movement overhead startled her so much that she cried out and flattened her back against the wall.

Birds poured out of the upper recesses of the cave, and she watched them soar away, moonlight silvering their wings—hundreds of rock doves, she realized, had been disturbed by her presence. They commonly nested in the caves and cliffs along the shore, but she had not heard their telltale cooing and rustling over the sounds of the incoming tide.

Drawing a shaky breath, she continued. The cave was enormous, its ceiling an inverted bowl over a wide pool, the entrance a low arch. Kelp and bladderwrack draped portions of the rock and floated on the surface of the water. A broken wooden crate floated past near her feet.

She stopped, uncertain where to look first. She had not expected to find cargo neatly stacked just inside, but she had hoped to see some stored goods upon entering.

As she drew out of the blue glow of moonlight, the darkness became inky. Jenny lifted the lantern's window a little and turned the wick higher, casting a golden bloom over the walls.

The creases and crevices in the rock walls took on new dimension. The cave was permeated with openings and passages into other recesses that looked like more caverns. Any of those spaces might be used for storage.

If she kept a cautious foot and a careful eye, as her father had advised her, she could locate his stolen whisky and make her way out of this place before anyone returned.

As she neared the blackness at the back of the cave, a shrill scream came from some shadowy recess. Jenny stifled a gasp and shivers rose along her neck and arms. The sound had not been the steady roar of the sea, nor the harmless chorus of rock doves.

The scream came again, reedy and eerie, while Jenny stood in the darkness, chilled to her soul.

HEARING DISTANT hoofbeats and the dense jangling that signalled the movement of many horses, Simon slowed his own mount and waited. Within a minute or so, a group of men and horses topped a hillock and came across the broad swath of moonlit moorland.

Thirty or more riders, each man leading a packhorse, traveled bold as brass in the clear light of the full moon. No harnesses were muffled, no lantern shuttered, no voice softened as they rode toward the cliffs that led down to a secluded beach and caves that were known smuggling haunts.

Free traders commonly moved through the countryside in groups as large as a hundred men and twice as many horses, Simon knew—he had done so himself, years past. The larger the band, the less likely that customs officers would attempt to stop them or take custody of their goods.

Although alone, he decided to introduce himself as the new excise officer. A group this large had no reason to harm a single officer who presented no threat. Guiding his horse forward, he held up a hand and waited. He had a primed pistol tucked in his belt under his coat, but he made no move toward it.

They stopped gradually, and then the leader urged his horse forward a few steps. He was a large man, burly through chest and shoulders, his hair and beard reddish even in the moonlight. Simon recognized him easily.

"Customs and excise," Simon announced. "Greetings, Captain MacSorley. I am Sir Simon Lockhart. Perhaps you remember me."

"Lockhart o' Lockhart?" MacSorley stepped his horse forward again, and grinned. He carried a long club across his saddle pommel. Smugglers with any sense never carried pistols—to do so was tantamount to rebellion against the government. "I do remember ye, lad—but not as a gauger."

"I'm now the resident excise officer for this part of the Solway shores. You'd best tell me your business here, Captain. I see those packhorses have full panniers."

"Och, there's no shame in a bit o' the free trade, as ye no doubt recall." MacSorley came closer on his horse, hands calm on the reins, no obvious threat in his manner. Behind him, his men waited and watched. "Years ye've been gone sir, and I see what brings ye back. Paid work, a secure position wi' some respect…and a fine chance to work both sides, eh?"

"That may be," Simon said cautiously.

"Clever lad to get the best of both. Though the pay for excise work is poor."

"It can be profitable," Simon said. "A fee is paid per each cask confiscated."

"But 'tisna so easy to get enough cargo to make good cash. Ye know well how it works here—if I dinna see ye, then ye dinna see me. A man can make a good living along these shores if he plays his hand carefully. There's a fair bit o' traffic." Angus smiled, and watched Simon closely.

"Aye, so I'm aware. Pot-still whisky is regularly brought south, and hides, as well, and there's trade in rum and brandy, silks and laces. There's wrecking, too, which I expect is still sometimes done under cover of darkness," Simon said dispassionately. "Not under bright moonlight like this."

"True, there's plenty to keep men busy of a night. And not enough king's men to keep up with it all, eh?" Angus grinned.

"We may be few, but we're a curious and persistent lot."

"Most gaugers play blind when it suits," Angus said.

"I see clearly when I want to," Simon said. "What are you all about on such a fine moonlit evening, Captain?"

"Och, just carrying a bit o' the finest whisky in the land to those that have the craving for it," Angus said boldly. With over thirty men facing one officer, Simon thought, MacSorley could afford to be bold—for now.

"Jock Colvin makes a fair whisky, too, as I recall."

"Glendarroch brew is fine stuff, I give him credit for it. But his stills are small, and he doesna produce as much as some do. Fussy about it, him and his lassie. They horde it too long. Aged whisky is good but doesna turn a profit for years. Besides, Jock's been arrested—as ye must know, being a preventive man."

"No doubt his arrest was good news for MacSorley's lads."

"Well, I'm sorry for him, and surprised to hear he resorted to horse snatching. But the magistrate's animals are fine ones, and valuable, and Jock's always been a bit of a daftie."

"Though never a thief," Simon answered, watching MacSorley.

"Ye never know what makes a man change. Look at ye, now."

Simon inclined his head in acknowledgement. With no proof and no protection, he could hardly accuse the man of committing the crime himself. But he resolved to look into it further. "So you're moving some whisky about? Taking it down to meet a ship?"

MacSorley grinned. "Could be, or could be we're taking it by land to Carlisle and over the border. Or we may be taking it back home to drink it all ourselves. Smugglers dinna care to move about much under a full moon.''

"Of course. I did hear a ship might be expected tonight.''

"I've heard none of that. Even so, what could one fresh new gauger do about it?''

Simon smiled. "Little enough.''

"Do ye have a taste for good whisky yerself, Lockhart?'' MacSorley turned and beckoned one of his men forward. The man dismounted, pulled a tin flask out of a pannier basket strapped to a horse, and came forward to hand it to MacSorley.

Angus offered the flask to Simon. "This is verra fine stuff. And ye might find a cask o' this stuff on yer doorstep…let's say at the full of every moon.'' He glanced upward. "There'll be a cask delivered wherever ye like tonight. To honor old friendship, o' course.''

Simon took the round flask, turning its weight in his hand. Tin, cheaply made and well-used by its dents and scratches—just the sort of vessel that smugglers used to transport whisky in quantity. He glanced at MacSorley. "And in return?''

"Ye'll be unobservant as the former excise officer. We had a fair agreement with that lad.''

"The man was shot while riding over the moor one afternoon.''

Angus shrugged. "We had naught to do with it. He let us alone, so we let him alone. It was Jock Colvin's lads—the Royal Defiance Bladder Band, they call themselves. Fools and ruffians, those lads, but dinna let their jovial ways convince ye that they're harmless."

"Captain MacSorley, I can look the other way if you and your lads smuggle a few gallons to pad your purses. The king's laws are harsh, and Scotsmen must find ways to make do." He leaned forward, the flask in one hand. "But should you harm innocent citizens or take what does not belong to you or betray good men for your own ends...I will see you then, by God, and I will pursue you." He straightened. "Fair warning, Captain."

Angus narrowed his eyes. "Perhaps one keg of whisky a month is not enough."

"More than enough. Too much, in fact." Simon did not care much for whisky—or for bribes.

"I heard an interesting rumor some time ago, Lockhart."

"What was that?" Simon asked warily.

"A fellow I met at a market fair mentioned that Lockhart o' Lockhart was a guest in the Edinburgh dungeons. Held for smuggling offenses, he said."

"I was held...for a while."

"Ah. I remember, years ago, that ye had some falling out with Jock Colvin. Did ye come back to repair that rift?"

"I returned because this commission was assigned to me. And some rifts...are not easily repaired."

"Well, if ye decide to go back to yer rapscallion ways, ye canna rejoin Jock's band so quick. He still has a grudge against ye. However, we might take ye...did we find ye trustworthy."

"I'll remember that. For now, Captain, I trust you and your lads to go home from here, put away whatever you've got in those packs, and take quietly to your beds for the night."

"And who will see that done? The excise man?" He laughed.

Simon tossed the flask quickly through the air, so that MacSorley barely caught it. "I cannot accept gifts while acting as an officer of the king. But your generosity is appreciated."

MacSorley narrowed his eyes, shoving the flask into the pocket of his coat. "Ye'll regret that, sir."

"Good evening." Simon turned his horse and rode off, leaving MacSorley staring after him. He could feel the bore of the man's eyes and dark thoughts as he rode over a hillock on the moor.

Glancing about, he saw no one else, including Felix Colvin and his kinsmen, or Jenny with her horse cart. He hoped she had indeed headed home. There were far too many rogues about, despite the bright moon, and he did not want her on the moorland.

Nearing the cliffs, glancing about, he decided to wait by the cliffside to watch the sea for ships, and the moor for smugglers. Excise men often set themselves up for waits of several hours, and he would be no exception. Besides, he had told Bryson to bring dragoons back to the area of the cliffs, and the fellow could be back within the hour.

Dismounting, he led the black stallion toward a dense stand of hawthorn trees and gorse bushes, surrounding a large clearing. The place had long been used as a hideaway by smugglers.

As he led the horse inside the screen of trees, he noticed another horse already there—a bay mare. Nearby was a small pony cart, concealed by straw and dry branches.

Jenny. He almost swore aloud. Tying his horse beside hers, he turned and went toward the cliffs. Where had she gone, and what sort of urgent business did she have here, alone?

She must be doing her father's work for him, while Jock sat in prison. Cursing Jock for sending his daughter out alone on a dangerous task, Simon made his way along an outcrop of boulders that overlooked the sea and the beach below.

The moon was a bright silver coin in the sky, its light pouring over surging tides, the sands along the shore, and the black creased rocks that formed the high cliffs.

Leaning his elbows on one of the boulders, Simon took a spyglass from his pocket, opened it, and looked through it.

He could see the silvery sparkling waves, and far out, the black reef where wrecks sometimes occurred. Water frothed on the surface of the sea, delicate as lace. Above, in the purple dusk, the moon's pale, mottled surface filled, for an instant, the circular window of the spyglass.

He might as well settle in for a long wait, he told himself. His mission for the customs and excise board involved the pursuit and capture of the smugglers who were running high quality whisky over the Scottish border and down along the coast. That in itself was not so unusual, but these particular rogues had a habit of killing men who balked at their high prices. And the whisky itself was of a very fine quality, mostly originating from Glendarroch.

Learning that in Edinburgh, he had volunteered for this post. If Jock Colvin and his men had resorted to the roughest means of making their living, then Simon wanted to be involved in their pursuit and capture. If they were innocent of those practices, he wanted to be involved in the proof of it.

And he had wanted to see Jenny again.

Training the glass along the shoreline, he watched the tides sweep toward the beach, creaming over sand, gushing in and out of coves and the sea caves that sprinkled the coast. He saw no one at all—and certainly did not see a slim young woman intent on some foolhardy mission.

Where the devil had she got to? Surely not into the caves below, he thought—but every instinct, and the rising hairs on the back of his neck, said that she had done just that.

He slipped the **spyglass** into his pocket and straightened. W**alking along the** upper cliff edge, breeze blowing through his hair, he scanned the shore.

Then, behind him, he heard the muffled sound of horses. Turning, he hunkered down and moved toward the stand of trees where his horse and Jenny's were hidden.

A sudden sound popped nearby, and he felt a tug on his arm, a sting like that of a bee. Looking down, he saw his torn coatsleeve, and with an odd, detached sense, realized that he had been shot.

Another pistol shot rang out, and Simon dropped to the ground, rolling as he landed. Strangely, the ground gave way beneath him, and he hit something hard, then tumbled down farther into blackness.

CHAPTER FOUR

JENNY STOOD TREMBLING in the darkness, but the eerie shrieking did not come again. She glanced toward the wide mouth of the cave, where the surging sea tide, rippled with froth and moonlight, was already higher. For a moment, she longed to run back toward the entrance and leave this frightening place.

The cave was haunted, they said, by the ghost of a long-ago piper who had lost his way, following the fairies deep into the maze of the caverns and tunnels beneath the cliffs. Haunted, as well, by the legendary sea kelpie that took the form of a graceful white horse, luring souls to their deaths in the water.

But she could not turn back. Her father had sent her here, and this might be the last favor she could ever do for him.

Drawing a breath, she forced herself to move onward. A narrow pass cut through the rock, and she followed it. The lantern's glow revealed the brown and rusty variations in the walls, and the stone felt damp and rough beneath her fingers.

Beyond the pool of lantern light, the blackness and silence seemed complete. The sea shushed in the main chamber behind her, the sound fading as she walked. Her footsteps crunched over gritty sand and broken shells, and her fingers touched slimy seaweed on the walls. So the tide came this far and this high into the caves. Shivering at the thought, she moved on.

Waving the light around, she saw crevices, caves and winding passages, just a portion of the honeycomb of tunnels and chambers beneath the cliffs. She would have to search until she found the caves where the MacSorleys stored their smuggled goods.

Turning down a wide, twisting channel, she noticed a sudden bloom of light, its source hidden. Then she heard men's voices, low and urgent, and she stopped, heart slamming.

Quickly she shut her own lantern and ducked into a nearby crevice, hoping that it was deep enough to conceal her.

Three men came into sight, the leader carrying a lantern with an opened window. He muttered to the others, and they halted near a protrusion in the wall, behind which Jenny stood hidden.

Hardly daring to breathe, she waited.

The men came forward, and she glimpsed them just past the concealing edge of the rock. The man with the lantern had a craggy face, harsh in the light. All three wore dark jackets and wide-brimmed hats, though she saw only the leader clearly.

"There's someone here, I know it," one of them growled. "I heard something."

"Och, it could be the piper making his way through caves. They do say he still roams," another said.

The leader snorted a laugh. "Ha! The full moon and the Beauty about in the night has made cowards out o' you brats."

"But the Beauty keeps us safe, here in these caves—we're glad for that legend. No one comes near here," one of the others said. "But I swear I heard footsteps and saw a light."

"You heard the sea, or the birds escaping. And you saw moonlight or the lantern's reflection."

"Could be our own lads."

"Aye, could be."

They moved again, and Jenny feared that they would soon see her. Turning, she wedged into the crevice, which was deeper than she had first thought.

Crunching footsteps came closer, and the lantern light spilled over the hems of her brown patterned dress and dark gray cloak, though the fabrics blended with the rocky surroundings. She held her breath, standing in the blackness.

Then a strong hand covered her mouth from behind, and a hard grip took her by the waist. She was pulled, hard and fast, into the crevice.

SHE STRUGGLED in his arms, thrashing so much that Simon thought sure she would give them both away. Keeping his hand over her mouth, he lowered his head. "Be still, Jenny, for love of God," he breathed. "It's only me. Hush."

She froze. Then her cheek moved softly against his own as she looked up him, wide-eyed. She quieted, but sank a well-aimed boot heel into his shin.

Grimacing, Simon tightened his grip around her waist, hugging her so that her back pressed against his chest, feeling her tense in his arms. The smugglers were only a few feet away, their lantern light spilling into the crevice. Simon held Jenny utterly still with him.

His left upper arm throbbed where the pistol ball had torn through fabric and flesh, though by some miracle it had not embedded. Every movement made it ache more fiercely. Although he had used his wadded cravat to staunch the bleeding, he felt a trickle down his arm and hand, and he realized that his blood was staining Jenny's cloak. He fisted his hand as he gripped her, though the flexion brought a fresh wave of pain.

He wondered if one of the bastards standing just out of arm's reach had shot him, or if MacSorley or one of his men had followed him to plant a pistol ball. That question was one among many that he meant to have answered before long.

Resting his cheek against Jenny's hair, he inhaled the scent of wildflowers in that silky coolness. Her slender body felt good in his arms, and he sensed the thud of her heart. She flooded his senses, filled his body with desire and gratitude just to be with her again, no matter the circumstances.

Four years ago, he had left his heart in her keeping, like some hidden treasure she did not even know she had. Now she was in his arms, but nothing was as he had imagined it would be. He had planned to take slow, measured steps to apologize, to confess his secrets, to win her love again and to regain the respect of all the Colvins, as well.

But Jock was sentenced to die, Felix and the others distrusted him and Jenny was angry and wary. Instead of careful wooing, Simon found himself hurtling headlong into danger with the very girl he had promised, however unwillingly, to let alone.

More than that, he was obliged as king's officer to discover why she was here among rogues and thieves. He could only hope that Jenny Colvin was not enmeshed with the smuggling criminals he had been sent to find and quell.

Hearing low murmurs and more footsteps, he opened his eyes to see the light pass by the crevice. Long after the steps faded, Simon stood motionless with Jenny, his heart pounding in rhythm with hers. Finally he let out his breath, and she did, too.

She turned. "You!" she snarled, and gave him a shove, so that his left shoulder thumped against rock. A stab of pain went through his arm, but he snatched her wrists, held them between her breasts and his own chest. "What the devil are you doing here?" she demanded. "Following me? Set on searching me again?"

"Should I?" he whispered. "Have you stuffed your drawers with bladderskins since last we met?"

"Insufferable gauger," she muttered, and twisted in his grip. He let her go to spare his wounded left arm the effort. She turned in the narrow space, her body brushing his through layers of clothing, and leaned to peer outside.

He looped his uninjured arm around her to pull her back against him again. "Be careful," he whispered.

"I'm not foolish," she retorted.

"You're here, aren't you?" he whispered. "I would not call that whip-smart, my lass."

"You're here, too, Simon Lockhart," she pointed out.

"Aye, but I'm a rogue. I've the right."

She made a little sound of disgust, then craned her head forward to look cautiously into the passageway. "They're gone."

"They could still be in the outer cave. Let me

see.'' He eased past her, his body rubbing against hers in a delicious way as he leaned out to look.

A faint glow showed far down the passage, and he vaguely heard voices above the constant roar-and-shush of the entering tide. Simon glanced over his shoulder. Jenny's face showed pale in the deep shadows, her blue eyes large, dark, so intent they nearly sparked.

''They're in the main cave,'' he told her. ''Who are they?''

''The older man is a cousin of Captain Mac-Sorley, but I dinna recognize the others. They're all MacSorley's men, I would say.''

''I met him with several of his lads out on the moor. They seemed to be quite busy tonight, too, though they denied it.''

''They're all rascals, and I dinna want to be any-where near them. But we canna stand here in this wee crevice all night.'' She began to squeeze past him.

He took her upper arm. ''You'll stay with me.''

''Go about your business—whatever that may be—and I'll go about my own.'' She tried to twist past him, but he blocked her with one arm and the leverage of his body.

''Just what is your business in these caves, Jenny?''

The effusive light in the outer passage reflected on her face as she stared up at him, frowning. Her eyes were two great dark gleams, and in sunshine, he knew, would be sapphire bright.

"My father sent me here," she said bluntly. "He asked me to find something for him here. I canna tell you more than that. Why are you here?"

He shrugged. "I have my secrets, too."

"You always had too many secrets, Simon Lockhart," she whispered intently. "Well, now I have some, too. When I've found what my father sent me for, I'll leave, and no harm to anyone."

"That sounds just the thing to interest the excise man."

"The de'il take the excise man," she said between her teeth, her face angled close to his.

"He probably will," Simon murmured.

God, he wanted to kiss her, suddenly, urgently. The feeling overwhelmed him, strong as the sea. He stood there, aware of her breath mingling with his own, feeling her taut arm under his fingers. His body flexed, heated, in response to her nearness. Gazing at her calmly, he fought the desire to pull her into his arms and kiss her as passionately and madly as he had done on the day they had parted, years before.

No, he cautioned himself. He had come back to woo her and win her. Snatching her up to kiss her with all the desperation and loneliness inside of him was neither wooing nor wise.

"I've missed you," he whispered, treading carefully.

"Not a letter in four years," she said. "Not a word."

"I sent word, I told you, in the first month after I left."

"We never got it. What about all the other months?"

"I was…busy," he said.

"And now I'm busy. I must go." Picking up her lantern, she slid open the shutter a little.

"No light," he growled, and snapped the window shut. "Those men saw your light earlier, and heard the doves."

"The what?"

"The rock doves," he said. "When you came in, the birds flew out the entrance. I heard it, and so did the smugglers. Bonny little sentinels, sounding an alarm whenever strangers approach the seaward entrance. That may be why MacSorley uses this place."

"That, and because people stay away for fear of seeing the Beauty, or the ghosts who haunts these caves." She tilted her head to look at him. "How long have you been here? When I left the moor, you were riding out after MacSorley's band. Yet you were in the cave before me, though I never saw you, nor saw any birds flying out of the cave when I entered."

"I did not come by the seaward entrance."

"There is no other," she said.

"So I thought, too, until I fell through a hole and found myself in the Kelpie's Cave. I made it this far down the passage before I saw MacSorley's lads, so I ducked in here. You came along not long after."

Jenny looked surprised. "There's a landward entrance?"

"On the moor near the hawthorn grove where we left our horses. I saw Sweetheart there with the cart."

She tilted her head. "Do you think MacSorley and his men know about it?"

"Quite possibly they dug the tunnel themselves. The opening was hidden by bracken and turf, and a stone at the entrance moved easily when I fell on it. Likely they use that access to move contraband in here when the tide is high."

She frowned. "If they go out now and see our horses in the hawthorn clearing, they'll realize we're in here."

"Aye, and there's your wee pony cart filled with empty crates, all ready for transporting...what was it again?" he fished.

"Nothing a gauger need worry about. Go on about your preventive work and leave me be—but first tell me where to find that landward entrance.

'Twill be hours before the tide recedes, so I canna leave here as I came in, after I—'' She stopped.

"Ah, your urgent matter of free trade.'' He regarded her soberly, and lifted his right hand to press on his wound, which ached and still seeped.

"I told you I promised to do something for my father. Nothing much, but if he wants this...I will do it.''

"Whatever it is, Jock would not want you in here with smugglers about.''

"He wouldna want me in here with *you*,'' she pointed out. "So just show me the landward entrance, and I'll be fine on my own.'' She neatly ducked past him to step into the passage.

"Ho, lass,'' he said, snatching her arm and drawing her inside the narrow confine again.

"Let me go,'' she whispered urgently, and smacked at him with a fisted hand. The blow caught the tender spot on his upper left arm that he had been trying to protect.

With a low, involuntary moan, he grasped at his shoulder. "Damn,'' he breathed, as pain exploded in his arm and strange lights dazzled in front of his eyes.

Jenny clutched his forearm. "What is it? Are you hurt?''

"I'm fine. I just—did not expect to be pummelled,'' he said, gathering his wits and straightening again.

"You're white as chalk. I didna mean to hit you so hard."

He laughed then, could not help it, and the sheer agony abated a little. He shook his head. "No, my dear. I'm pistol shot." Sucking in a breath, he pressed his hand over his torn sleeve, where the blood seeped.

She gasped. "Let me see," she insisted.

"It's fine," he said, shaking his head.

"You're bleeding," she whispered. "I didna notice in the dark." Her hands encircled his arm, and a little blood leaked through her fingers. "Oh, Simon! My God. That must be tended, and soon. But we must find some place better than this—we need light, and you need to sit down."

"There's a spot back there—I found it just before you came." He tipped his head to indicate the darkness behind them. "It's very well hidden. Come on."

Taking her arm, he guided her farther into the narrow channel in the rock where they stood. The crevice appeared to end at a sheer rock wall, but a horizontal split in the rock leaked fresh sea breezes.

"Climb through," he whispered. "There's a little cave on the other side."

Jenny slid quickly through the crack in the rock and out the other side, while Simon followed, ignoring the burst of pain in his arm.

He emerged to stand in a small natural balcony

formed by a pocket in the massive black rock of the cliff face. The little terrace was open to air and light and provided a magnificent view of sea and sky.

Jenny stood looking out over the sea, where breakers creamed like lace and moonlight spangled the water. Twinkling lights showed all along the black line of the hills beyond the shore.

Simon crossed to join her in two or three steps. The sea air felt good as it wafted through his hair and fluttered his shirt and jacket. He stood beside her and breathed in the freshness, resting his right hand over the aching wound. The indigo sky sparkled with stars, and the round moon glowed like a white fire, casting its pure light over the sea.

"It's beautiful here. So peaceful." She smiled up at him in the moonlight.

"Aye," he agreed softly. "And it's safe here. No one will find us—providing we're quiet."

"Good. Then I can care for that wound properly. Sit, you," she directed, steering him toward a low protrusion in the wall that could serve for a bench, "and take off your coat."

CHAPTER FIVE

EASING OUT OF HIS COAT, Simon sat, brightening the lantern to cast a golden wash of light in the moonlit interior of the little hidden terrace. Jenny turned her back to him, and he realized that she was tearing a length of cloth from her chemise.

Coming toward him, she set to work, neatly—and rather heartlessly, he thought—ripping the length of his bloody sleeve to the shoulder.

"That was good lawn," he muttered.

"And will make a fine bandage," she said. Her touch was soothing as she wadded his torn sleeve to clean his bared arm. Then she pressed with both thumbs on the wound.

"Ow!" He sucked in a breath.

"There's no pistol ball in there," she pronounced.

"I knew that," he rasped. "You had only to ask."

She dabbed at the wound, a deep gash through skin into muscle that bled freely. "Oh, my dear...it needs cauterizing."

"Bandage it tightly. We've no time."

Quickly she wrapped fabric around the taut muscle of his upper arm. In the moon's blue light, he studied the pale grace of her profile and the gleaming sweep of her hair.

Closing his eyes briefly, ignoring the searing pain in his arm, Simon smelled the copper tang of his blood, the salt air and the faint sweetness of wildflowers in Jenny's hair. He felt comforted by her fragrance, by her gentle touch.

He still loved her, always had, always would, no matter if she returned it. The blend of fire and gentleness in her, together with her serene beauty and graceful shape, still captivated him. Memories of her had sustained him through two years in a dreary prison cell, and through two more years while he worked off the rest of his sentencing and strived to improve his circumstances, all the while planning to return a new man in her regard—and in his own.

"Who shot you?" she asked in a tight, low voice. He saw her frown.

"I do not know."

"You said you spoke with MacSorley out on the moor. Did you see guns on his men?"

"No guns, but they would not be so foolish as to show them to a preventive officer. Clubs and blades are one thing—pistols are regarded as wholly another. Then the law would be after them for rebellion and treason over smuggling. Most free traders respect that as too great a risk."

"My father's lads never carry them, but Mac-Sorley and his pirates might well have them."

He nodded as she tied off the bandage and drew the remnant of his sleeve over the wound. "That will do for now. But you must see a doctor and have that cauterized, or it will continue to seep."

"Later. Thank you, lass." He eased back into his coat with her help, and stood. A wave of pain and dizziness passed quickly enough. "We cannot stay here."

"But you said we couldna be found here."

"We're well hidden, aye, but as cozy as our little secret place is, we must go. I intend to get you back home to Glendarroch as soon as possible."

"I willna leave the caves just yet. I told you so."

"Jenny Colvin," he said sternly, "these sea caves will soon be filled with the worst smugglers on the Solway shores, and I do not want you here."

She leaned toward him. "Show me where that landward entrance is, and I'll see to my errand and be gone before the rest of MacSorley's ruffians come around. And you can tend to your work and then go find yourself a doctor."

"You haven't changed." He glared down at her. "Still as stubborn as a stone."

"And a good thing," she retorted, "or I might

have crumbled, years ago, when someone I once loved betrayed me and mine."

He deserved that, he knew, but it still hurt.

Jenny crouched and slid through the horizontal gap. Watching her slender bottom wriggle through, followed by her neatly shaped limbs and booted feet, he lifted a brow and enjoyed the sight.

Her hand stretched toward him. "Come on!" she whispered.

Following her into the narrow crevice, he eased past her to peer out into the passageway. Seeing a faint light moving over the walls down toward the main cavern, he frowned.

"They're still there," he whispered. "We'll have to go the other way to avoid being seen. Some of these passages loop around—we may be able to find the land exit this way."

Tugging her along, he hoped he was right. When he had fallen through the opening, he had been stunned by the pistol shot and was disoriented in the caves at first. Even now he did not feel quite himself. He willed the dizziness to pass.

Her arm came round his waist to support him, and he let her think he needed it. Better to have Jenny Colvin's tender regard than her temper, he knew.

He liked, too, the feel of her hand at his waist, and her shoulder tucked beneath his arm—for a while, at least, he could feel as if Jenny truly cared for him.

"WHERE ARE WE?" Jenny asked, grasping Simon's hand as they hurried along in the darkness. They had stumbled past black and slimy walls to turn down dark tunnels that ended abruptly, and they had peeked into several cavelets that had yielded neither exits nor stored contraband. Jenny still carried the tin lantern, its shutter raised just enough to provide a dim light.

"We're deep under the cliff by now," Simon answered. "There's a passage to the right that may circle around. Come on." He led her along, his hand firm over hers. "I came here often as a lad, but I've never explored the whole of it. The caves are like a labyrinth, reaching for miles under the moor, they say."

"They also say this place is haunted." Jenny shivered, remembering the eerie screams she had heard earlier. Glancing around in the looming darkness, her step slowed. She was suddenly very glad for Simon's presence. She had not really wanted to explore the caves alone. "Do you know the way?"

"Not really, but I remember some of this from years ago. I used to come here with my father—he may have been a local magistrate, but he took a hand in the free trade, too."

"I remember," she said. Simon's father had died fifteen years earlier, and Jock Colvin had taken Lockhart's young heir under his wing in the smuggling trade, but for the few years that Simon had spent away at school and university. A provision in Lockhart's will had gained his son an education in the law, although Simon had returned to Glendarroch afterward to remain three years more, until his disappearance.

Simon strode so fast that Jenny hurried to keep up. "I hope we willna see the ghost of the piper, or meet the sea kelpies," she said, meaning to make a jest, but her voice trembled nervously.

"What is it...are you frightened?" He glanced at her and squeezed her hand.

"Of course not."

"We're in more danger from MacSorley's rogues. They have goods hidden in here somewhere."

Jenny nodded, thinking of the cargo she must find for her father, if it was here at all. She slowed to peer into a low cave, but it was very black inside, and she saw no shapes of crates or casks, smelling only damp stone and seaweed.

"Simon, is that why you came down here? To look for contraband?" she asked as they walked on.

"Not intentionally—I fell like a rabbit down a hole. But if I find illicit taxable goods and a bonny lass in the bargain, then it's worth it."

"Worth a pistol shot?"

"Almost," he said. Stopping suddenly, he

stretched out his uninjured arm to block her progress. "Shh—there's a light."

She saw it then, a faint golden spill on the rocky sheer ahead of them, where the walls soared to a high natural vault. Simon moved forward furtively, and Jenny followed, silent and alert. All she heard was the grit of their footsteps on sandstone, and the quiet power of the sea far behind them.

As they came cautiously around a bend in the channel, she saw a lantern, its flame fluttering, hung from a protrusion in the rocky wall. Nearby was the rough arch of a cave opening, its interior dark but for the wash of lantern light.

Inside the cave, Jenny glimpsed movement—a pale shadow shifted, ghostlike and eerie. She heard the clap and ring of metal on stone. Gasping, she clutched Simon's shoulder.

"A ghost!" she whispered.

He motioned for her to stay back, but she went with him. A few discreet strides brought them near the chamber's entrance. Simon flattened against the wall, keeping Jenny behind him as he peered into the chamber. "What the devil?" he murmured.

"What?" she whispered fervently.

"There's your ghost," he said. Slipping his arm around her, he let her look past him. Beyond the pool of light, the pale shadow took form.

Jenny gasped. The ghost flicked its tail and whinnied, stepping backward nervously. It turned its great, beautiful head and gazed at her with soft, dark eyes.

"A horse?" She looked at Simon in disbelief. "Here?" Pale as milk, huge in a cave the size of a large stall, the horse swung its head and whickered anxiously. It backstepped, iron shoes ringing on stone.

She stared, dumbfounded, realizing that the scream she had heard earlier had been the horse neighing.

Simon smiled at her, his eyes vivid blue in the strong play of light and shadow. "Here's your Beauty, my lass. I suspect this is the legendary beast that scared the wits out of Nicky Colvin earlier tonight."

"The Beauty? The sea kelpie that rides out under a full moon to warn of danger at sea? But this is a real horse. The other is a vision, or a magical creature."

"A real horse, my dear, and likely used by MacSorley and his lads to warn others away from these caves on nights when they plan to move smuggled goods." Simon frowned, watching the horse.

Whickering again, the animal stepped sideways, tail flashing like sea foam in the darkness. Jenny noticed that the Beauty was tethered by a headrope to an iron ring embedded in the wall. A trough of oats and another of water sat within easy reach, and the floor of the natural chamber was covered in straw and smelled of muck. Jenny wrinkled her nose.

"Easy, my love," Simon crooned.

Jenny glanced at him quickly, heart leaping unbidden, but his attention was focused on the horse. "Easy, bonny lass," he repeated as he moved into the cave.

He whistled softly, a soft and easy sound, as he stroked the mare's muzzle, then patted her broad neck. Jenny joined them, the horse blinked at her with disinterest and blew into Simon's palm. He laughed softly and glanced at Jenny.

"You always had the touch for horses," she said, smiling. "Mares especially loved you, as I recall."

Taking the headrope, he led the horse toward the entrance arch, coaxing her into the pool of light. He checked her bite and her ears, murmuring gently, then dropped to one knee and ran his hands gently down her forelegs, then stood to trace his hands over her back and withers. Jenny noticed that he kept his left arm close to his side much of the time.

"Is she healthy?"

"She's fine. But I'm puzzled about something…ah. Look at this." He held out his palm, which was chalky white.

"Is that powder?" She touched the horse's back,

and brought her own hand away whitened. She sniffed it. "Limestone chalk."

"Aye. She's been made to look white." He rubbed a spot vigorously on the horse's shoulder. "See, her skin is dark, and her coat is dappled— she's actually a gray, with a white mane and tail. Not much work to make her look like the legendary Beauty."

"But why?" Jenny asked. She patted the horse's muzzle. "They wanted to keep people away from the sea caves, I suppose."

"Aye, so that they could move their goods about undisturbed. But there's another reason." He smoothed a gentle hand over the horse's neck, and the mare snuffled affectionately at him. "This is a Connemara, about three years old," he said. "I recently read a description of a horse like this one. Dappled gray, with one dark foreleg. I think we've found the magistrate's missing horse."

Jenny looked at him, stunned. "The horse my father is accused of taking?"

"I read the sheriff's report, and this horse matches that description."

"Oh!" She reached out to touch the mare's muzzle in awe. "Then this proves my father's innocence! Oh, Simon—"

She surged toward him, looping her arms around his neck in an impulsive and joyful hug. Though surprise registered on his face, he circled his uninjured arm around her waist and leaned close, accepting the embrace.

As she looked up at him, he turned his head, and in that moment, his mouth accidentally brushed her cheek. He touched his mouth to hers tenderly, his hand at her lower back pressing her against the hard planes of his body.

Her breath faltered, her knees went weak, and in that one swift, blessed moment, Jenny felt hurt and resentment melt a little under the deep magic of his kiss, the comfort of his arms. Joy bloomed in the space between one breath and the next.

And then the barriers fell back into place, slamming down like iron gates. Jenny broke the loop of her arms and stepped back, blushing. "I am sorry," she said.

"I am not," he replied softly, watching her. "Not for that."

She looked away, flustered and stunned by the surprises of the last few moments. The simple kiss still lingered on her lips. *Do not be a fool,* she told herself. *Do not let him charm you again.*

"Are you sure," she said, gulping, "that this is the magistrate's horse?"

"Aye. She's a Connemara—see the proud shape of her, and the height? By her teeth, she's three or so. And she's a gray. Just how many three-year-old female Connemara grays are there along this coast, do you think?"

"Perhaps just one."

"Aye, then." He looked at her sharply. "Jenny Colvin, be honest with me, now. Did Jock take this mare, and stash her here? Is that why you've come to the caves? To find the horse?"

"No!" She folded her arms in sudden, indignant anger.

"Hush," he cautioned. "Our comrades will come running to join our little celebration." He cocked a brow.

"No, he did not steal the horse," she hissed, "and no, he did not hide her here, and no, I did not—"

"Fine," he said curtly, holding up his palm. "The question remains, who did, and what do we do with the horse now?"

"We take her to the magistrate, of course, before they take my father to the gallows in the morning for—" She stopped.

"I agree this might keep Jock from a hanging, but I wish it were guaranteed. And how are we to get her out of here?"

"Oh, the tide!" She frowned, then began to pace back and forth. "If we wait until the MacSorleys leave the cave—do you think the Beauty could swim in the sea far enough to get out of the cave to the beach? Some horses can."

"I won't risk it," he said. "And we've no boat for us, even if she could swim alongside it. The tidal pull in the Solway basin is treacherous, especially under a full moon. I might see you both go down, and...I couldn't live with that."

She sent him a sharp glance. "You let years go by without knowing what became of us," she pointed out.

He sighed, his arm still resting on the horse, and regarded her. "I knew," he said quietly. "I always knew."

"How?" she asked.

"I have my ways, love, and my secrets, too." His voice, quietly heard in half shadows, sent a thrill through her. "I worked as a solicitor for the Customs and Excise Board in Edinburgh. I read the reports from the Solway officers. I knew when your kin were sighted, when they were questioned or fined, when goods were confiscated. And I knew when your father was arrested. I came back...to do what I could, if he was innocent of the charge."

"He is." Tilting her head, she watched him, heart beating hard. She remembered that sudden, heart-melting kiss. Her thoughts and emotions tumbled, and she suddenly wanted to know what had happened to Simon. Until then, she had clung desperately to her anger. Now she felt it beginning to dissolve a little.

Yet there was no time for questions. "Simon— we must get the horse out of here quickly. But the tide will not pull out for hours yet."

He took the headrope and led the horse back to the troughs. "There, my bonny. We'll get you home to your owner somehow," he murmured. He stroked her again, whistling that same gentle tune, and the horse snorted with contentment.

Simon looked at Jenny. "We may be able to take her out through the landward entrance."

"Is it possible?" Hope flashed within her, and she smiled, but resisted the urge to give him another hug. That, and the kiss, had aroused strong, insistent feelings in her that left her head and heart whirling.

He must have felt it, too, for his gaze was hungry and intent on hers. In the silence, she felt something powerful pass between them, as strong as a tide, as mysterious as moonlight. A blush heated her cheeks, and she glanced away.

"We must find that other exit soon, before MacSorley's men come back for the horse," she said quietly.

"We'll need to wait a bit before we take her out. I want to know what MacSorley's men intend to do with her."

"They mean to ensure that my father hangs, that's what."

"They might mean to sell her down to England, or over to Ireland or France. Felix Colvin mentioned a ship coming in tonight." He strode toward the entrance, grabbing Jenny's hand as he passed, tugging her with him into the corridor. As they went, she took up the lantern she had set down, and followed.

CHAPTER SIX

"MY FATHER NEVER used these caves," Jenny said. "That proves that he did not take the magistrate's horse." She held the lantern as they walked and he took her other hand, his grip strong. Although the cave was chilly, she was troubled by the distinct coolness of his fingers. He was paler, too, she thought, glancing at him. A trickle of blood ran over his left hand.

"Dear God, Simon. Your arm—you must let me tend to it again."

"It's nothing," he said, jamming his hand in his pocket. "Jenny, finding the horse could help Jock, but the authorities already have enough quarrel with him for distilling and trading illicit whisky."

"But horse thieving is the hanging crime. He'll be saved from that, at least, if we can get the horse to the sheriff in time, before the morning—"

"We'll have to prove someone else took her. Jock could have put her there himself."

"He never comes to these caves. He's afraid...of

sea kelpies and ghosts, though he would never admit it.''

''I never knew that.'' He smiled faintly. ''We'll watch what MacSorley means to do with your Beauty. If we can catch them about to sell her or ship her off, that will be proof enough.''

''We canna wait.''

''How can we walk out of here leading that horse? There's smugglers all about. Here, this way.'' He tugged her along a narrow artery through the stone where the walls were clearly marked with traces of chisel work. ''It looks familiar now...I think we may find the landward exit. Aye, there,'' he said, as they reached a fork in the corridor.

He pointed toward a short, third spur off the two routes. At the end of that tunnel, raised a little above the level of the floor on a ramp of stone, Jenny saw a smooth slab fitted into the rock wall.

As large as a door but rounded, the slate was fixed with an iron pull-ring and iron hinges, the whole neatly set in the shadowed recess of the back wall. On a side wall, two iron hooks protruded from the stone, ready to hold lanterns or other gear. A shovel and an axe leaned in a dark corner.

''I came through there by accident,'' Simon said. ''I happened to fall through the brush that conceals the hatch on the moor. It opened easily enough when my weight fell against it.''

"I think we can bring the horse through there," Jenny said. "It looks large enough. Let's go get her." She turned.

"Not yet." Simon grabbed her arm. "I'll wait here to see what they intend to do with her. You go through there, and home," he ordered, turning her toward the short tunnel.

"Oh, no," she said, rounding back. "I told you I'm staying."

"You'll not," he said, taking her shoulder to turn her.

"I will," she said firmly, and shrugged off his hand, stepping away. "Thank you for showing me the exit." Swinging the lantern, she strode back toward the horse's cave.

"Stubborn lass," he muttered as he followed.

She smiled and glanced over her shoulder.

He caught up to her, and as they passed the horse's cave in silence, Jenny took Simon's arm again, a gesture of compromise as much as a bid for simple comfort in the gloomy, eerie recesses of the underground labyrinth. At a turn in the tunnel, Simon held out his right arm to keep Jenny behind him.

She glanced around. Behind them lay the horse's cave, and several yards in front was the little crevice where they had hidden earlier. Beyond lay the great hall cave, open to the sea. From that direction, a faint light washed over the walls.

"They're coming this way," she whispered.

"Shut the lantern," he growled. She did so, and he looked at her. "I'll go ahead to see what they're doing. There's a wee cavelet just here—wait inside, lass, and do not move."

"But you—"

"Jenny, listen. If I do not return for you soon, go back to our little moonlit balcony. You'll be safe there." He gave her a gentle shove toward the low mouth of the small cave just behind her. Then he sprinted away, quick and quiet.

She eyed the low, dark opening dubiously. Earlier, she and Simon had peered into the small cave, which had seemed unremarkable. Ducking, she stepped inside.

Once past the low-hanging entrance arch, she found with surprise that she could stand upright in the blackness. The space seemed higher and larger than she had thought. Tracing her hand over cold stone, she moved deeper into the cave, following the curvature of the wall. A moment later, she knocked her shin against something hard, and bumped her hip against some other object. Reaching out, she felt a wooden object under her hand, and groped around to find several more, all of similar size and shape.

Opening her lantern, she saw casks neatly stacked all along the walls, and more kegs and wooden crates on the floor. Moving around, she saw round iron-banded wooden kegs in the small and portable size that smugglers, including her father, often used. Shifting one of them, she heard liquid slosh inside.

Whisky casks. She had found the smuggler's cache of goods.

Then light infused the entrance and she heard footsteps. Sliding the lantern shut, she crouched behind a stack of boxes next to the wall. Long shadows fell across the entrance, and she heard voices as several men entered the cave.

Curled behind the boxes, she waited silently. Glancing through a narrow space between crates, she saw six men in all, including the three she and Simon had seen earlier.

With low murmurs and brisk directions, they set to the task of lifting and carrying casks and boxes. A few of them hoisted the small, heavy wooden casks to their shoulders, while others carried out two or three boxes in a stack, and some took a few of the sacks.

Within minutes, they were gone. When she was sure of safety, Jenny crawled out of her hiding place. She opened the lantern a little and moved around the crowded cave, searching for anything that bore the Glendarroch symbol, a tiny design of an oak leaf burned into the wood.

She found boxes of laces, silks and other fabrics, and kegs of brandy and rum, as well as whisky that was not Glendarroch make. Sighing in frustration, she glanced anxiously toward the cave entrance. The smugglers might be back soon. Lifting the lantern, she scanned the cave one last time, and suddenly glimpsed the tiny, familiar oak leaf design branded on some wooden casks.

Sighing in relief, she hurried to the other side of the cave to discover several stacks of small, portable kegs at the back of the cave, hidden by a tall pile of boxes, so that Jenny could not get to them easily.

Enough, for now, to know that Colvin goods were here. She had to let her kinsmen know.

But she did not want to leave Simon with his wound bleeding again, although she knew he would insist that he was fine.

Realizing that some whisky would be useful for his wound, she tried to get to one of the Glendarroch casks but could not reach them. Examining the wooden boxes stacked nearest her, she pried open one nailed lid with a broken bit of stone. Inside she found tin flasks filled with liquid, most likely Highland whisky.

Removing one flask, she wedged it down her

bodice, above the ties that snugged beneath her breasts. Shivering from the cold touch of the metal, she slipped out of the cave and ran down the empty passageway.

WHAT THE DEVIL had become of her?

Simon paced the little balcony area feeling an increasing sense of alarm. He had seen the smugglers go in and out of the very cave into which he had shoved Jenny, and had to duck deep into the crevice to avoid being seen himself. Now he was fraught with concern for her, and angry with himself for leaving her.

And he had seen that the smugglers were moving illicit cargo, while he, the excise officer, was trapped, one man unable to stop them. Despite their presence, he had to find Jenny.

Bending to crawl back through the gap in the rock, a wave of dizziness took him with such force that he paused while the little cliffside niche seemed to swing crazily. He broke into a clammy sweat and his arm throbbed painfully. He knew it was bleeding again, felt the warm soak of it through the bandages.

Still, he could not sit here panting and reeling. He had to find Jenny, either to save her—or stop her from whatever madness she had planned that night. He suspected Jock had sent her here on some illicit chore.

Head swimming, he looked through the gap again, and saw a slender dark shadow slipping through the crevice to come toward him. Relief washed over him, and he realized again how very much she meant to him.

He waited while she emerged sideways through the gap and placed her booted feet on the floor, skirts rucked over her stockinged legs to her knees. Then he took her arm to assist her.

"Jenny, thank God," he murmured, and pulled her into his arms, feeling an undeniable force, relief and love and a sudden, inconvenient surge of desire. He pressed his cheek against the sweet wildflower softness of her hair as he embraced her.

Her arms came around his waist, and she rested her head on his shoulder for a moment. "The men came to that cave. I had to hide there for a while. There were six of them this time."

He nodded. "And more than that in the main cave. I saw them loading goods into two rowboats." He did not want to let go of her, he realized, nor did she seem inclined to pull away.

As he held her, something cold and oddly shaped pushed into his chest. Frowning, he set her away from him, glancing down at the tantalizing swell of her breasts. A strange bulk rested beneath the fabric of her bodice. Keeping that awareness to himself, he glanced at her. "And just what were the smugglers doing there, lass?"

She laughed, at once sultry and mischievous. "I found their store, Simon. Casks, boxes, sacks—there's whisky and West Indies rum, French brandy, laces, silks, all in one cave."

"Aye?" A wave of the accursed dizziness he had tried to ignore hit him again, and he leaned against the rock wall near them. A cool, reviving wind blew against his neck and through his hair. Moonlight poured over his shoulder to show Jenny's face.

She looked at him with concern. "The cave looks small from the outside, but inside 'tis spacious—and full of cargo."

"Including tin flasks?" With deft fingers, he reached inside the neck of her dress, grabbed the flask and drew it out. The metal felt warm where it had touched her skin, and he could not help but notice the firm, luscious shape of her breasts. "You did not have this on you earlier. Do I need to search you more thoroughly?"

She watched him in surprise, then drew a long, deep breath.

He dangled the flask between his fingers. "What's the meaning of this?" he asked in a low voice. "Are you in league with these smugglers after all?"

She blinked at him and licked her lips, an unconscious gesture that revealed her nervousness.

He wanted desperately to kiss her in that moment, wanted to take her in his arms and explore every part of her, touch and savor her as he had done years ago. His body throbbed with the need, despite their situation, despite the dizziness and pain that plagued him.

"No," she said firmly, at last. "I brought that for you."

He frowned. "I do not accept bribes."

"Nor do I give them. Sit down over there." She motioned toward the ledge of stone that served as a seat. "Your wound is bleeding again. Are you fevered?" She touched his forehead, then his cheek. Her hand was cool, the sensation delicious and soothing, as if he was fevered—but surely there was another reason that he felt overheated in her presence, with his heart slamming and his body hardening.

"I'm fine," he said, and let out a grunt as she shoved him gently downward.

"Sit. And give me your coat again." She assisted him as before, being careful of his wounded arm. Kneeling beside him, she gasped softly. "Oh, Simon," she whispered.

He glanced down. The bandage she had applied earlier was a dark mass in the moonlight—surely

An Important Message from the Editors

Dear Reader,

Because you've chosen to read one of our fine romance novels, we'd like to say "thank you!" And, as a **special** way to thank you, we've selected <u>two more</u> of the books you love so well **plus** an exciting Mystery Gift to send you — absolutely <u>FREE</u>!

Please enjoy them with our compliments...

Pam Powers

Lift here

How to validate your Editor's "Thank You" FREE GIFT

1. Peel off gift seal from front cover. Place it in space provided at right. This automatically entitles you to receive 2 FREE BOOKS and a fabulous mystery gift.

2. Send back this card and you'll get 2 brand-new *Romance* novels. These books have a cover price of $5.99 or more each in the U.S. and $6.99 or more each in Canada, but they are yours to keep absolutely free.

3. There's no catch. You're under no obligation to buy anything. We charge nothing—ZERO—for your first shipment. And you don't have to make any minimum number of purchases—not even one!

4. The fact is, thousands of readers enjoy receiving their books by mail from The Reader Service. They enjoy the convenience of home delivery...they like getting the best new novels at discount prices BEFORE they're available in stores... and they love their Heart to Heart subscriber newsletter featuring author news, horoscopes, recipes, book reviews and much more!

5. We hope that after receiving your free books you'll want to remain a subscriber. But the choice is yours— to continue or cancel, any time at all! So why not take us up on our invitation, with no risk of any kind. You'll be glad you did!

GET A ***Free*** *MYSTERY GIFT...*

*SURPRISE MYSTERY GIFT COULD BE YOURS **FREE** AS A SPECIAL "THANK YOU" FROM THE EDITORS*

The Editor's "Thank You" Free Gifts Include:

● *Two BRAND-NEW Romance novels!*
● *An exciting mystery gift!*

Yes! I have placed my
Editor's "Thank You" seal in the
space provided above. Please
send me 2 free books and a
fabulous mystery gift. I
understand I am under no
obligation to purchase any
books, as explained on the
back and on the opposite page.

PLACE
FREE GIFT
SEAL
HERE

393 MDL DVFG   193 MDL DVFF

FIRST NAME	LAST NAME

ADDRESS

APT.#	CITY

STATE/PROV.	ZIP/POSTAL CODE

(PR-R-04)

Thank You!

The Reader Service — Here's How It Works:

Accepting your 2 free books and gift places you under no obligation to buy anything. You may keep the books and gift and return the shipping statement marked "cancel." If you do not cancel, about a month later we'll send you 3 additional books and bill you just $4.74 each in the U.S., or $5.24 each in Canada, plus 25¢ shipping & handling per book and applicable taxes if any.* That's the complete price and — compared to cover prices starting from $5.99 each in the U.S. and $6.99 each in Canada — it's quite a bargain! You may cancel at any time, but if you choose to continue, every month we'll send you 3 more books, which you may either purchase at the discount price or return to us and cancel your subscription.

*Terms and prices subject to change without notice. Sales tax applicable in N.Y. Canadian residents will be charged applicable provincial taxes and GST.

not how it should look, he thought, feeling almost befuddled, swamped by dizziness again. He leaned back against the wall, aware of damp, cold rock.

Gingerly she peeled away the sodden strips of cloth to reveal the wound, and wiped his arm with the previously torn sleeve that she pulled from his coat pocket. Reaching for the tin flask he had set down, she handed it to him. "You'd better drink some of this. I'll do what I can to stop the bleeding."

He glanced down at his arm. "Damn," he murmured.

"It needs to be cauterized." She sighed, looking worried.

"I'm not happy about it, but I'm not keen on bleeding to death, either. Have you ever done this?"

"No. But I've seen it done. But how...in here?"

"I have a knife, and we can use the lantern flame." He withdrew the little black-handled *sgian-dhu* that he carried sheathed at his waist beneath his vest. Silently, he laid it on the ledge of rock beside her.

She opened the lantern shutter and turned up the wick so that the flame flared. Simon lifted the flask and drank.

Mellow fire slid down his throat, faintly sweet, its inner heat flaring quickly. "Excellent," he said, mildly astonished, distracted for the moment from the dreaded task ahead.

He had been raised around illicit whisky production in pot-stills hidden from the king's men, yet somehow he had never developed a taste for whisky himself, despite its ubiquitous presence in every Scottish household he had ever known. He found the stuff unpleasant at best, harsh and undrinkable at worst. But the contents of the tin flask surprised him—delicate and subtle, its delicious warmth was invigorating and intriguing. He took another sip.

"This is...rather good," he admitted.

"Have a little more," she suggested. "You may need it." She pushed his hand, holding the flask, toward his mouth.

He sipped. "I confess I've never tasted whisky quite like this. There is something...faintly sweet about it, almost soft, yet the burn is strong. It's like...honey and flame mixed together. A superb choice in stolen peat-reek, my dear," he said, and raised the flask in salute.

"Superb? Then I wonder—let me taste it," she said, and took the flask from him. Setting her lips around the neck, she drank.

"Careful, lass, it's powerful," he cautioned. "I can already feel it in my blood after just a few sips."

"Aye," she said, frowning thoughtfully, and

swallowed again. "Oh, aye…this is indeed the best whisky in all of Scotland. It's Glendarroch make."

Disliking the stuff as he did, Simon always found it a challenge to distinguish one whisky from another. "How do you know it's Glendarroch?"

Jenny swallowed again. He watched the delicate ripple of her throat muscles, saw the pink tip of her tongue touch her lips. She closed her eyes, savored, then sighed. Watching her, Simon felt his body fill and harden, but he ignored the sweeping urge of desire as he waited for her answer.

She looked up. "Because I know my own. I made this whisky."

CHAPTER SEVEN

"YOU?" HE STARED at her in disbelief. "You are responsible for Glendarroch whisky?"

Had he come here searching for the men who were smuggling Glendarroch whisky only to discover that it was not MacSorley, not even Jock Colvin, but Jenny herself he was after, and Jenny he must arrest?

"Aye, for the most part it's my doing," she said, as if there was nothing wrong in producing illicit whisky. "I oversee the production in the stills, while Da and Felix sell and move our goods. Our stuff is in great demand these days."

"So I've heard," he drawled.

"We can hardly make enough to meet the requests." She shook her head. "You'd best drink a bit more."

"And you'd best tell me more about your illicit whisky business," he said sternly.

She frowned at him. "Will you arrest me if I do, gauger?"

He leaned forward, right hand still pressing his

left arm. "Whatever we do or say in this place," he murmured, "stays in this place. Will you trust me in that, at least?"

She nodded slowly, then touched the blade of his *sgian-dhu* to the lantern flame. "You've been gone a long while, Simon," she said as she worked. "Not long after you left, I took over the production of several of Da's pot-stills. He had so many that he couldna keep up with them all—and dinna ask me how many, or where they're hidden, excise man." She glanced at him.

"I wouldn't dream of it," he drawled. "Go on."

"I had watched the process since I was a child, so I knew a good deal about whisky-making. Da thought me old enough to taste the batches. I had a knack for knowing one kind from another, and for judging the best of it."

"How did you come to do that?" he asked, looking at her curiously. "I remember that you were fond of wandering the hills when the heather and summer wildflowers were in bloom, and I know your da had pot-stills hidden in those slopes. But I do not recall that you were fond of whisky, though you had some now and then, as we all did from childhood on."

"And I know you never liked it much at all, but you must drink it now, regardless." While he did, she tilted the *sgian-dhu* and let the bright flame pour along the steel blade, which took on a limpid shine. "Wandering the hills gave me the knack, I think," she said. "The hills, the heather, the flowers and grasses and burns, all of it are part of me. I know their scents, their tastes, their feel, and I sense it in the whisky somehow." She shrugged. "I can tell when the flavor of the drink is too peaty, or if there were heather bells mixed with the barley mash, or if primroses or wild onion flavor the water of the burn. If there's wild garlic, for example, we throw the batch away—I willna accept it." She wrinkled her nose.

"I doubt I could tell the difference."

"Ah, you would have been able to if you had stayed with us. I might have taught you myself."

"I would have liked that," he said softly.

She glanced away. "Aye, well, drink it now— even though you may loathe it."

He laughed. "Your brew is very fine, I assure you." He sipped. "Go on. What sort of magic do you conjure over Glendarroch whisky?"

"When I began supervising the production, we tried different kinds of barley, different containers, varying the distilling times, and so on. I made more and more suggestions, and one day," she went on, reaching out to urge the flask toward his lips again, "we discovered that some whisky that had been stored in some old oak sherry casks, and left alone for a year, was better than anything we had ever produced. It had a lovely golden color, and all the strength and whimsy of Scotland itself in its flavor. Drink another wee sippie, now,'' she urged him.

He did, then lifted a brow. ''Do you want to make me fou?''

''A little,'' she admitted.

Simon half smiled, contemplating her beautiful, sparkling eyes. He did not feel drunk. It took a lot of any sort of drink—ale, wine or other—to take him down, but he had relaxed enough to realize how tense he had been in her presence, overly cautious and concerned he might misstep, missay himself.

Better to be himself and take his chances, he told himself. She would either love him or not, regardless. And no matter what happened, he could never stop loving Jenny Colvin, rogue's child, whisky smuggler, nurse and more bright and dazzling to him than that full moon over the sea, he thought, glancing past the cave.

Oh, aye, he was a wee bit fou, he thought.

''Is this the aged whisky, then?'' He lifted the tin flask.

''Aye, that batch is a little over three years old by the taste of it.''

''If it's such rare stuff and so much in demand, the excise man should not be drinking your store.''

''We'll make an exception for you. And Mac-Sorley had no right to this batch—oh,'' she finished suddenly, biting her lip.

He paused in lifting the flask to study her. "And just how did Glendarroch's finest batch turn up in MacSorley's cargo? Is your father in league with them? Answer me," he added, when she looked away, still and silent.

She sighed. "Captain MacSorley stole it from us," she admitted. "After my father was imprisoned, Uncle Felix discovered that fifty casks of whisky were missing from the place that we had stored this stuff for aging. Da asked me to come here and see if 'twas here, so then we would know for sure that MacSorley took it. So...my father can die in peace." She blinked back tears.

"Och, Jenny," he murmured in sympathy. Then he shook his head. "But why is this so important to Jock?"

She lifted her chin. "That whisky will earn a fortune in trade. The longer it ages, the more it's worth. Da wants his kin to have the benefit, not MacSorley. He also suspects that MacSorley stole the magistrate's horse and blamed him for it, and he was right. Cap'n MacSorley is an evil rogue," she went on. "He wants to control the smuggling along this coast, but my father has the greater share of the business." She scowled.

"I see. Now that you've found the whisky, what then?"

"Felix and the lads will deal with MacSorley."

"The excise men should take care of that," he said grimly.

"Aye, and they'd take care of my father, too, in their way. No, Felix and the lads must do this. Remember, preventive man," she warned, "this was all spoken in our place of secrets. And whatever we do and say here is never to be known by anyone else."

"Agreed," he said softly, and felt a surge of desire thrill through him unbidden. "Besides, you have the knife," he teased, smiling at her.

"Aye, and it's hot now. We must see to your arm."

He frowned. "Aye then. Get on with it."

She reached under the hem of her dress to rip another length of fabric from her petticoat. Then she thrust the *sgian-dhu* into the lantern flame again, heating it one last time.

Simon watched, waited. The whisky's power heated his blood, warming him head to foot, baking out the clammy feverishness he had felt earlier. He did not intend to get truly drunk—he had never enjoyed the drunken state much, and he would need a clear head to face MacSorley's lads.

The flame spilled over the shining blade. Simon cleared his throat, sat straighter and angled out his left arm.

Jenny looked at him then, her face lovely in the blue-shadowed moonlight, the lantern light showing sparks in her eyes. For a moment, he saw an incandescence in her, saw the beautiful and compassionate spirit that had drawn him back here, despite distance and years, despite grief and secrets, doubt and hope.

He saw the tenderness of love.

Then she lowered her glance.

He wanted to kiss her. The feeling roared through him. He wanted to hold her, and explain what he had held in his heart for so long. Instead, he said nothing, waiting while she poured a little whisky on a wadded cloth and leaned forward.

"This will sting," she said.

When she pressed the spirit-soaked cloth to his arm, it burned like fire. He sucked in a hissing breath.

Quickly Jenny leaned forward and kissed his mouth. Tasting her sweet lips, he forgot physical pain for an instant. He cupped the back of her head, deepened and savored the kiss, felt his hunger for her burn hot and insistent.

She tilted her face and let the kiss renew, and he felt his soul begin to stir in him. Secrets long-held clamored for release. He had carried them for so long.

Then she pulled away in the darkness, sat back.

He blinked in surprise. "What was that for?"

"To hush you. I was afraid you might cry out when the whisky touched the wound."

"I'm a tough lad." He grinned, though his arm stung like the devil.

"Aye, but the rest of this will hurt much more."

"Do your worst, Jenny Colvin," he murmured, his gaze steady, "if it means you'll give me a healing balm like that afterward."

In the lantern light, her cheeks blushed deep pink. She twisted a cloth in her hands and handed it to him. "Bite on that. This will not be pleasant."

"Though you think I deserve it." He slid the rolled cloth between his teeth.

"Hush, you," she said, smiling faintly, shaking her head a little. Once again she thrust the blade into the lantern flame, then brought the knife toward him. When he sensed the heat, he closed his eyes. He felt her hand rest on his own, and her fingers knotted in his. Drawing a breath, he squeezed her hand.

The hot blade seared his gaping wound, sending a lightning strike of pain through him. He grimaced, jammed his teeth into the cloth, felt sweat bead on his brow. As the knife lifted away, he suppressed a deep groan. Leaning back against the relief of cold, damp rock, he closed his eyes while the world spun.

"Oh, Simon," Jenny whispered, as she began to bandage his arm again. "I didna mean to hurt you so. I'm sorry. Oh, Simon."

He said nothing, leaning his back against the rock, eyes closed, as he mastered pain and dizziness. Finally, when he felt her tying off the new bandage, he opened his eyes. The world had righted itself a little. White moonlight, brighter for the darkness he had just seen, showed Jenny kneeling at his feet, leaned against his knees as she worked on his arm.

When he saw the raw anguish on her face, he felt as if pain, and the dealing of it, had bonded them. In silence, he touched her cheek, tracing his fingers over her jaw.

"No matter," he murmured wearily. "It needed to be done, and you had the courage to do it."

Jenny tipped her cheek into the palm of his hand, and he saw tears glimmer in her eyes. "I'm so sorry," she said again.

"I should be the one asking your forgiveness," he murmured.

"When I brought the knife to your arm, then I knew…" She stopped, closed her eyes.

"What, love?" he asked quietly.

"That I…never wanted to cause you pain, though all these years, I have been so angry with you."

"I am truly sorry if I hurt you," he whispered.

"And I you." Her chin trembled, and tears pooled in her eyes. "Here," she said abruptly, shoving the flask toward him. "Drink a bit more. You need it, for the…the pain." She wiped her hand under her nose as if to stave off her tears.

He lifted the flask and swallowed again. It burned smoky-sweet as it went down, its fire dulling the sharp ache in his arm, filling all of his senses keenly for an instant. "My God," he murmured. "You really do make magnificent whisky, Miss Colvin. Only the rarest brings tears to the eyes like this, and makes a man want to sing hallelujah."

"Oh, dinna sing," she said hastily, laying her finger on his lower lip. "We canna risk attracting the smuggling sort."

He chuckled, entranced, and kissed her fingertip. She slowly traced her fingers over his lips, his chin and jaw, then dropped her hand away. "You had better make sure I stay quiet then, as you did before," he suggested.

She smiled. "Shh...perhaps you've had enough after all."

In the luminous moonlight, she leaned so close that he felt her breath caress his lips. His heart pounded, slow and hard, and he forgot why he was here with her, why the whisky warmed his blood. He forgot about pain, and secrets, even forgot that enemies were elsewhere in the cave.

He was aware only of the magic conjured by moonlight and dreams, aware only of Jenny. She heated his blood more potently than drink ever could.

"White fire," he said suddenly.

"Wh-what?"

"Your whisky," he said. "It goes down like white fire. Like moonlight transformed to some magical potion." He glanced toward the full moon, visible through the split in the rock.

"I like that," she whispered, still closer to him. Her eyelids lowered as she looked at his lips.

"And you, love," he said softly, "are like white fire, too." Stretching out his right hand, he cupped the back of her head and sank his fingers into the gleaming mass of her dark hair. She angled her face toward him, suffused in luminous moonlight.

Stay away from my daughter.

Jock's words intruded, reminded. God forgive him, he could not keep away from her. Tonight she had the allure of moonlight on her, and he had fallen under her spell long ago. Years had not abated that power. She had filled his dreams all that time, and now he was with her at last. He could not stay away from Jenny Colvin, no matter what her father wanted.

Lost in her lovely eyes, caught with her inside the intimate space in the rock, he felt as if they had found some secret pocket in eternity. Here, the sea whispered below them and the moonlight poured its gentleness upon them. Here, fear and grief and close-kept secrets held no power over hope, and love.

Jenny drifted shut her eyes, and Simon touched his mouth to hers, lingered. Her lips softened beneath his, and she breathed out a sigh, a poignant sound that fueled his desire. Pulling her toward him with one arm, he felt her arms slip around his neck, felt her body curve to his. Through layers of fabric, her breasts were soft, firm, warm against his chest.

Leaning toward her, for she still knelt beside him, he slid his fingers deep in her hair, felt the braiding loosen. Her hair spilled, rich and silky, over his hand and down her back. Gathering her to him, he kissed her as he had wanted to do for years, since the day he had left.

Then suddenly she pulled back. "Your arm—"

"It's fine," he whispered, drawing her toward him to kiss her again. "I have wanted to kiss you like this for so long...."

"If you wanted that so much," she said, her lips touching his, "why didn't you come back and do it?"

"Hush." He kissed her then as he had dreamed of doing, hard and fierce, his heart beating fast against hers, while kisses rained, and his body surged, and his love for her raised his soul in him until he hardly knew where he ended and she began.

Her lips were warm and soft, and he tasted the sweet fire of the whisky between her mouth and his. Touching his tongue to hers, he heard her gasp a little with the pleasure of it, felt her sink more deeply against him.

A moment later she drew back. "No," she whispered, her breaths coming as fast as his own. "No, Simon Lockhart. You can always make me melt—like strong whisky, every time you touch me. But there are too many questions between us now."

He lifted his hands away from her abruptly, palms up. "Very well," he said curtly. "No more. I apologize, Miss Colvin. You have my apology for all of it—the hurt, the worries, the waiting. But do not ask me why, not yet... What is it?" he asked, as he saw her eyes grow wide, heard her gasp. "What's wrong?"

"Your hands," she said. "Your wrists!"

Damnation, he thought, and lowered his hands quickly. He had forgotten about the scars.

She grabbed his wrists and turned them toward the moonlight, running her thumbs over the glossy, healed ridges of skin, rotating his arms to look at the fine, scarred grooves that ran across his forearms below the wristbones. "You did not have these scars years ago. What happened?"

He frowned, looking at the familiar striations. He had forgotten about them, having lived with them for years. And he had forgotten that Jenny had never seen them.

"Simon." She looked up at him, brows drawn tight, her fingers cool and soft upon his wrists. "These were made by manacles."

CHAPTER EIGHT

THE TRUTH had asserted itself despite his secrets. Simon realized that the time had long passed for honesty. "Manacles, aye," he said gruffly. "I was in prison."

Her hands tightened on his wrists. "Why?" she breathed. "When? We heard you were briefly jailed in Edinburgh. But this—"

"I was in the dungeons—for two years."

"Oh, God," she whispered. "What were the charges?"

"I was arrested—" he drew a breath, steeled himself to deliver more of the truth that he had withheld so long "—for taking in a cargo of French laces and West Indies rum, and trading twenty casks of Scottish whisky."

"But—" Jenny stood quickly, turned away, pacing a few steps in the little niche in the rock that held them safe from the rest of the world. "But...that night you left...my father had traded a load of twenty casks of whisky for a cargo of laces and rum."

"I know," he said quietly.

She whirled. "And you were the one he entrusted to watch the goods, while he went in search of Felix, who had wandered off."

"I remember." He watched her steadily.

"He left you there," she said, "and then you disappeared."

Simon nodded. "After your father and the others left, several revenue men came with dragoons. The chief customs and excise officer was with them, sent from Edinburgh to intercept that shipment. They had already caught the free traders on the cutter out in the firth, but they did not know who else was involved. They found me with the goods, but could find no one else that night."

"And they never proved who else had a hand in that cargo. I remember—but we thought you took it. We were never told the whole truth of it. After my father and Felix saw the dragoons that night, they went back to their houses and their beds, so when the king's men knocked on their doors, they were sound asleep, or seemed so. My father thought you had done the same. When he and the others went back to the cliffs, you were gone. We heard no word from you, and the excise officer said only that my father was a lucky man to have avoided the king's men that night, and lucky to be rid of you."

"That particular officer was a sly fellow who

loathed me," he said. "I found out later that he wanted Jock to believe that I had betrayed him, to help ruin me."

"My father assumed you had taken off with his cargo."

"In a way I did. They loaded it in a cart and we went off to Edinburgh. It was a merry convoy," he said bitterly.

"Did you tell them who the goods belonged to?"

"Why would I do that?" he asked softly.

"Surely they asked."

He lifted his wrists in silence, to let the scars serve as evidence of his resistance. Someday she would see the scars on his ankles from iron cuffs, and the lash marks on his back.

"You never told," she whispered. "My father traded that cargo, arranged everything that night. You only guarded it. Yet you went to prison...to protect him, and all my kinsmen."

"Jock would have hanged if they had taken him," he said quietly. "He had been arrested too often for similar crimes. I had never been taken before, so they were lenient with my sentencing. Not death, but two years in the Edinburgh dungeons."

"In chains."

He shrugged, folded his hands to cover the scars. "I was not always...cooperative. I was glad to spare Jock's life, but I cannot say I was content to be there.''

Jenny let out a little sob and rushed toward him, sinking to her knees. ''Oh, Simon,'' she said, and wrapped her arms around him. ''Forgive me, please.''

He bent toward her, resting his cheek on her hair, gathering her close with one arm. Closing his eyes, he breathed in the scent of flowers and sunshine in her hair, savored it. How he had missed that.

''There's nothing to forgive, love,'' he murmured. ''It's I who should ask that of you.''

She shook her head. ''All this time we thought you had betrayed my father and had stolen from him to suit yourself. And I thought…that you didna love me after all.''

He made a gruff sound. ''From that day to this, I have never stopped loving you. Never, Jenny Colvin,'' he whispered. He tipped his head to rest his brow on hers. ''I came back to tell you so.''

THOSE WORDS, on his lips, seemed almost like a dream, for she had yearned for them so long. A sob caught in her throat as she gazed up at him.

''And I never stopped loving you,'' she whispered. ''Never, even though I tried—'' She looped her arms around his neck and pressed into his embrace. Lifting her face for his kiss, she felt his sigh, felt his arms tighten around her.

He brushed a hand over her hair. "I had no choice that night, Jenny. I hope you believe that."

She nodded and tilted back her head, accepting his kiss again, his lips warm and firm on hers, so that she felt his love, his strength, surround her.

His face in the moonlight was precisely cut, his eyes vivid blue, his beard a dusky shadow on his lean jaw. His mouth was full cut and gently arched, with a hint of mischief. She had always loved the shape of his lips, and she kissed them again, a quick savor. But she could not shake the taste of sadness in it as she thought of what he had endured for her, for all of them.

"Two years in prison," she whispered. "I cannot imagine...but what of the rest of the time? You've been gone four years in all."

He looked down at her soberly. "Did your father ever tell you what happened that night? Did he tell you that we argued?"

"He said only that you had a dispute over some strong differences. We assumed—my kinsmen and I—that you wanted a greater share of the smuggling profits, since you took the cargo...but then, you didna take it," she added thoughtfully, frowning up at him. "So what was the dispute over?"

"You," he murmured. "I asked your father for your hand in marriage that night—and he refused to allow it."

Her heart beat fast and hard as she gazed up at him. "What?"

"He told me that he would never allow you to marry a rogue and a smuggler. He told me to stay away from you."

She tilted her head, trying to comprehend. "He never said so to me...what if you had not been arrested that night?"

"I would have gone away for a bit, I suppose. I was already thinking of changing my circumstances. My father had insisted on my education, but as a headstrong lad, I had not used the benefit of the education, and returned to the free-trading life after university. But when I realized that I loved you and wanted to settle down into a more normal existence, I realized that I did not want to be a smuggler all my life. I wanted to make more of myself."

"Why did you not come back? I would have understood."

"Damned fool pride. When your father told me I was not good enough for you...that stayed with me a very long time. I had to prove him wrong, and prove to myself, too, that I was more than a rogue with a ruined castle and no fortune, with the law always one step behind me."

"I didna care whether you were within the law or outside of it." She slid her arms around his waist. "I wanted you, and nothing more."

"But my pride was too strong, Jenny," he murmured. "Your father thought I had betrayed him...and I felt betrayed as well. I was hurt, and proud, and determined to stay away until I could better myself."

"What did you do those two years?"

"An acquaintance of my father's befriended me in Edinburgh, a judge in the Court of Sessions. He had been present at my sentencing, and he saw to it that my treatment improved in the dungeons. When I was free, he found me a position in the customs and excise offices—I knew the law, and I knew smuggling." He shrugged. "They needed my...unique expertise."

"You never let us know." She frowned.

"I sent word at first, through my friend. I took your silence for a reply," he said.

"We never had a message. If I had known, I would have gone to Edinburgh myself, with or without my father's blessing."

He smiled and brushed a hand over her hair, then bent to kiss her again, and the tenderness and power in it threatened to melt her limbs out from under her. She grabbed his forearms for support. From the press of his hard body against her own, she knew that he felt as she did, overcome with passion, with relief, with desire long held in check.

He cupped her jaw, traced his fingers down her throat and over her upper chest, so that her heart leaped. She arched against him, ached for him, every part of her hungry for what had been so long denied, snatched away and now restored to her.

She savored his kiss, the supple touch of his tongue upon hers, his fingertips tracing lightly down her throat and over her collarbones, delicate yet firm touches that made her heart soar. When his hand moved over her bodice, she moaned softly with delight and passion.

His mouth was hungry on hers, his hands compelling as they gentled over her breasts. She gasped, sucked in her breath, felt a lightning stroke of desire plunge through her. Pressing her hips tightly against him, she felt the hard evidence of his passion for her, matching, complementing her own.

Her heart hurt to think about what he had suffered for those he loved, and she felt a surge of love so complete, so full of compassion and patience that it brought tears to her eyes as she stood wrapped in his arms.

And she wanted him to feel loved, wanted him to know how much she wanted him, and how much she still cherished him.

''Simon,'' she breathed, slipping her hands along his shoulders, then up, sinking her fingers into his thick, dark hair. She could not say more—there were no words good enough to express what she felt in her heart. She could only let her hands, her lips, her body speak for her.

As his fingers found the hidden buttons that opened the front flap of her bodice, she drew in her breath, felt her heart quicken. He pulled away the bodice and slid his hand over the chemise beneath it, and she felt the first exquisite touch of his hand upon her breast, gentle as moonlight. She drew in her breath in ecstasy, for she had not felt that sensation since he had left her heartbroken, years before.

Now, beneath his touch, she pearled for him, nipples firming, her body crying out for more, her soul radiant within her, filling with love for him. He bent his head to touch his mouth to her breast. The world seemed to shift beneath her feet, and she clung to him, ran her fingers deep into his hair.

Suddenly all of it came full circle for her—on the night he had left, she and Simon had met secretly, their kisses torrid, his hands hot upon her, and she had wanted to give herself to him completely, wanting to be with him forever. And he had told her then that he loved her. But he had refused, in a tender and gentlemanly way, to take her completely—not yet, he had said, though her body had pleaded for release with him—not yet.

Tonight she would be his at last, her finest dream come true. Wrapping her arms around his neck, she felt his hands like a blessing upon her, and she sighed into the depth of another kiss, while the moonlight sparkled over the water and the sea surged beneath the cliff, and she felt its rhythm echo within her, washing away resistance and old anger, filling her anew.

ALL THE PASSION he had saved for her poured through his soul, fired his blood. He kissed her and could hardly believe he held her like this at last. Through two years of prison, he had watched sun and moon through iron bars, and dreamed of Jenny. He had imagined her voice, her laughter, her touch, and had remembered her beautiful dark blue eyes. Now she was here in his arms—warm and willing, sweet and lush.

He had intended to take his time wooing her, for he wanted her love again, fiercely, though he would wait a lifetime if it took that. He wanted the respect of Jock and her kinsmen again, wanted all that he had lost restored, for the Colvins were like family to him. He had been lost after his parents' deaths, and Jock had given him affection and guidance and a sense of belonging. And Jenny had charmed and captivated him from the first moment, and continued to do so.

Stay away from my daughter.

God, he could not. Not when she wrapped her arms around him like this, her wildflower scent driving him mad with its elusive delicacy…nor when she tilted her head just so, touching her lips to his, opening so that he tasted the inner moisture of her mouth. Not when she sighed into his ear, spoke his name like a prayer, pressed her body against his, until he filled and pulsed hard and hot for her.

She was magic to him, part of the elemental passion that set his heart to beating, made his blood surge, kept his soul bright. Since the first day he had met her, she had been part of his life. He would not stay away, if she wanted him.

He swept his hand over the sweet curves of her breasts, felt her mouth soften and open under his. She moaned into his mouth, and her pleasure echoed in him, so that he ached deeply, hardened further for her.

He adored her fire and her innocence, her will and her purity. He wanted her so intensely that it whirled through him, body, blood and soul, like a storm he could not withstand.

Urgency rushed through him, and fire built inside of him through shared kisses and caresses. Yet he reminded himself that they might have only minutes here, for the slow sweep of the moon through the night sky would turn toward dawn soon. Outside this small pocket in the cliffside, danger lay all about, and he wanted to keep her safe.

But if she yearned for him as he did for her, he could no longer hold back. So long as they must conceal themselves from the smugglers, they would be protected by the perfect solitude of this place.

"Tell me," he whispered in the small, perfect shell of her ear. "Do you want this between us, here and now? If we go on, it will not be easy—" he kissed her, dragged his mouth from hers "—to stop. I will honor you...only tell me."

She drew back, her gaze searching his own. He let go of her, held up his hands, let her decide for herself.

Then she gave a little sigh and curled her arms around his neck, pressing against him, touching her lips to his. All the answer he needed.

"Aye," she breathed. "What we say in here, and what we do, will stay secret in this place. This is only for you and I to know."

He glanced up at the moon, pale and bright as it hovered over the glittering sea. "Aye, my love."

She opened her lips under his, touching her tongue to his. The thrill of that tenderness spiralled through him, crown to foot, as did the ecstasy of knowing that she wanted him, that she loved him.

Freedom was at hand at last for him, after so long in a prison of his own making. He pulled her to him, framed her face in his hands and let the kisses go wild, let them grow fiery and mellow, as certain and hot in their power as the finest whisky on the tongue. Kisses like white fire, sinking straight to the heart, hot and powerful.

She sighed and rubbed his wrists where the scars marked the pain he could finally release. The wound in his arm was forgotten already, its dull ache fading in a tapestry of caresses and kisses. Her hands soothed over his body, and his gentled over hers. He traced his lips along the sweet column of her throat, pulled her fast into his embrace, drank deeply of her with lips and with all of his senses.

Moving a little, he braced his back against cold, black rock, felt as if he could draw strength from the massive cliffside. The whisky still warmed his blood, but it was Jenny's own natural fire that heated him, heart and soul.

She leaned with him, and he slid his hands to her waist and downward, cupping her behind and pressing her tighter against his hardness. He was more than ready for her, but he made himself go slowly, for he did not want to rush her, or rush this.

But she seemed impatient, for she slanted her hips into his boldly. "Do not stop now," she whispered against his lips. "We have been apart so long, and no one can find us here. Simon," she whispered, as he dragged his mouth from hers, "the moon is magic tonight, and the dawn will bring too many changes—please, love me now, while the world is far away, and our secrets are safe."

He groaned, swept his hands over the curve of her back, flared over her slender hips. He pulled her against him and she tightened her arms around his neck and kissed him deep and slow and tender. He burned for her touch, ached for it, when he cupped her breasts together, stroking the nipples to firmness. Moaning, she arched toward him, and her hands traced a path along his back and his arms, gently avoiding the wound she had tended for him.

Then he turned her with him, leaning her against the dark inner wall of the snug crevice that held them so intimately. He entwined her fingers in his and lifted her arms, held her captive while he kissed her, explored her with his lips, kissed her cheek, her throat, her breasts, a rain of all the kisses he owed her for his absence, flowing over her like hot stars.

She swayed with him, rocked against him, her hands straining under his. Then he released one of her hands to slide his fingers down her skirt, lifting the dark printed cotton, seeking beneath gauzy underclothing, torn for him, until he touched her inner thighs gently, where the open slit in her drawers emanated the warmth of her body. His heart beat faster, his body surged, and for a moment he thought of the search he had been forced to make of her earlier.

He would have killed any man who had touched her like this. Pausing, he closed his eyes, breathing hard. But she gave a moan like kittenish fire, sweeping herself against his fingers, pleading. His fingers discovered her, teased, delved into honeyed softness, so that she cried out, moving against his bold touch.

She fumbled at his waistband, pulled at his buttons, shaped the hard contour in his trousers, and soon she freed him, pulled him against her. Her gown rucked up between them, fabrics sliding, and they impatiently pushed at clothing, tugged, until flesh met flesh, and hearts and breath joined in a hard, fast rhythm. He lifted her slightly, her back against the rock.

The moonlight showed her clearly to him for a moment, her eyes closed in ecstasy, the pale oval of her face blissful. The sight made him wild for her, and he kissed her lips, deep and lingering, then lifted her a little in one arm.

She wrapped her legs around him, muscles firm and strong, and then she opened for him. A moment later, her heat sank over him so exquisitely that he groaned, but kept himself still.

Unable to bear it any longer, he moved with her, and she welcomed it with a moan. Slowly, surely, he went deeper, then began to thrust, until the power of his love for her, and his need for her, burst through him like the sea pounding the cliff rocks below.

Wrapped in his arms, she tossed her head back and began to cry out, shivering with him, and he kissed her into silence, taking her cry into himself.

CHAPTER NINE

FAINT BUT DEFINITE, the noise startled Jenny so that she jumped a little, resting in Simon's arms. Held safe there, filled with a deep, blissful sense of comfort and love, she had nearly fallen asleep, as he had.

Now she heard the eerie, high-pitched scream she had heard hours ago, when she had first entered the sea cave. Shivers ran down her spine. Sitting away from the drowsy shelter of his arm, she looked around. "Simon, listen—the horse!"

"Aye." Simon went to the inner split in the rock to look toward the passageway. "They're moving her."

Listening, Jenny heard the chink of iron shoes on stone, and heard the muffled low tones of the men's voices. "Oh, God," she said. "If they take her away and sell her off, we'll lose the chance to free my father. We have to stop them somehow."

Standing, Simon went to the opening in the cliff side to look over the half wall toward the sea. Removing a spyglass from his inner pocket, he extended it and held it to his eye.

Joining him, Jenny looked far out over the sea, where dark, gleaming waves were touched with a lacy froth. The moon, round as a silver coin, hovered closer to the horizon than before. Hours had passed, and all too soon dawn would brighten the sky.

And then her father would be led to the gallows.

"Damn," Simon murmured. "Just as I thought. Look." He handed her the sleek wood-and-brass tube. ":A ship is approaching from the southwest. It's not a cutter, which could belong to smugglers or the revenue board, but a lugger, by the set of the sails."

She peered through the spyglass and found the dark shape skimming the ocean horizon. Square sails marked it as one of the small, blunt-nosed luggers often used for transporting cargo along the coastline of England and Scotland.

"Damnation," she whispered.

Simon glanced at her. "Do you recognize it?"

"It looks like one of the ships that come across now and then from the Isle of Man," she said. "My father and my kinsmen may have met that ship before. It's heading toward this shore." She handed the telescope back to him. "If it's the ship and captain I'm thinking of, they regularly trade with France."

He closed the spyglass and slipped it into his pocket. "Then that's why they're so busy this evening moving cargo down to the sea cave. They mean to meet this ship to trade those goods."

"And the horse."

"So it seems. They could easily sell the Connemara off to France, and no one could ever trace her. They only need to wait for the tide to pull out some to get her out there. And it's already receding," he added, leaning over the breast-high rock ledge to look down. "In another hour or so, the horse will be able to wade far out."

"There's a sandbar out there, where they can set a plank to bring the horse into the lugger." Jenny laid her hand on his sleeve. "Simon, please—I know you're an excise man now, and you gave up a good deal for my father's sake once before…but please help him again. We must stop them from taking that horse away."

He watched out to sea, his handsome profile clearly defined in moonlight and shadows. Behind them, in the passage, the horse neighed again, faintly heard through layers of rock. Simon turned his head to look down at her in pensive, grim silence.

"You know Jock is innocent," she said.

"Aye." He paused. "I sent Bryson and the dragoons to fetch reinforcements before I was shot, and fell into the caves. I was to meet them near the cliffs. Even without me, they should spot the activities in the sea cave, and send men down there.''

"Felix was planning to come, too. We canna chance waiting.''

He nodded. "If we can escape by the landward passage, we'll have plenty of willing assistance to stop MacSorley.''

"I wish we could bring the horse out, too—but they have her now." Jenny sighed.

"Wait here." Simon bent to enter the narrow gap. Jenny rushed to kneel there, and Simon reached out to touch her cheek. "I mean it, love. Stay here, where you'll be safe. I'll be back.''

"Simon—''

"I'll be back for you, Jenny. Nothing could keep me away.''

"I know, love," she murmured. "Your leaving doesna worry me. I just want to be with you, to help you.''

He touched her cheek for a moment, then turned to disappear into the shadows.

Once she heard his faint footsteps out in the narrow crevice, Jenny rucked up her skirts and slid through the gap.

SIMON WAS hardly surprised when Jenny came up silently behind him. He had not expected her to wait docilely—that simply was not in her nature. For good measure, he sent her a scowl, then lifted a hand to keep her safely in the shadows behind him.

Leaning to peer out in the passageway, he heard the horse neigh, then saw the mare buck, tail sweeping the air, shoes ringing on stone. The men around her were preoccupied with calming her and moving her along.

Simon turned to Jenny. "Wait...please," he whispered, and kissed her lips swiftly, feeling a sudden tender rush of love, desire and a hint of fear, as well, on her behalf. Seeing that the horse's side-stepping had thoroughly distracted the smugglers, Simon moved into the passageway and dipped into the shadows.

"What was that?" One of the men turned, holding up a lantern. "I saw something."

"'Twas naught—damn this devilish beast," the older MacSorley answered as he struggled with the lead rope. "We've got to get her doon to the water, whether she wants it or nay. The *Jupiter* has been sighted—'twill soon be close to shore, and they'll be expecting this fine cargo."

"Aye, and that beast and Jock Colvin's best whisky will fetch us a good price," one of the men, a new arrival, said.

Hearing that gruff tone, Simon peered out from the shadows and saw Angus MacSorley.

"Though I wonder where the de'il that new gauger got to," Angus said then. "I didna tell ye to wound the man, just keep him away from the cliffs.''

"He ran off somewhere—likely to find himself a physician, and fetch more dragoons. We'll take care o' this cargo afore he returns.''

"Besides, by dawn he'll want to stay in town to see Jock Colvin hang,'' the eldest man said, holding the lantern high.

That was all he needed to hear, Simon thought. But one man and one woman could do little to stop them just now. He had to get out through the landward entrance to meet Bryson and the dragoons—and he had to get Jenny out of here quickly.

He peered past the out-thrust in the rock that hid him from sight. Not fifteen feet away, he saw the white horse, her lead held by the older man he had seen earlier. Four other men came from the direction of the storage cave, hoisting two casks of whisky each on their shoulders. They paused hesitantly, unable to make their way around past the Connemara, while the older MacSorley and another man struggled to tug her along.

"We'll get her onto the lugger, and she'll be sold off soon enough and no longer our problem,'' the older man said.

Angus nodded. "Shame to give her up—she's done well for us these months.''

"Aye, the legend—but we'll find another white horse to continue it,'' his cousin answered. "I wish we'd thought of it years ago. It keeps the locals away, and the excise men, too.''

"Well, the beast will be off to France, and Jock will have his hanging," the older man said, "and we'll own the whisky trade along the Solway shore." He gave a celebratory whoop, which echoed in the passage, and only startled the horse further. She kicked out, forelegs beating the air, her cries reverberating.

Simon glanced back at Jenny, who stood in dark shadows. He could see her wide eyes and angry, tightened mouth. She had clearly been listening, and took a step forward as if she meant to do something about what she had heard.

Simon held up a cautioning hand. Then he removed his coat, dropping it into the shadows, and reached upward to grasp the rock. Testing the strength of his left arm, he found it still painful but capable enough with the bleeding stopped.

Stealthily, bathed in shadows and unnoticed by the men, Simon swarmed up a toothy section of the rock wall.

JENNY NEARLY gasped aloud when she looked up to see Simon balanced on a lip of the rock. Pressing close to the wall inside the narrow crevice, she watched him climb upward through the darkness. Glancing toward the passageway, she saw the elder MacSorley cousin pulling the horse along the corridor. And she saw that Angus MacSorley was with them.

Wondering what Simon intended to do, she watched, biting her lip anxiously. Blending into the shadows high on the wall, he slowly stood, booted feet precariously balanced on a ledge about eight or ten feet above the floor of the cave. The smugglers, focused on the behavior of the restive horse, ducked to avoid her whipping hooves. None of them noticed the man who inched along the ledge above the level of their heads, hidden by darkness.

As one of the men yanked on the lead rope, pulling the Connemara down the corridor, the mare advanced a few steps, then whickered and stomped the ground.

Simon crouched and whistled softly, the sound reverberating eerily in the cave. Then he stepped out into plain air and dropped neatly onto the horse's bare back.

Pandemonium erupted as the horse reared, pawing the air, and the smugglers staggered frantically out of the way. One dove down the corridor, and Angus stumbled to his knees while the eldest man fell over him. Those who carried casks dropped them hastily and ducked, so that kegs and men seemed to roll on the floor.

Heart pounding, Jenny watched, fisting her hand against her mouth to keep from crying out. One of the smugglers fell near her and slid past with a grunt, knocking his head against rock.

She looked up again to see Simon winding the fingers of one hand in the horse's mane. Reaching out with the other hand, he snatched at the head-rope. The older smuggler still had hold of it, though he had been thrown back against the wall. Leaning forward, releasing his hold on the Beauty's mane, Simon slipped the little knife from his belt, cut the taut rope and freed the horse from the smuggler's hold.

Jamming the knife into his belt, he used the shortened bridle rope, the mane, the strength of his knees and sheer instinctive skill to control her as she bucked and whirled about.

"Jenny!" he called, as the horse kicked out, knocking over another man who began to rise to his feet. "Jenny!" He glanced over his shoulder, then turned the horse's head.

Dashing into the corridor, skirting two men who lay dazed or unconscious on the ground, Jenny ran the few feet toward the horse. Whistling, cajoling, pulling with the headrope so that the horse was forced to circle and could no longer buck, Simon calmed the horse enough so that it stood, breathing heavily.

Leaning to stretching out his right arm, Simon beckoned urgently to Jenny. She ran toward him, leaping upward as he grasped her forearm and pulled. A moment later she was seated astride the horse's flanks behind Simon, holding on to his waist as he turned the horse again.

Leaning forward, he urged the Connemara down the corridor. Iron shoes echoing loudly against the rock, breath bellowing, the horse plunged into the darkness.

Jenny clung to Simon, bent low with him. Glancing back, she saw some of the men get to their feet and begin pounding after them in pursuit, their shouts reverberating from the walls.

As Simon guided the horse around the crazy turns in the maze of tunnels, Jenny kept her head low, as he did, too, for the ceiling heights varied from one channel through the rock to the next. As they turned down the short stem toward the landward exit, Simon turned to look at her.

"The door," he said. "You'll have to open it." He slowed the horse, which stomped and snorted. While Simon soothed the Beauty with a stroking hand and a calm voice, he gave Jenny support as she slid from her perch, feet smacking on stone.

Stumbling to her knees, she rose and ran for the end of the tunnel and the ramp of rock that led upward to the stone that blocked the exit. Behind her, Simon brought the horse closer, dismounted and walked the animal the rest of the way.

Hearing shouts and stomping feet as MacSorley's men came down the tunnel in pursuit, Jenny tugged on the iron ring embedded in the stone door. She threw her weight back until the stone yielded and swung inward on its hinges.

Pushing it wide, she felt cool, fresh air and glimpsed moonlight above layers of earth and grass. The ramp in the tunnel continued past the stone slab to the level of the moor. The exit opened out of the side of a hillock amid a heavy cluster of boulders, screened by bracken and grasses.

She stepped aside to allow Simon to pass as he tugged the Connemara forward with the rope. Suddenly the animal snorted, sensing fresh outside air, and tried to barrel past Simon to escape. Holding the lead to avoid losing the horse once it got outside, Simon managed to climb out first, then turned to coax the horse through. Avoiding the dangerous hooves and the powerful flanks, Jenny helped guide the horse from behind.

Little cajoling was needed, for the Connemara gave a desperate neigh and clambered out quickly, if awkwardly, soon planting its four feet on soft turf, lifting its head to whicker in clear relief for a moment.

While the horse grazed a little, Simon reached down to help Jenny scramble outside. She fell to her knees in cool, dewy grass, then looked up. Bathed in moonlight, the moor seemed a magical, wondrous place. Jenny glanced around, feeling as if she had never seen it before, or saw it with new vision.

Then, through the opened hole slanted into rock and earth, she heard the angry roars of men pounding along the tunnel. Simon dove for the slab and pulled on its iron handle, groaning with the effort as he yanked it closed on its hinges. Just as the smugglers streamed toward the door, he slammed it into place. Their shouts were suddenly muffled and then silenced.

Simon grabbed a nearby rock and jammed it through the handle for a makeshift lock. "That will hold them, but only for a bit," he said. "Now where is that—" He turned where he stood, looking at the ground, walking in a circle around the concealed entrance.

"What are you searching for?"

"My pistol," he answered. "I dropped it when I fell—here it is, thank God." He bent to retrieve his gun carefully from under a patch of gorse, and slid it into his belt. "Come on, then," he told Jenny, holding out his hand.

Nodding, she rose from the damp grass. Overhead, the bright moon hovered on a velvety field sparkling with stars. But along the horizon, a faint blue-gray line already glowed.

"Dawn," she murmured. She turned to Simon. "It's nearly dawn! We have to get to the Tolbooth—"

"Aye." Holding both her hand and the mare's rope, he tugged them toward the nearby hawthorn copse.

"There's no time to put Sweetheart back in her harness," Jenny gasped. "And we've got to bring the Beauty to the sheriff—Simon, wait. Help me up—I'll ride her."

Without protest, Simon cupped his hands for her foot, and she vaulted onto the Connemara's bare back. Pressing with her knees to keep her seat, she twisted her hands in the long, thick white mane. While Simon bolted into the hawthorn grove, she waited impatiently, the mare echoing her anxiousness by prancing and pawing, although accepting Jenny as her rider.

Simon rode out of the grove, mounted on the black stallion that he had left there earlier, and drew up beside her. His own horse shifted restively, sensing the urgency.

"Can you do this?" Simon asked.

"Aye," Jenny answered, and leaned forward, legs and hands gripping tightly, to surge past him.

Simon followed her through the fading moonlight.

CHAPTER TEN

CANTERING BESIDE Jenny, Simon soon glimpsed men running through the darkness along the cliff side. He shifted the reins to his left hand, ignoring the ache in his wounded arm, and rested his free hand on the butt of his pistol. With a glance at Jenny, he urged the stallion ahead of the Connemara.

"Who goes there?" A man emerged from behind a cluster of rocks. "Is it you, Lockhart?"

"Aye." Seeing Bryson, Simon slowed his mount and turned, while Jenny followed, her horse a pale shadow on the dark moor.

As the revenue officer approached, Simon saw three dragoons with him. In the shadows beside an outcrop of rock, several other men walked under the guard of more uniformed dragoons.

"Where have you been?" Bryson complained as he came toward Simon.

"In the sea caves," Simon answered. "Who's that with you?"

"We caught the rascals who were parading over

the moor earlier," Bryson said, gesturing toward the group, who approached with an escort of four dragoons holding bayonets.

"Uncle Felix!" Jenny said, turning to look.

"Aye, Felix Colvin and his band," Bryson said. "They claim to be innocent of wrongdoing, but we caught them—"

"They're not the men we want," Simon said. "Let them go."

"But they were leading a convoy of men and packhorses—"

"The rascals we want tonight are down in the sea caves, readying cargo to take out to a lugger in the firth. In fact," Simon said, gesturing behind him, "if you post a few dragoons near that rocky hillock near the hawthorn copse, with guns at the ready, you'll soon see rascals come up through the ground, and into your trap."

"What?" Bryson said.

"I'll explain later. And send some men down the cliffs to the sea caves, if you will, to nab some lads who are about to row out of there to meet a lugger out in the estuary."

"What about Felix Colvin and his lads? We were taking them to the Tolbooth."

"Oh, I'd wager they'd be glad to go after the rogues down in the caves—aye, Felix?" he asked, as Jenny's kinsmen walked up in the company of the dragoons.

"Fetch MacSorley's lads for ye? Och, aye," Felix replied.

"They're carrying a load of whisky stolen from Miss Colvin's legitimate still, with plans to sell it off for a profit," Simon said. "You might want to reclaim that for your niece."

"We surely would," Felix growled. He looked at Jenny. "What's that horse you've got, lass? Looks familiar." He frowned.

"This is the Beauty," she said, smiling, as she patted the horse's neck.

"The Beauty!" Felix gaped. "How could ye catch her?"

"She's the very one Nicky saw earlier tonight," Jenny said, as the Connemara sidestepped nervously. "And she's anxious to bring good fortune to my father." Smiling, she rounded away with the mare and urged the animal to a brisk canter over the moor.

"What the devil—" Bryson said.

"Has the lassie gone daft?" Felix asked. "What horse is that?"

"The magistrate's horse," Simon replied. "We found her in the caves—MacSorley had her all along, after stealing her weeks ago. That horse will bring very good luck indeed to Jock Colvin."

"If ye get there in time, lad—the dawn is breaking," Felix said, pointing toward the pink blush on the horizon. "Hurry! D'ye think ye can catch that lassie?" He peered past Simon.

"Oh, I think so," Simon drawled, as he turned his horse's head to urge the stallion forward.

Jenny was not so easy to overtake this time, for the Connemara was swift and strong and desperate for a good run, but Simon rode with consummate skill and a light hand. Soon he drew the black stallion alongside the pale mare. Jenny glanced over at him, her hair and cloak whipping back, and she smiled, slowing so that their horses could keep pace.

"Greetings, Miss Colvin," he said pleasantly.

"Sir Simon," she said. "Will we have enough time to get there, do you think?" She glanced upward anxiously.

The wide bowl of the sky was still dark overhead, scattered with stars, and the full moon rode like a pearl on that sparkling field. Where the sky met the horizon, rosy pink light glowed.

"Sun and moon together," he said, looking at the beautiful sight. "Surely that must be a good omen for us."

"I hope so." She frowned.

"We have time, Jenny love," he said. "If you're worried about your father, that fine horse will take you to him in a hurry."

She slowed the horse and halted. A little surprised, Simon followed suit with the stallion, and maneuvered close to Jenny's horse, about to ask her what she needed.

Leaning toward him, Jenny kissed his lips, quick and tender. He slid his fingers deep into the silky thickness of her hair, renewed the kiss, and drew back.

"What was that for?" he asked. "I thought you were in a great rush."

"I am," she said. "I just want you to know how much I love you, Simon Lockhart, and how very grateful I am to you. And I wanted to ask if you were coming with me." Twining her fingers into the horse's long white mane, she watched him.

"I'll be right beside you, love," he said. "Always. I swear it." He leaned down and kissed her again, embracing her in the circle of his arm. "And Jock Colvin will have to learn to live with that."

She laughed, a silvery sound, and drew away, riding swift as the wind. Simon easily kept pace, smiling to himself, deeply glad to know that Jock's life was about to begin anew.

And so was his own, for he had wooed Jenny Colvin after all, and in the span of one moonlit night.

Dear Reader,

There's always been something special about a full moon. Whether worshiped as a goddess by ancient Egyptians, praised in verse by lovesick Elizabethan poets, or regarded as a gift of light by farmers hurrying to harvest a crop, a full moon glowing in the night sky is a powerful sight. Even jaded New Yorkers will slow down long enough to gaze up at a full moon as it rises majestically between the skyscrapers.

In "The Devil's Own Moon," the full moon becomes a kind of celestial matchmaker for two long-parted lovers determined to stay that way. While childhood friends Sophie and Harry first discovered the joy and passion of love in a moonlit stable, well-meaning parents conspired to separate them, and their very different lives keep them apart as adults. But years later another glorious full moon draws them together once again, and this time the power of love won't be denied.

The idea for this anthology was concocted by several good friends sitting beneath a beautiful full moon in Harper's Ferry, West Virginia, surely one of the most romantic spots in America. As you read these stories, I hope you can share some of the good times and laughter that inspired us on that moonstruck night.

Please look for my next full-length book, *The Passionate Princess,* coming this fall from Harlequin Historicals.

Happy reading, and happy spring!

Miranda Jarrett

THE DEVIL'S OWN MOON

Miranda Jarrett

For my dear friends and moon-maiden sisters,
Merline and Susan (and a special nod to Cathy!)
Who else could be more deserving?

CHAPTER ONE

LORD HARRY BURTON, the fifth earl of Atherwall, gazed from the window at White's, and wondered restlessly how the devil he was going to pass one more interminable night in London.

The gray afternoon, still more winter than early spring, was already fading away into dusk, and over the rooftops and chimney pots an icy pale full moon was rising to stake its claim in the sky. A chilly wind licked through the streets and alleys, swirling dead leaves and old newspapers against the legs of the few hapless pedestrians. Most Londoners of his class would be perfectly happy to forgo any entertainment on such a night and so unfashionably early in the season, and spend the evening instead snug in their own elegant drawing rooms, warm and cozy before their smoky coal fires with brandy and hot China tea to keep away the rest of the chill.

But then the Earl of Atherwall had never behaved

like the rest of his class, and tonight would be no exception.

"Mark that plump little hussy down there on the pavement, Harry," said his friend Lord Walter Ranford, standing at the window beside him. "Singing for her supper, I'd say."

Harry lowered his gaze from the rising moon to the street below, where a young ballad singer was bravely continuing her trade despite the wind and cold. Her round face was ruddy from the chill and her body was swathed in so many layers of woolen scarves and shawls and petticoats that she resembled the sparrows in the park who fluffed their feathers to keep warm. The basket at her feet held only a handful of coins to show for her songs, and the few passersby on the street were too eager to reach their destinations to linger and listen. Yet still she sang, her head thrown back and her mittened hands clasped before her.

"I'll wager a guinea that her voice is sweeter than that fat old cow we heard at the opera last night," continued Walter, rhapsodizing over the girl with the same romantic eagerness that he showed toward most women. "With a face as sweet as that, how could she sing other than like an angel?"

"Only if the clouds of heaven are spun from ice," said Harry idly. The girl was pretty enough, with an upturned nose and curly ginger hair, though her tenuous life on street corners was already beginning to harden her face. No matter how Walter might idealize her, Harry was too realistic not to suspect that she'd likely be on another street practicing another trade later that night, making up the difference after the small day's take from her singing alone. "If I take your wager, how do you propose to judge her voice?"

"I could have her brought inside," said Walter, his enthusiasm bounding ahead of common sense. "She could sing for us as we dined, and we could judge her that way."

"What, and risk spoiling my meal if her song isn't as sweet as you want it to be?" said Harry. "No, better to judge from here, I think."

"You'll take my wager?" asked Walter with surprise, for Harry seldom accepted anything Walter proposed, especially where women were concerned.

"Oh, why not," said Harry indulgently. Walter could be a bit of a fool, but at least he was a good-natured one, and besides, what else did Harry himself have to do for the next quarter hour or so? "Let's test your fair angel's talents."

Without waiting for Walter to answer, he unlatched the sash and threw the window open, the curtains billowing inward with a gust of cold, gritty wind. Ignoring the indignant protests of the other gentlemen in the room, Harry leaned out the open window, his elbows on the sill and his dark hair tossing around his forehead. The cold felt good on his face, sharp and *real* in a way that too few things did for him these days.

"Good day, sweetheart," he called. "My friend here has wagered that you sing better than the celebrated Signora di Bellagranda."

The girl turned her face toward them and grinned widely enough to show the gap where, young as she was, she'd already lost a tooth, or had it knocked out.

"G'day, m'lord," she called cheerfully, assuming correctly that if Harry were leaning from the club's window, he must be a nobleman. She dipped a curtsey, her patched skirts sweeping the pavement. "Do that be your friend beside you, th' one what has most excellent taste in music?"

Eagerly Walter crowded in beside Harry. "I am that friend, dearie," he declared. "Would you grace us with your favorite song?"

The girl tipped her head to one side. "Not for nothin', I won't, m'lord."

"Win or lose, you'll have the guinea that's been wagered," said Harry, and the girl's eyes widened with awe. A guinea was likely more than she'd earn in a month of songs. "But you will have to sing, so we can judge."

"Aye, m'lord, that I will." She nodded, and cleared her throat self-consciously. "'The Sorrowful History of the Highwayman Dick Turpin,' m'lord, if you please."

She closed her eyes, clasped her hands together again, and began. Her voice *was* good, clear and on key and easily rising over the sounds of the street. If she lacked the trills and frills that Signora di Bellagranda had acquired on the Continent, then that was not necessarily a bad thing to Harry's ears.

Yet what truly captured his attention was neither the girl's voice, nor her face, but the song itself. Each verse catalogued another step of the famous highwayman's career, from humble beginnings to glory and love and finally, the inevitable capture, trial and trip to the gallows. The song couldn't have been that old—there were people still living who could recall Turpin's hanging—nor did it likely have much basis in fact, romanticizing the life of a common horse thief and highway robber. Yet in the girl's robustly melancholy voice Harry could hear all the differences between the dash and adventure of Turpin's day, and the dull constraints of his own modern times.

"I say, Atherwall," whined one of the gentlemen in the overstuffed chairs behind him. "I've had about enough of that infernal arctic blast of yours. Shut that window directly, I say, before we all perish."

"Oh, yes, we shall *all* perish," declared Harry from the window, raising his voice so everyone would hear him. "But it will be boredom that does us in, not some paltry April breeze. Blinding, blistering *boredom*."

"That's putting it a bit rough, Harry, isn't it?" asked Walter uneasily. "Likely you've already heard enough of the girl's song to judge her, anyway."

"I've heard enough to judge her exactly as you say, and agree that her voice is far superior to the signora's." Harry reached into his pocket for a handful of coins. "Here, missy. You've more than defended England's honor."

"Thank'ee, m'lord, thank'ee!" The girl grinned and curtseyed, then swiftly gathered the coins Harry tossed down to her. He could hear her astonished gasp clear up at the window: he'd given her four times the guinea he'd promised. She curtsied one last time, then, while Harry still leaned out the window to watch, she scurried away with her new wealth before he might change his mind.

"She's gone, Harry," said Walter, shivering beside him. "Now you can shut this wretched window."

"What, on such a balmy April evening?" Harry smiled back over his shoulder, pointedly keeping the window open. "It's so fine, Walter, I've half a mind to go out riding."

"Don't be an ass," said Walter crossly. "No

sane man would ride anywhere tonight if he didn't have to."

"I've never claimed to be sane, Walter," said Harry easily. He slid the window closed and turned, folding his arms across his chest. "That girl's song made me think, that is all."

At once Walter's expression turned wary, an expression Harry recognized readily enough. He was always making other people wary like this; it was something of a habit with him, albeit an unintentional one.

"What the devil are you plotting this time, Harry?" asked Walter uneasily. "Not another breakneck race to Edinburgh on hired nags, I trust, or driving a curricle blindfolded. No more shame to the good name of this club, yes?"

"Oh, certainly not." Harry shrugged elaborately, well aware of how many of the others were now listening, too. No doubt the whispers were already starting, and the wagers in the betting book with them. He'd never set out to make his reputation as a daredevil, or to feed the scandal pages of the newspapers. All he'd wanted to do was test the limits of his own skill and resourcefulness, and test and try himself as well.

And if, in the process, he also recklessly courted danger, disaster and death, then so be it. It was no one else's business but his own, and he simply didn't care. He was unburdened with a wife, a family, a mistress or any other mortal who might genuinely care what became of him. The only two people who had brightened his life—his younger brother George and the only girl he'd truly loved—had long ago left it, and him, forever. He'd yet to see his thirtieth birthday, he was strong and reasonably handsome, rich beyond reason and titled beyond reproach, and yet there were far too many mornings when he stared up at the pleated canopy over his bed and wondered bleakly why fate had let him—*him*—wake to another day.

Walter cleared his throat self-consciously. "Then what's this about, Harry? How exactly did that chit's song set you to thinking? Damnation, but I hate it when you turn mysterious!"

Harry glanced past him, to the large looking glass that hung over one of the fireplaces. There the reflection of the rising full moon seemed to be a silver beacon to him, beckoning him to—to what?

"How long ago did Dick Turpin ride his famous Black Bess across Hounslow Heath, anyway?" he mused. "Our grandfather's time, no more, yet how much has changed since those days!"

Walter snorted derisively. "What's changed is that now a gentleman can travel in peace, not fearing for his life and pocket watch."

"But consider the adventure that's been lost!" said Harry with a sigh of regret. "What's become of gallantry, I ask you? Those old gentleman of the road knew how to steal a lady's heart along with her locket, just as they could share the purse of some fat country squire with orphans and widows.''

"What's become of them is that they've all been hanged," said Walter. "Just like you will be if you try this."

"One night, Walter," coaxed Harry. "One ride, that is all. A black scarf and cloak, a brace of pistols and the darkest horse in my stable to be my own Black Bess. How can I let a moon such as this one go to waste?"

"You will if you value your life," warned Walter earnestly. "Harry, these days every mail coach has a man with a blunderbuss on the box beside the driver, and they won't pause to ask your name or leave before they shoot you dead."

But Harry only smiled. "Who said I'd stop a mail coach? A private coach, one with a pretty lady inside—that's more to my fancy."

"A full moon's no guarantee of anything, and neither is a pretty lady," said Walter, shaking his head. "You, of all men, should know that."

"And I, of all men, do not care." Harry reached out to clap Walter heartily on the shoulder. "You must know by now what a perverse creature I am. The surest way to make me do anything is to tell me I can't."

"Of course you *can*," said Walter with obvious frustration. "It's just that you *shouldn't*."

"But I'm giving you a chance to win more than a guinea tonight, Walter," said Harry easily. "I'm sure a good many of the gentlemen in this room will show more faith in my abilities, and be eager to place a few coins on my head to match yours. Being so certain that I'll be scattered into oblivion by a blunderbuss, you're bound to triple your money at the very least."

"For God's sake, Harry," sputtered Walter. "I've no intention of betting against you, even when you insist—"

"Gentlemen," announced Harry, sweeping his arm grandly before him, a showman as well as an earl. "Lord Ranford has challenged me to re-enact one of Dick Turpin's famous rides across the heath this night."

"The devil he has!" exclaimed another man with obvious delight. "What are the terms this time, Burton? How shall we know if you've done as you've said?"

"I'll bring back my victim's purse as proof," promised Harry, "before I deposit it into the poor box, in true Robin Hood fashion, and if there's a lady in the carriage I stop, I'll capture her handkerchief as well. As for knowing beyond that—I cannot imagine that the return of a dashing highwayman will remain a secret for long in this city, can you?"

"Ten pounds says you'll get away with it, Burton,'' declared another man. "No constable will ever catch you on those devil-bred horses you favor.''

''And I say you'll be stopped before you start,'' called someone else. "This is 1803, Burton, and thieves of that sort aren't to be tolerated.''

''Address your opinions and wagers to Ranford,'' said Harry with a farewell bow that encompassed the entire room. "I've much to do to prepare for tonight.''

He left in his wake both cheers of encouragement and mutters of disapproval, the way it usually was with him. Yet the excitement of what he planned raised his spirits, and the sharp evening air that struck his face as he stepped from the club's door only increased his anticipation. No matter how unfashionable it was for a gentleman to walk anywhere in London, to Harry the distance between White's and his own house in St. James's Square seemed far too short to bother with the display of a carriage, and his stride was long and purposeful as he cut across the cobbled streets. The wind was dying with the day, yet still the first lamplighters were struggling with stray gusts as they tried to steady their ladders against the posts.

Looking once again up over the rooftops, Harry wondered why the lamplighters bothered. The full moon now glowed round in the sky like a disc of polished silver, nearly as bright as the golden sun itself. A moon like this would cast shadows on the moor as if it were day instead of night, and briefly Harry questioned the wisdom of his plan. No highwayman could be properly mysterious in such conditions.

But perhaps being seen was not so very bad after all. A black-clad figure on a dark horse, washed in silvery light—what could be more daring and romantic than that? For him the best part would be the chase, racing through the night at a breakneck pace to ambush a solitary carriage. He intended to carry a brace of pistols for effect, and to defend himself if it came to that, but as for the capture, he hoped to be able to rely more on surprise and charm for success than on force and threats, especially if a lady were involved.

He smiled to himself, picturing some fair creature begging prettily for his mercy, which he, ever gallant, would gladly give. Wide-eyed, she'd lean from the carriage's window, where the moonlight would find her face, and—

And what? His imagination stopped abruptly, brought to a halt by a memory as brilliant as the moonlight itself, a memory so shockingly sharp it made him swear aloud.

Another April moon such as this one, ten years ago, his last night home at Atherwall Manor before his journey across the Continent began: he was eighteen again, and Sophie was sixteen, the age she'd always remain for him. They'd met in their special secret place up the ladder and over the stables, where they knew they'd be alone except for the sleepy horses below.

But still the moonlight had followed, slicing in through the square single window to find the thick golden blond of her hair. Sophie's hair had always reminded him of a new-mowed shock of hay, straight and shining and resisting her aunt's efforts to make it curl for fashion's sake, and she'd smelled like new hay in the sun, too, sweet and wild, with freckles like cinnamon scattered over the bridge of her nose.

She'd promised to be brave and not to cry, and she'd kept her word to the last. But the sadness in her eyes had been inescapable, as if she'd already realized how final their farewell would be, and when they made love one last time, it had seemed to him that every touch of hers, every kiss, had carried a bittersweet tenderness. She'd known then; she'd known. But he, great strapping fool that he'd been, had understood only when it was too late, when she'd sent back his letters unopened, unread, unwanted.

They had been friends, it seemed, since she'd been born, and he'd always expected her to be there with him until he died, and he'd never, ever dreamed instead that she'd end everything so completely the first time fate had separated them.

"Good evening, my lord," said the butler as he opened the door, his expression swiftly changing to concern as Harry stepped into the light of the night-lantern in the hall. "My lord, are you unwell? Should I fetch—"

"Of course I'm well," said Harry, striving to recover his earlier bravado. No one could undo the past, least of all the past he'd shared with Sophie Potts, and the sooner he could finally make himself accept that, the better. "Well enough, at any rate. Now come, Hargraves, and hurry. I've much to do this night, and precious little time in which to do it."

CHAPTER TWO

"BETTER YOU SHOULD spend the night here, miss," said Mrs. Lowry, the innkeeper's sturdy wife, her hands folded over her apron and her broad face wreathed with concern. "It's not safe to begin such a journey after dark. It's courting bad luck, miss, plain and simple."

Deliberately Sophie set the stoneware teacup down on the table. Believing in luck, bad or good, was a luxury she'd never granted to herself. "I thank you for your concern," she said, "but the moment the wheel on the carriage is mended, I must be on my way."

But Mrs. Lowry pretended not to hear, instead openly appraising Sophie's plain travelling dress and gauging her ability to pay. The inn was small and old, with only this single public room, and from the lingering haze of last night's tobacco to the bare, battered tables, Sophie guessed that most of the Lowrys' business came from local farmers coming to drink when their day was done, and not from weary travelers staying overnight.

"I won't charge you much for the night, miss," said the innkeeper's wife finally, deciding Sophie was worth her trouble. "You being respectable and all, I could put you in with the widow. She's small, and won't take more than her share of the bedstead."

What a sorry compliment, thought Sophie wryly, that she was now considered such a well-aged spinster at twenty-seven as to be safe company for poor widows! Yet what else would Mrs. Lowry make of her? She was dressed in somber, serviceable clothing, a gray wool gown with a dark blue wool spencer buttoned up close beneath her chin, and her hair was drawn back so tightly under her untrimmed bonnet's sugar-scoop brim that not a strand of it showed. She looked like an old maid because circumstances had made her one, and she'd long ago abandoned any impractical, impossible dreams of a husband and children of her own.

Yet still she wasn't so old that she'd forgotten when she'd been regarded as a beauty instead, when gentlemen in the street would turn to watch her when she passed them by, when one handsome young man in particular had called her the loveliest girl in the kingdom, and given her his heart to prove it....

"I am sorry, Mrs. Lowry, but I cannot linger," Sophie said, her bittersweet smile more for her memories than the woman before her. "I am expected to arrive as soon as is possible."

Mrs. Lowry sniffed. "That's if you arrive at all," she said darkly. "There's things that happen out upon the road that no young woman such as yourself should have to suffer."

"Oh, I'm a practical creature, Mrs. Lowry," answered Sophie confidently, "and I'm not easily frightened, particularly not by goblins and ghosts hiding in the shadows. I'm accustomed to making do for myself. I've come clear from Lincolnshire thus far without mishap, and I expect to reach Winchester the same way."

But Mrs. Lowry only shook her head. "It's not the ghosts I'm speaking of, miss. It's the flesh-and-blood dangers. I cannot speak for Lincolnshire, but this close to London and Portsmouth, things are different. Times are unsettled on account of the French war. There's all manner of thieving ruffians about on the roads, deserters from the army and those who've run from navy ships and the good Lord knows what else. And considering the sorry state of your carriage, miss, why, I'd—"

"*Thank* you, Mrs. Lowry," said Sophie as firmly as she could, determined not to listen to any more. "I appreciate your interest in my welfare, but my plans remain unchanged."

Of course her plans wouldn't change, no matter what Mrs. Lowry urged. How could they? A governess between positions had no say in such arrangements. In the best of circumstances, a governess was little more than an elevated housemaid, expected to obey her employers' wishes without question. If Sir William, her new master, wanted her to begin her responsibilities as soon as possible, then Sophie would. He had even insisted on sending a hired carriage to fetch her from Iron Hill, her last place in Lincolnshire, to be sure she arrived safely.

Sophie had appreciated his concern, until she'd seen the carriage itself: an ancient, spavined specimen on rickety wheels, and driven by a large, gruff man whose name she still hadn't caught. The worn springs and patched seat cushions that smelled like nesting cats had been a not-so-subtle indication of how Sir William already regarded his sons' new governess, as were the second-rate horses that were acquired at each change along the road. When earlier today a spoke on the left lead wheel had cracked on a large rock, Sophie had been startled, but not surprised.

But she *would* cope, and once again make the best of the lot she'd been given. She would not be intimidated by Sir William or his rickety hired carriage, or frightened by the possibility of phantom thieves. She would adapt, and she would persevere, the way she always did. It was one of her greatest strengths, something to take pride in. Every one of her references praised her for it: "No challenge is ever too great for dear Miss Potts."

"Please yourself, then, miss," said Mrs. Lowry, pointedly gathering up Sophie's empty tea cup without refilling it another time. "Risk your life to oblige your master's whims. Leastways you'll have the moon for company, even if your common sense has fled."

And how much more agreeable company that moon would make than an ill-tempered innkeeper's wife, thought Sophie wearily as Mrs. Lowry stalked back toward the kitchen. Sophie would take the moon any day, hands down. With a sigh, she pushed the bench back from the table and stood, smoothing her skirts as best she could. After three days of travelling, her clothes were rumpled and wrinkled and filmed with a fine coating of road dust that no amount of brushing seemed able to budge.

But if she and the carriage were spared further accidents, she should reach her destination by tomorrow morning, and with that knowledge to fortify her, she retied the ribbons of her bonnet beneath her chin and resolutely headed for the door.

And gasped out loud.

The moon rising over the roof of the inn's stable was more like a set piece on the stage, all candle-light and silver foil, than a real feature of the evening sky. As round and silvery bright as a new-minted Spanish dollar, this moon managed to make the sky itself seem too small to contain it, clamoring for attention from everything grand or small that now basked in the glorious glow of its light.

Only one other time have I seen such a moon. Only one other time, another April night, and that so long ago it could have belonged to another life....

"There you be, miss." The carriage's driver tugged on the front of his broad-brimmed felt hat. "Will you be going now?"

Reluctantly Sophie looked away from the moon to the man before her. This was a sizable speech for the driver, but it still left questions unanswered.

"You were able to find an acceptable wheelwright in this village, then?" she asked briskly. "Is the wheel mended to your satisfaction?"

"It'll do," said the man. "Well enough."

"That is not convincing," said Sophie. "I've no wish to have my neck broken in the middle of the night because of a poorly done repair."

He shrugged, as if to agree that he wasn't entirely convinced, either, but what else could be expected?

"Might I see the wheel for myself?" Dealing with uncommunicative boys was a specialty of hers—she was as good at coaxing them to speak as she was at teaching them to write in a fine, gentlemanly hand without blots—and though the driver was far older than any of her charges, she guessed the same direct approach would apply. "Would you please show me the repair?"

"Aye, miss." He led her to the gig in the court-yard, a drowsing horse already waiting in the traces. "There it be."

She leaned over to inspect the wheel, though be-yond the newness of the replaced spoke, she hadn't much notion of what she was inspecting.

"We can stay 'til morning, miss," said the driver. "On 'count of you not wantin' to go."

"But I do." She rose, brushing her hands to-gether. "If you are satisfied with the wheel, then we shall leave directly."

The man scowled stubbornly. "It don't be the wheel, miss."

Sophie sighed, her impatience growing. "Then what exactly *is* it?"

"That moon," he said, solemnly pointing up in the sky like some Old Testament prophet. "Strange mischief happens wit' a moon like that one."

Strange mischief: was that all it had been with her and Harry beneath that other long-ago moon?

"Moon like that be same as midsummer night," he continued. "No matter that it be April. The fairy queens and such will be about, no mistake, ready t' fright the horses."

"Butter and beans," declared Sophie soundly, folding her arms over her chest to reinforce the strongest oath she ever used. "My father was a cleric in the Church of England, and he would have told you that the only place fairies and goblins and other heathen nonsense exist is in an empty head, especially a head made more empty by a full belly of gin below it. Now shall you drive me as you were hired to do, or must I climb up top and take the reins myself?''

Grumbling what was doubtless a great many oaths toward Sophie and her ancestry, the driver finally took his place on his seat and Sophie hers inside, and the gig rolled slowly from the inn's yard and onto the open road. Once again Sophie settled herself as best she could against the flattened cushions, her sore muscles protesting at resuming the same uncomfortable position as they had these last days.

She drew the carriage robe over her legs against the evening chill, and tucked her hands beneath her arms for good measure. If she hadn't been so busy arguing with the driver over the fairies and the moonlight, she would have asked at the inn for a jug of hot tea to bring with her, and perhaps a light supper to last her through this final leg of her journey.

Well, she'd be the one to pay now, not the driver, and it would serve her right if a random fairy or two did cross their path this night. She sighed, curling her feet up on the seat beneath the robe, and gazed out at the moon, still rising in the evening sky. How much her life had changed since that long-ago April full moon, she thought drowsily, and how much she'd changed herself, while Harry—ah, Harry would never change, because he'd never had to.

She couldn't remember a time when Harry hadn't been there for her, whether they'd been hunting frogs in the rushes near the pond, or pretending to translate Latin fables while her father dozed in the next room, or climbing the apple trees for the sweetest fruit in the orchard at the manor. He had been her best friend and companion for so long that when they'd finally, awkwardly, blissfully kissed, the summer she'd turned sixteen, it had simply seemed like one more glorious adventure to be shared with Harry.

But her father, his health failing, had seen the peril in such adventure. Sorrowfully he blamed himself for his inattention, and for allowing Sophie to become so familiar with the family at the manor. He understood what Sophie herself was too young to comprehend: that when Harry's father died, Harry would become the fifth earl of Atherwall, while Sophie would be no more than the penniless daughter of a country cleric, with no fortune or future, especially not with an earl. Sooner or later—more likely sooner—Harry would inevitably leave Sophie and any child she might conceive, and take as his wife a more suitable girl of his own class.

The bitter, heartbreaking truth of that had hurt, hurt worse than anything Sophie had every imagined. Harry could never be so faithless—to love, to friendship, to her—and she'd tearfully refused to believe such a grim prediction. But she'd been practical even then, hadn't she? Once her tears were dried, she'd done what was best for everyone. At last she'd listened to her father's reasoning, and by the time Harry had left for his two years' tour travelling the Continent, she'd come to see how inevitable their parting must be.

Her father had written to Harry on her behalf, and returned every one of Harry's letters unopened and unread. Then to put her father's worries about her future to rest, she'd accepted her first position as a governess. She didn't doubt that she'd done what was right, even if it never, ever would be fair....

It was the jolt of the sudden stop that woke her, tossing her forward clear off the seat into an inglorious heap of petticoats. Still more asleep than awake, Sophie clumsily struggled upright on the carriage's floor, shoving her hat back from where it had been knocked across her face. Not another broken wheel, she thought with dismay as she struggled to untangle her legs from her skirts. At this rate they'd never reach Winchester.

But then she heard the stranger's voice, and froze.

"Keep your hands where I can see them," he was ordering the driver. His voice sounded muffled, as if he were disguising it behind a scarf or mask. "No foolishness, or you'll be the one to pay."

Her heart pounding, Sophie kept low, not wanting to draw attention to herself. Through the window, she could see they were stopped beneath the dark shadows of trees, the branches a black tangle against the night sky. They'd been ambushed by some low sort of thief, trapped like a drowsy chicken by a fox, and her temper flared at the foolish indignity of it. Hadn't enough happened on this miserable journey without *this?*

"You bloody thievin' coward," snarled the driver. "You've stopped th' wrong carriage, you have."

"What, because you're the brave fellow with the reins?" asked the other man, clearly bemused.

"Nay, because I've only th' one passenger," said the driver stubbornly, "and she don't be what a bastard like you wants, not at all."

The man chuckled, and Sophie's anger simmered, hot with indignation. Though the thief's voice seemed purposefully disguised, from his manner and words Sophie was sure he'd been raised a gentleman, accustomed to being obeyed. But what sort of gentleman would have become a highwayman, stopping carriages on the road at night? And what *gentleman* would enjoy distressing a woman travelling alone, laughing at her plight like this one was doing to her this very moment?

"So you wish to be the fair lady's champion?" he asked the driver. "You would defend her?"

"Nay, *I* won't do that," answered the driver quickly, and without a hint of gallantry—not that Sophie had expected any. "She be plain, an' poor and sharp-tongued, too. If it weren't for what her master'd say if I lost his new gov'ness, I'd give her t' you outright, an' save th' horse instead."

"A plain, poor governess." The disappointment in the man's voice was so palpable that Sophie wrinkled her nose. He was a fine one to show such scorn for her position, considering how dishonorably he earned his living! "Ah, well, better I should judge for myself, yes?"

Sophie could hear him coming closer, the puffing of the horse's breathing and the jingle of its harness. The man might be disappointed in the prospect of *her*, but he still would have an interest in her purse—the purse filled with her hard-earned coins that she'd no intention of surrendering to a lazy rascal like him.

Think, Sophie, think! Don't just sit here cowering like a helpless head of cabbage, waiting for the stewpot. Show a bit of backbone. Think of how to save yourself, then do it!

He was on one side of the carriage, and she on the other, and swiftly, before that changed, she reached up to unlatch the door, shoved it open, and scrambled out to the ground. With so much moonlight, she'd need to use the carriage as a screen between her and the man as long as she could. She bunched her skirts to one side, freeing her legs to run, and began clambering up the embankment, her shoes sliding in the soft, damp soil. If she could just get to the bushes, she could hide there in the shadows, until the thief lost interest and rode away. She'd already disappointed him by being poor; how much more time would he be willing waste on her, anyway?

But she'd forgotten her ungallant driver. He'd turned to look when he'd heard her open the carriage door, and as soon as he realized she was fleeing, he lashed his whip over the horses' backs, making them jump forward in their traces.

"Stop, you miserable coward!" she shouted furiously after him as the carriage rattled away. It wasn't only that he'd abandoned her; he'd absconded with the two trunks with her clothes and books and other belongings, as well. "Stop at once, you—you—*ohh!*"

Suddenly the man on the horse loomed up in the road before her, a menacing black silhouette made sharp in the moonlight. He was a large, powerfully built man, made larger by the horse dancing lightly beneath him and the dark cape billowing around his broad shoulders.

What a great blustering bully, observed an unimpressed Sophie, trying to intimidate a lone woman on an empty road. She'd known five-year-olds with better manners—at least after they'd had her as their governess.

"Stand and deliver," he ordered through the dark scarf wrapped around the lower part of his face, giving his voice an extra growl for effect. "Now, miss. Be quick about it."

"No, I will not," she answered irritably, folding her arms across her chest to stand her ground on the sloping embankment. After all, *he* was the one who should be on his guard, not her. Because of him, she was going to be late to arrive at Sir William's house, and she hated being late to anything. She was tired and hungry and cold and in a perfectly foul humor after watching most of her worldly goods go rumbling off into the night, likely never to be seen again. Oh, yes, *he* should be the one on his guard from her.

"First, I will not 'stand and deliver,' because I am already standing," she continued, "and secondly, because I do not oblige great hulking bullies simply because they say I must."

Without answering, he shifted slightly in the saddle, turning so she couldn't miss the moonlight glancing off the long barrel of the pistol in his hand.

But she also didn't miss how he'd left the lock on the gun uncocked. She'd grown up in the country, and thanks to Harry, she knew all about guns—far more, apparently, than did this sorry excuse for a highwayman. He was like an oversized watchdog without any teeth, all bark and bluster but no bite.

"Hand me your money," he ordered gruffly. "That's all I want. To give to the poor."

"For the *poor?*" she repeated, incredulous. "You expect me to believe that?"

"You should, because it's true," he said, more than a little defensively. "Give me your pocketbook, and then you shall be free to go."

"Oh, butter and beans," she said crossly. "This being England, I'm free to go now, if I please, and with my pocketbook, too."

"Wait," he said softly. "Please."

To her own surprise, she did. She wasn't exactly sure what it was in his voice that made her pause, but she heard it just the same, and waited as he'd asked.

"Take off your hat," he said in the same soft voice, strangely more potent to her than all his earlier menace. "Let me see your face."

Instantly her wariness returned. "Why? So you might see for yourself if I'm as plain as that infernal driver deemed me to be?"

"Please," he said again. "For the sake of beans and butter."

"Butter and *beans*." She narrowed her eyes, not understanding why he'd quoted her own nonsensical words back at her. But once again, she found herself obeying, untying the wide ribbons of her bonnet and sliding it back from her head. She wasn't ashamed of her face, plain though it might have become, and she raised her chin to the moonlight to let him look his full.

"Sophie," he said. "My God, Sophie, it's you."

CHAPTER THREE

FATE, THOUGHT HARRY with wondering amazement. It had to be fate that had brought them back together after so many years.

She'd changed, of course. Who wouldn't, in that time? The angles in that lithe, coltish body he'd remembered so well had softened and grown more womanly, her movements less impulsive and more assured. She'd grown into her face, too: the passionate mouth that was too full for accepted beauty, the tiny crescent-shaped scar on one cheek left from a childhood fall from an apple tree, the quizzical dark brows that still didn't match her fair hair. But even before he'd seen her face, he'd known it was her. He hadn't believed it at first, his heart racing even as he'd denied the possibility to himself, but still somehow he'd *known*.

But what had given fate such a damned peculiar sense of humor as to play this sort of trick on him? To deposit Sophie Potts back into his life here, on this deserted road, with him gotten up as a highwayman for the sake of some infernal wager and her dressed as—well, he couldn't put a decent word to the hideous, unflattering way she was dressed, could he?

But it *was* her, and that was really all that mattered.

"Sophie," he said again, tucking the pistol back into his belt and swinging down from the saddle to join her. "Sophie, I—"

"Stop," she said sharply. "Stop where you are, sir, and come no closer."

Belatedly he pulled the scarf from his face and pushed back his hat so she'd recognize him. "Sophie, look," he said. "Look at me. I'm not a 'sir.' I'm Harry."

Her frown became more perplexed as she searched his face. Even in the moonlight her eyes were exactly as he'd remembered them, a deep, intense blue framed with thick golden lashes, beautiful eyes, but intelligent, too, and always filled with questions.

Including, it seemed, now. "Harry? It cannot possibly be you, can it? Can it? *Harry?*"

"The same." He grinned, unable to help it, and scarcely able to wait for the moment she'd throw her arms around him like the old days. He almost— *almost*—expected next to see his brother George come bounding from the trees. Indeed, seeing Sophie again was making him feel as if the past ten years and all their sorrows had magically vanished, a grim weight lifted from his back. "Tell me you'd know me still, lass. Tell me I'm not so vastly different as all that."

"Actually, you are," she said evenly, frowning a bit as she looked him up and down. "You're a great deal larger than I recall."

"I'm not the stripling I was at eighteen, no," he admitted confidently. He was still lean, but now there was muscle and strength to his body and limbs, as well. "But that isn't such a bad thing for a gentleman."

For the first time she smiled, her face softening with amusement: another reminder of what he'd lost when she'd disappeared from his life. "You haven't changed so very much after all, have you, Harry?"

"Seeing you again makes all that time feel like nothing."

"Nothing?" she asked, the bittersweet regret in her voice unmistakable. "It's been nearly ten years, Harry. So much has happened to us both since then, hasn't it? I was only seventeen when you sailed, you know, and you'd just passed your nineteenth birthday."

"The fifth of May." He smiled crookedly, wondering exactly how much else she was remembering along with his birthday. God knows it was all coming back to *him:* her taste, her scent, the way she'd laugh with gleeful triumph when she'd outrun him through the orchard, then sigh with contentment afterward when they'd lie in the tall grass and he'd hold her close. "You would remember the dates and such. You were always far better than I at ciphering and logic."

"Yes," she said, smiling still as she glanced down at the gun in his belt, "and I always knew enough to uncock the flintlock on a pistol if I intended to use it."

He followed her glance down to the pistol, as if seeing it for the first time that evening. "But I didn't intend to use it," he said sheepishly, "not truly, and never against you."

"Then what precisely *were* you doing, Harry?" she asked, her smile fading. The breeze was tugging at the tight knot of her hair, pulling tendrils free to dance across her temples and cheeks, and impatiently she brushed them aside with her gloved fingertips. "What manner of cruel masquerade would reduce you to stopping hired carriages to rob the women passengers?"

"I don't know how to explain it, Sophie," he said slowly. She'd scoff at his wager with Walter as foolish and idle, and though she'd be right, he didn't want to spoil things by hearing her tell him so.

But how could he have guessed that when he'd stood at the window at White's, watching the moon rise, that it would somehow lead him back to Sophie Potts?

"It was the moon, *this* moon," he continued, grasping for the right words. "Likely you won't believe me, Sophie, but you have been in my thoughts ever since it came over the rooftops."

Ever skeptical, she tipped her face to one side. "The *moon,* Harry?"

"Yes, the moon," he said, his voice low, confidential, as if wooing her all over again. He took a step closer in the road, pulling off his glove before he reached out toward her. "It's almost as if that infernal moon were haunting me, making me think of nothing but you and the past. Remember, lass, remember the last night before I left for Dover? That was April, too, with another moon exactly the twin to this one, and—"

"No, Harry, don't," she interrupted abruptly, shaking her head. "Please. Don't."

"Why not, Sophie?" he said, undeterred. He swept his hand up toward the sky, so grand a gesture that his horse whinnied uneasily behind him. "Can't you see for yourself? It's fate that's brought us back together, lass, fate and this moon that—"

"But I don't believe in fate, Harry," she said, purposefully looking away from the sky and moon to the rutted road beneath them. "If you can remember that I had skill at ciphering, then you should likewise recall that I don't believe in fate, or destiny, or anything else that claims we cannot have will over the lives God gave us. I never have, Harry, and I'm not going to begin now, not even for the sake of your moon.''

''I'm not asking you to begin anything new.'' Gently he touched her chilly cheek with his fingertips, not wishing to startle her as he coaxed her to trust him again. Yet still he could feel the little tremor that rippled through her, a shiver of—of what? Fear or excitement or uncertainty, anticipation or dread or the wildest joy, all the same things he was feeling himself?

''I'm only asking you to be the old Sophie from the manor,'' he continued, ''the one who seized whatever life tossed her way, and claimed it as her own. Remember who you are, lass, and what we had together. That's all I'm asking.''

''That's a great deal.'' Though she didn't pull away from his touch, her eyes were troubled as she searched his face. ''We were scarce more than children then.''

''We were far more than that, Sophie,'' he whispered, leaning closer to kiss her. ''We were lovers.''

''No, Harry, don't,'' she cried softly, twisting away from him just before his lips found hers. ''What we were then no longer matters.''

''Damnation, Sophie, it does,'' he said, hoarse with frustration. He reached for her again, and once again she pulled away, her heavy woolen skirts swinging out from her legs like a bell. "Why won't you admit it?"

"For the same reasons I left you before," she said, her words coming in such a painful rush it was almost a sob. "Because I'm good at calculations and logic and seeing which things can be combined with success and which cannot. Because we were never meant to last together, Harry, and all the moonlight in this sorry world cannot alter that truth."

"What if I said I cared for you still?" he demanded. "That's the truth, moon or not."

But she only shook her head again. "You should have forgotten me, the way I forgot you."

"But you didn't, Sophie," he insisted. "Damnation, I've only to look at your eyes now to know that. Why can't you admit you still care for me, as well, the way I know you do? Why can't we take this night that's been given us, and leave the rest until tomorrow?"

"I won't, Harry," she whispered, her voice breaking with a long, heartbreaking sob. "I can't. Not even you could make me do that. Because you will always be the Earl of Atherwall, and I will never be more than a mere country governess, and neither of us a match for the other."

But before he could answer, to his shock, she *changed.*

There on the moonlit road, she swallowed back the sob and visibly steeled herself, straightening her back and composing her features into severe propriety and blinking back any stray tears. Through sheer willpower alone, she put everything to rights. Briskly she tied the bonnet ribbons beneath her chin, using the broad brim like blinders to shutter and shadow her face, and the transformation was complete. In no more than a minute, she'd smothered both her beauty and emotions as surely as if she'd hidden them behind a mask. She became exactly what her driver had declared her to be: a poor, plain governess that no man would ever notice.

"Do you understand, my lord?" she said. Even her voice now seemed to carry a governess's schoolroom authority, while the use of his title—damnation, he never thought he'd hear that from *her!*—served to accentuate the gulf between them even more. "Have I made myself clear, my lord?"

He nodded silently, too stunned to find words for his response—at least not words he'd want to use to her.

How in blazes could she possibly believe he gave a fig about his rank over hers? How could she do that, when she was the one who'd thrown up a wall of scratchy wool and propriety between them, as impenetrable as one of stone and mortar?

Yet here she was, wanting him to believe she'd no interest left in him at all, that she'd prefer her life as a lowly governess to whatever he offered. Of course if she truly wanted to be free of him, then he'd let her go. He had never forced a woman to do anything she didn't want, and he wasn't going to begin now.

But the memory of the other Sophie, the laughing, bold, adventurous girl that he'd loved with such passion and delight—that Sophie wouldn't let him leave. God knows he'd seen glimpses of her tonight, little bright flashes behind the severe facade that proved she still existed.

One more night with her was all he was asking. One more night together…

She claimed she placed no value in fate, and proudly made her own choices for how she ordered her life. Well, then, so be it. Let her be stubborn; let her be proud. He wouldn't argue, because that, too, was part of what made her Sophie, and besides, she'd never give in.

But before this night was over, he'd play the ruthless highwayman again. He'd use every scrap of charm and persuasion and passion to steal away her heart for keeps. This time, when she made her final decision, he'd leave no doubt that she'd make the right choice: the one that would include him.

"You do understand, my lord?" said Sophie again, striving to keep the anxiety from her voice along with every other emotion. She wished he would answer, instead of simply *standing* there. "I have made myself clear?"

The tall man before her was Harry, and yet he wasn't. He'd changed, her Harry, and this elegant, self-possessed gentleman in black was a far cry from the boy she remembered. His smile was the same, and so was his laugh, but the well-muscled chest and arms beneath the tailored coat were new, as was the lordly imperious air that, she guessed, must have come with his title. There now was a darkness to him, too, that was harder to explain, a moody undercurrent that seemed as black as his clothes.

It worried her, this black streak, just as she was worried by whatever foolishness had inspired his masquerade as a highwayman. Over the years, she'd read enough newspapers with accounts of fashionable London to know how his boyish impulsiveness had grown dangerously into reckless dares and wagers. It had been one thing to see how high he could climb up a tree when they'd been children, and it was quite another for him to drive a phaeton blindfolded at breakneck speeds. If the driver on her own carriage tonight had been armed, he very well could have killed Harry outright. Then the fact that Harry's pistol hadn't been cocked would have been as meaningless as his intentions. It was almost as if he wished to die, a final, flamboyant gesture to show the world he was beyond caring.

And he'd been right, painfully right, about one thing: God help them both, *she* did still care for him.

"Do you understand, my lord?" she said again, feeling like a desperate parrot with only one question learned by rote. "Do you—"

"Yes, lass, I do." His voice was low, careful and now intentionally devoid of the emotion he'd shown before. "I do not care for your decision, but I shall abide by it."

"Thank you." She knew she was making the right choice. Along with Harry's wagers and exploits, those newspapers had also linked him to scores of women, titled, wealthy beauties all, and each one of them proof that he'd never keep a lasting affection for a humble country spinster. A duchess might indulge in an dalliance with Harry, but a governess would only be ruined.

Of course she'd made the proper decision.

But suddenly Sophie felt the evening's chill, making her hug her hands around her folded arms. At least the walk ahead would warm her, even if it could never be as satisfying as the kiss she'd rebuffed. She looked down the road where her carriage had vanished. "Do you know how far it is to the nearest inn? I was asleep when we stopped, and did not notice how far we'd come."

"Not far," said Harry, pointing in the opposite direction. "Perhaps a quarter mile at most."

"But what about that way?" she asked. "That's where that wretched driver went with all my belongings."

"Oh, at least five miles," said Harry. "That is, if that rattletrap of yours can travel so far without falling to bits."

"It already very nearly has," she said, her unhappiness growing by the second as she stared down the road, as if staring alone would somehow bring the carriage back. "A pox on that lazy coward of a driver! He has not only robbed me of my trunk, but now I'll never make Winchester when I promised. Even if Sir William doesn't dismiss me outright before I've properly begun, then he'll still regard me as an unpunctual laggard, unfit to be trusted with his sons."

"You, Sophie, a *laggard?*" asked Harry wryly. "Oh, my, my. Pray not a *laggard,* of all things base and unspeakable. Whatever is this kingdom coming to?"

She turned back toward him, glaring. "This is your fault, too, my lord. Don't pretend that it isn't. If you hadn't startled that dullard of a driver with your—your *foolishness,* then he wouldn't have bolted in the first place."

But Harry only shrugged, unconcerned. "You

should be glad to be rid of the man. He certainly was happy enough to shed you.''

"I'm so very pleased you're amused, my lord,'' she said, snapping off each word like a brittle icicle. "What better use for my troubles than to entertain you?''

"Oh, Sophie, I am sorry.'' He smiled ruefully, open repentance that licked at those icicles. "I *have* caused you trouble. I admit full responsibility, freely and openly.''

She sniffed. Things were seldom so direct with Harry. "Thank you, my lord.''

"I should be the one thanking you,'' he said, his cloak giving a grand flourish to his bow, "for being so forgiving. Now you must let me make my amends, as any gentleman should.''

"You needn't do anything, my lord.'' she said quickly. She couldn't allow herself to become indebted to Harry, not for so much as a shilling. "You are not obligated to me in the least.''

But he swept aside her objections as if he hadn't heard them, and perhaps, now being an earl, he hadn't. "I'll take you myself to the closer inn and see that you are fed and settled there for the night. Tomorrow we'll find that rascal with your trunk, and then I'll have my own carriage come take you wherever you please.''

"No!'' she exclaimed, appalled that he'd assume such responsibility for her welfare. For years she had been an independent woman, perfectly capable of looking after herself, and she most certainly did not wish to be ''settled'' anywhere by Harry. ''That is, thank you, my lord, but I can manage perfectly well for myself.''

She curtseyed with the deference owed to earls, then turned and began walking briskly down the road, toward the closer inn.

''You needn't walk, Sophie,'' he called after her. ''It's a chill night for a forced march.''

''Thank you, my lord, but both my feet and my shoes are equal to the challenge,'' she called back without turning. She suspected he was following, but she wouldn't give him the satisfaction of looking over her shoulder to be certain. ''It shall take more than a bit of a breeze to stop me.''

''But why walk at all,'' he reasoned, ''when you might ride instead?''

Instantly she recalled riding with him on a summer morning so early that the sun had just begun to rise. They hadn't bothered with a saddle, but had ridden together on one horse with only a blanket beneath them. With no grooms yet in the stable to watch, she'd hiked up her skirts over her bare legs and sat astride, nestled back against Harry while his arms had held her steady, and she'd felt like some wild, pagan princess, racing with him across the open fields....

''The saddle will not accommodate two riders,

my lord, nor would it be a proper arrangement for us,'' she said, striving to push away the unruly memory. *Blast* him for making her thoughts go down such paths! ''I shall walk, thank you.''

''But I didn't mean to ride with you,'' he said, coming up to join her as he led the large black gelding by the reins. ''You shall have Thunder here to yourself, and I'll walk.''

She flushed with guilt, wondering if he'd been remembering their wanton summer mornings, too, or if they'd only been in her own wicked head.

''I meant that it's not a sidesaddle for a lady's use, my lord, and besides, I've no wish to deprive you of your own horse,'' she said, quickening her steps even though she knew she'd no hope of outpacing his long stride. ''You ride, and I'll continue as I am.''

''Then I shall walk with you,'' he said, easily falling into step with her, the way he'd done in the old days. Though he made no move to take her hand again or otherwise touch her, she was still so acutely aware of his nearness that the sensation was almost painful.

''At least, I will, Sophie,'' he continued, ''unless you have an objection to sharing the road with another traveler. But beneath this moon it's quite companionable for old friends like us, don't you agree?''

She stopped abruptly at that, making him stop, too.

"It's not going to be the same as it was, Harry," she said urgently. "You can just put that notion aside right now. What we had when we were young is long past done, finished, and it won't ever be the same again."

With his face patched with moonlight, his smile came slowly, almost lazily, and so filled with his old charm that she simultaneously wished to shriek with protest at the unfairness of it and purr with pleasure like a happy cat feeling its warmth.

"Oh, Sophie," he said fondly. "Of course it won't be the same. It will be *better*. Much better, if I've any say. But never the same, lass. Never the same."

"Oh, butter and *beans*," she muttered defensively, and with every last shred of resolve, she turned away from him and kept walking.

CHAPTER FOUR

"THERE'S THE INN NOW," said Harry, pointing toward the long, low house with six chimneys, sitting in the crook of the road. He had been walking beside her like an unwelcome specter; he might as well be useful, and point out the local landmarks. "The Peacock. Known for its turtle soup and tamarind punch, and a blind fiddler named Orlando who knows every song ever written."

Sophie paused for a moment, studying the inn. "You are familiar with this place, then?"

"I've dined there, yes," he admitted, and no more. The truth was that, when he'd been younger, the Peacock had been a favorite spot of his in the spring and summer. Tables and benches were brought out beneath the trees and along the stream that ran behind the inn, and the fiddler had played for the dancers under the starlit skies, long into the night. The inn was near enough to London for Harry to bring a lady for supper, yet sufficiently far away as to make the trip seem like an adventure to the lady, and far enough, too, to justify taking a room for the night if the supper went well.

Not that Sophie needed to learn any of that.

He glanced down at her, at how she was brushing the dust from her hem before she'd go farther. He didn't remember her as being this overly concerned with appearances, or so determined to do what was right and proper. Perhaps that had come of being a governess, but for her own sake, he'd like to see her relax and be more at ease with herself as she was, and less concerned with how others might judge her. In other words, he wanted her to be like the old Sophie—the Sophie he was sure was somehow still beside him, retying the bow on her grimly unfortunate bonnet for what must have been the hundredth time this evening.

"The Peacock, you say," she said, sounding like a general reconnoitering the field of battle. The inn seemed uncharacteristically busy for the middle of the week, with light streaming from its window and patrons noisily coming and going through the yard. "I suppose it looks well enough from here. The inn has a respectable reputation among travelers?"

"I've never heard any complaints," he hedged, which, while true, was not perhaps what she meant. "If the same host is there that I recall, then he'll see that we're welcomed most handsomely."

She looked up at him with surprise. "'We,' my lord? I know you have walked with me this far—"

"And a rare pleasure it has been," he said gallantly, though in fact it hadn't been, not really. They hadn't exchanged more than a dozen words in the entire half mile they'd walked: scarcely the witty conversation he'd hoped for. All he'd really wanted to do was to stop the infernal trudge and slip his arm around her waist and pull the bonnet from her head and the pins from the tight knot so her glorious golden hair would spill down her back.

And then, with her face turned up toward him and moon, he'd kiss her and she'd kiss him, for as long as it'd take to compensate for the ten years they'd lost.

"I'd hoped I'd made my wishes clear, my lord," she was saying. "I do not require welcoming or anything else from this innkeeper. Rather I intend to make the necessary arrangements to retrieve my belongings, and continue on my way to Winchester, all as swiftly as possible. I am a most capable woman, my lord."

"Yet even the most capable women know when to accept assistance," he countered. "The keep is an old acquaintance of mine, and will be more inclined to help you after a word or two from me."

But such an offer was a mistake with her, a bad one, and she bristled accordingly.

"I do not need your *words,* my lord," she said. "Not one nor even two of them."

"Sophie, please," he began. "Blast, I didn't intend it like that!"

But off she went again without him, showing far more endurance than he'd given her credit for.

Far, far more, indeed, than did his horse, who decided that moment that he was too weary to walk another step.

"Hell, Thunder, not *now*," said Harry, leaning forward as he yanked as hard as he could on the reins. Sophie had nearly reached the inn's signpost, painted with a cross-eyed portrait of the inn's namesake bird. "Move yourself, you damned wretched beast!"

With a snort the horse suddenly complied, catching Harry so off balance that he fell stumbling backward into the dust. By the time he—and Thunder—had managed to recover together, Sophie had already disappeared inside the inn.

With the *whoosh* of the opening door to draw her in, Sophie felt as if she'd plunged into a river teeming and swirling with people of every age—people laughing, eating, shouting, flirting, toasting, singing, drinking, and dancing and everything being done at the loudest, most boisterous level possible, from the front tap room to the hall and up the stairway and down again. Overwhelmed by so much merriment, Sophie pressed back against the door frame, leery of being swept off into another room and never seen again. Crowds always made her uneasy, which was likely why she'd never cared for London. But she could cope with such challenges; any truly *capable* woman could.

"Ah, mistress, good day, good day!" called the red-faced innkeeper in his green apron, elbowing his way toward her. "John Connor, mistress, your servant. You've caught us on quite a night, haven't you? I trust the lads have seen to your horses in the yard?"

"Thank you, sir," shouted Sophie, standing very straight and striving to make herself heard over the fiddle player who'd just begun a fresh tune. "But I've no horses to be seen to. That's my problem, you see. I need to find—"

"Beg pardon, mistress?" the man called, apologetically tapping his forefinger beside his ear to show he couldn't understand her over the din. "You've a problem with your horses?"

"No, no, no!" she shouted, then lowered her voice as the man pushed his way to her. "No, Mr. Connor. My driver has left me, and now I must hire a carriage or chaise to take me to Winchester. As soon as can be arranged, Mr. Connor, if you please."

Connor tucked in his chin and frowned as he shook his head. "Not this night, mistress. I am very sorry to disappoint you, but with all this drinking and frolicking, there's not a man left sober enough to climb onto the box, let alone drive clear to Winchester.''

Sophie squared her shoulders with determination. ''I am willing to pay what is necessary, Mr. Connor,'' she said, holding her reticule before her to reinforce her words and her credit. ''But I must reach Winchester tomorrow.''

The innkeeper only shook his head again, his jowls swinging beneath his chin.

''Not from here, you won't, mistress,'' he said firmly. ''It'd be worth your life to go with one of these—why, my Lord Burton! How long it's been since you've graced us here at the old Peacock! Welcome, my lord, welcome!''

Sophie didn't have to look to know that Harry had joined her. Why should she, when Connor's greeting was as good as a royal fanfare?

''How are you, Connor?'' said Harry warmly. ''And your wife and the little ones? Ah, I've been away too long, that's a fact.''

''Well, well, we cannot complain,'' beamed the innkeeper, and then his smile vanished, his face turning solemn as he noticed Harry's dress. ''Oh, my lord, I am sorry! Here I am a-babbling on, and you in deep mourning. My sympathy on your loss, my lord.''

Now Sophie turned, ready to scoff at the notion of Harry's highwayman's black being mistaken for mourning. But to her shock, Harry's expression had suddenly gone shuttered and sorrowful, as if he truly did suffer from the deepest grief possible. She didn't have to know who he'd lost. Automatically she reached for his hand, pressing her fingers around his to offer whatever comfort she could to ease his suffering.

"Forgive me, mistress," said the innkeeper, quick to notice their linked hands—though not so quick to hide his surprise, his brows raised as he glanced over her rumpled wool travelling clothes and judged her frankly unworthy of the earl of Atherwall's attentions. "I did not realize you were with his lordship."

"Oh, Miss Potts has known me even longer than you have, Connor," said Harry, threading his fingers more closely into hers, acknowledgement of her gesture, and comfort returned. "Friends from the nursery, you could say."

And unexpected though it was, Harry's hand in hers *was* a comfort, one she'd missed more than she'd realized. The only hands she held these days belonged to children, and once again to feel Harry's familiar touch, his fingers so strong and sure as they curled around hers, connecting them together, brought a shock of pleasure she thought she'd put aside.

But neither comfort nor pleasure was proper for her to accept from him, and carefully, reluctantly, she now slipped her hand free of Harry's.

"As his lordship says, Mr. Connor, we are friends, but nothing more," she explained carefully, reminding herself of all the other women Harry must have brought here before her. "Nothing more at all."

But Connor wasn't listening to her. "Perhaps you can make the lady see reason, my lord. We've a great wedding feast here tonight, with all the county come to celebrate, and though this lady wants to go to Winchester, I haven't a man here I'd trust with a horse to take her."

"But have you a horse you'd trust with me, Connor?" asked Harry. "One fit for a lady to ride?"

"I am an excellent rider, Mr. Connor," said Sophie, seizing the idea. "Most any horse in your stable would do, so long as it could carry me to Winchester."

"Only if you're riding with his lordship here, mistress," said the innkeeper firmly, looking past her to the other room. "There's too many rascals on the road for a lady to travel by herself. Now, my lord, would you be wanting a bit of late supper for you and the lady, and your usual bedchamber? As crowded as we are this night, my lord, for you I can—"

"No bedchamber," said Sophie quickly. It would be one thing to share the road with Harry, but a bedchamber was another matter entirely. "No supper, either, Mr. Connor. We must be on our way as soon as possible.''

''Ah, Connor, you hear the lady's wishes,'' said Harry with a rueful sigh. ''No charming supper before the fire, no private room upstairs.''

The innkeeper frowned, studying the crowd that filled the front room. ''I know we're full to bursting, my lord, but I could make places for you and the lady by the fire, if you wish to warm yourselves.''

''Thank you, no,'' said Sophie quickly, unnerved by the prospect of squeezing in with so many others. ''We are perfectly fine as we are.''

Harry sighed again, more dramatically this time. ''You see how it is, Connor,'' he said. ''No matter how agreeable I try to be, Miss Potts cannot abide to keep my company.''

The innkeeper nodded with pity, commiserating as if Sophie weren't even there. ''Isn't that always the way with women, my lord?'' he said. ''But I'll have the cook fix you a nice supper to take with you in your saddlebag, my lord. We'll look after you proper, just the same. Maybe a supper by the light of that moon outside will change her heart, yes?''

''Ah, Connor, you're too kind,'' said Harry with a conspirator's grin that Sophie found intensely irritating.

''Not at all, my lord.'' The innkeeper bowed, already backing away to fill Harry's requests. "And pray come back to us at the old Peacock again soon, my lord, mind?"

"Why did you say I can't abide your company?" asked Sophie, more wounded than indignant. "You know that isn't true."

Harry looked down at her, and though he was smiling, she knew him—and that kind of smile—well enough not to trust it. "How the devil would I know that, given how you've grabbed at every chance you've had to try to run away from me?"

"Because it's—it's not true, that's why," she said, wincing inwardly at how inadequate this must sound as an excuse. But inadequate or otherwise, what else could she tell him? That she had to keep her distance because she enjoyed his company too much, not too little? That if she didn't, she'd tumble back into his arms as if nothing—not everything—had changed? "Because I say it isn't true, that's why."

"And that is supposed to be enough for me to believe you?" he asked lightly. "Your word alone?"

Before she could answer, a man with two tankards of beer in each hand came reeling past them, bumping into Sophie. At once Harry put his hands to her shoulders to keep her from falling, steadying her, but at the same time drawing her closer to him.

Not to kiss, not to embrace: merely to hold her there, close enough, close enough.

"Yes," she said finally, startling herself by how that single word had become a breathy sigh. "Because I don't lie, Harry, not now or before, about this or anything else. You *know* that about me, or at least you should."

His smile relaxed, and so did Sophie. The fiddler was playing a quick-paced reel, the floorboards beneath them shaking from the dancers' feet. "Lord Higginbotham's Reel"—she'd never hear it again without thinking of this moment. It was vastly strange to her that they could be standing in the front hall of this inn, with scores of people around them, and yet all she saw was Harry before her.

"That is true," he mused. "You couldn't lie to save your own life. Look, lass, there's the fair bride."

Sophie turned to follow his gaze, through the open doorway into the front room. To the raucous cheers of the guests, the young bride had been lifted onto a table for all to admire and toast, her eyes bright and her cheeks flushed with both exhilaration and nervousness at being the centerpiece of so much attention. She was dressed in a white sprigged gown with more white ribbons in her hair, and, like so many country brides, she was visibly pregnant. Her groom clambered up beside her, and with beer-inspired boldness, he took his new wife in his arms and gave her a loud, smacking kiss to the whooping delight of their guests.

"How pretty she is!" said Sophie wistfully. "I hope they'll be happy together."

Harry chuckled, leaning close over her shoulder. "From the looks of her, I'd say they've already found some degree of bliss with one another."

Sophie smiled, still watching the couple. "They look so young, don't they?"

"No younger than we were," he said, slipping his arms loosely around her waist as if he'd every right to do so. "Or have you forgotten, pet?"

"No," she said softly, letting herself sway back against him. "How could I?"

How could she, indeed, standing here in the circle of his arms with her head resting against Harry's shoulder? Even if she could have forced herself to remove such pleasurable thoughts from her memory, her body would always remember the passion she'd discovered with this man, and her heart—her heart would safekeep the rest for eternity.

Oh, she knew it was wrong to be so familiar with him here in such a public place, wrong to be so openly affectionate, and if any of her employers could have seen her like this, she would have been dismissed outright, without references. But the happiness of the wedding party and the young bride and groom made her forget such hard realities, and instead made her think back to when her world had been this full of love and promise, when the giddy measure of life's joy could be contained in a single stolen kiss.

"Do you remember watching the parish weddings with me?" she asked. "I had to be there, because of Father, but you always came, too, to keep me company."

"And for the sweet biscuits that were served afterward," he said, tightening his arms to draw her closer against his chest. "The shortcake ones shaped like shamrocks were the best, and I'd always be sure to take some home in my pockets for George. You know, Sophie, that when I watched those weddings with you, I always believed you'd be my wife."

"You did?" She twisted about, wanting to see if he was teasing, but to her surprise, he wasn't. "Boys aren't supposed to think of weddings, especially not boys who will become earls."

"Oh, but I did," he confessed, his smile lopsided and his blue eyes full of fond recollection. "I thought it had all been arranged, and deuced practical it seemed, too. I'd figured that was why you were so often at the manor with us, that you were practicing to be part of my family. Then, once we were old enough, your father would marry us in that same parish church, just as he did all the other couples who came to him. What ripe foolishness *that* was!"

She smiled in return, even as his confession stung her heart. He was right, of course. Such a fantasy *was* ripe foolishness, yet she could hardly find fault for him for wishing the same wish she'd secretly had herself.

"Your father would never have permitted such a match," she said swiftly, wanting to protect herself once again with the armor of facts and reason. "As much as he liked playing chess with my father, I would still have been too low-born for his elder son. He never let pass any chance to remind me of that. I was *common*."

"You were my *Sophie*," he said firmly, slipping his hand inside the brim of her bonnet to cup her cheek against his palm, and gently turn her face up toward his. "That was more than enough for me."

"Beg pardon, m' lord," said a pockmarked young man from the stables, "but Mr. Connor said t' tell you your horses an' your supper both be ready in th' yard."

"Oh, hell," muttered Harry, his hand still cradling Sophie's face. "My horse and my damned supper, ready exactly as I asked."

"Yes, exactly so," said Sophie, her cheeks burning as she drew back from his hand. She swallowed hard, composing herself as best she could before she looked at the stable boy. "Thank you, and please thank Mr. Connor, too, for being so prompt."

"The devil take Mr. Connor," said Harry darkly,

fishing in his pocket. "Wait, boy, here. Give this to the bride and groom with my best wishes for their future."

Three golden guineas glittered in Harry's hand before he pressed them into the grubby palm of the stunned boy.

"Go on, lad, take it to them," he said. "And pray don't be tempted to keep any out for yourself, else you find yourself turned into a croaking toad as a reward for your greed."

"That was very generous of you, Harry," said Sophie as she followed him through the open door and into the stable yard. "At least your gift was. What you said to the boy wasn't charitable in the least."

"Boys don't deserve charitable thoughts," said Harry. "I know. I was one myself, and for a good long time, too. That must be your mare, there next to Thunder. Will she do for you?"

"Oh, yes," said Sophie, rubbing her hands together to warm them. After the overheated inn, the night air seemed even chillier than before. "She's a good deal better than most hired horses, I should say."

"Likely that's because she's not a nag for hire, but instead belongs to one of the ladies inside." Harry stroked the white blaze on the mare's nose. She was a neat little chestnut with white feet to match her blaze, tossing her head and eager to be gone. "But we'll leave that to Connor to sort out, won't we? Come, lass, let me help you up."

But Sophie paused beside the horse, patting her hand on the mare's rounded side. "Tell me, Harry. Inside there. You would have kissed me, wouldn't you?"

He looked at her evenly. "Yes," he said, "and you wouldn't have minded if I had."

"No," she said, troubled by her own answer. "No, I do not believe I would have minded in the least."

"Ah, Miss Potts," he said, his laugh warm with indulgent affection. "Miss Potts, you are the most wickedly honest woman I ever have known."

"I cannot help it, Harry," she said forlornly as she climbed the two stone steps of the block while he held the horse steady for her. His profile seemed all angles in the moonlight, dark shadows and stark pales. The innkeeper had warned her about rascals on the road, but by agreeing to travel with Harry, she'd likely thrown in her lot with the most rascally one of the pack. If she were wickedly honest, as Harry had declared, then he was honestly wicked, his black hair tossing across his forehead and his cape blowing out behind him in the breeze. "I'm sorry, but I cannot help the way I am, not at all."

"Don't try, sweetheart," he said, waiting for her to gather her reins and settle into her sidesaddle before he swung himself up onto the big black gelding. "Especially when I mean to try kissing you again, I wouldn't wish you any other way."

CHAPTER FIVE

"You're tired, said Harry, slowing his horse so that Sophie would slow, too. They must have been riding at least an hour by now, though at night it was hard for him to know for sure. "There's another inn not far from here where we can stop."

"Not on my account," said Sophie quickly, visibly straightening her back. "We've scarce begun."

But she *was* tired. She could deny it all she wished, yet he could see her weariness in every drooping inch of her posture. She was entitled to her weariness, of course. He'd guess that her day had begun far earlier than his, no doubt at some uncivilized cock's crow rather than his genteel noon, and that as good a rider as he knew her to be, she must still be finding the lopsided seat of a lady's sidesaddle growing more and more uncomfortable as time passed, even though he'd kept their pace purposefully slow along the empty road to spare her as well as the horses.

But what had struck Harry the most was how quiet Sophie had become. Not the prickly, don't-

touch-me-or-die quiet that she'd made him endure
as they'd walked to the Peacock, but the kind that
came from being so tired that each word became a
trial to speak. She'd had to concentrate so hard on
not falling asleep in the saddle that she'd precious
little wit left to spare on conversation, even with
him.

He smiled at her fondly. She was being either
very steadfast and brave, or very pigheaded and
stubborn, or more likely, given that it was Sophie,
an equal measure of both.

"There's no sin to admitting you're tired, Sophie," he said. "You're not being a weakling if you
do."

"I am perfectly fine," she said, raising her chin.
"We squandered Heaven knows how much time at
the Peacock. The last thing we need now is to stop
at another inn, not if we wish to make any progress
at all."

"But I'll wager most nights at this hour you're
already abed, aren't you?"

She glanced at him suspiciously. "Most nights I
am *asleep,* yes," she said. "But on most nights I
do not have to reach Winchester by the next day.
We've been graced with a full moon that makes
everything bright as day, and it would be shameful
not to make use of it."

Harry sighed impatiently. Here while he'd been
pleasantly considering the romantic possibilities of

the moonlight, she'd been regarding it as little more than a glorified lantern to light her dogged way.

"But if you don't ease your journey, then—"

"I'm not going to another inn with you, Harry Burton," she said firmly. "I don't regret stopping at the Peacock, because we found a horse for me, and listening to the music and watching the wedding party was enjoyable. But what if anyone had seen us together? A governess like me, alone in the company of a nobleman of your reputation? For you do have a certain reputation with—with ladies, Harry. You cannot deny it."

"Of course I won't," he said righteously. "Damnation, you should be more concerned if I did, for it would mean I spent my days like an old woman, reading sermons and eating shirred eggs with a tortoise-shell teaspoon. A gentleman *requires* such a reputation."

But she didn't laugh the way he'd intended, instead looking away from him to stare down at the reins in her hands. Hell, how had he misstepped *now?*

"I am very sorry to hear that, Harry," she said, her disappointment palpable. "Though it does prove what I—"

"All it proves is that the wretches who write the scandal sheets are far better at fiction than fact," he said firmly. "Sophie. Sophie, look at me. If I squired even a quarter of the ladies attributed to me, then I'd scarce be able to hobble about, I'd be that taxed and riddled with pox."

She looked at him sadly, her face shaded by that wretched bonnet. "I cannot believe you are a saint, Harry."

"Damnation, Sophie, I'm not saying I am," he said. He couldn't begin to guess what answer she sought, any more than he could deny that there'd been other women in his life. Sophie wasn't a fool, and for that matter, neither was he. The best he could offer her now was what she deserved, and that was the truth. He could only hope that was enough.

"When I returned from France," he began again, "and you were gone, and—and another time as well, I was—well, then I was no saint. There, that's the truth. But women like that don't help beyond a night or two. I know that now. And it's what I *was,* lass, not what I *am.*"

"Thank you, Harry. Thank you for telling me that, but I'm still not going to another inn with you." She sighed mightily, twisting the reins more tightly around her fingers. "If I did, I might as well scatter my references to the winds for all the good they'd do me then."

"No inn, then. But what of that bridge ahead?" he asked, pointed toward an old, low stone bridge over a stream not far in the distance. The banks sloped gently, with ancient willow trees dipping their long branches into the stream on either side. "We could stop there and water the horses, and leave your governess's reputation as unbesmirched as ever."

Her mouth twisted, considering. "We could pause there, yes," she said slowly. "For the sake of the horses, not for me."

"Oh, entirely." He guided his horse ahead, leading Sophie to the bridge and down the sloping bank. The grass had just begun to come back with the spring, the sprouts soft and new near the water, and the reeds were starting to grow again beneath the mossy stone arch of the bridge. The water rushed and gurgled, echoing back like elfin laughter from beneath the curving stones, while the moon's reflection became a fragmented disc glittering on the dappled surface.

He climbed down and turned to help her from her horse, but she'd already slipped down on her own and was leading her mare to the stream to drink. She'd never needed much coddling when she'd been a girl, and clearly she still didn't, he thought wryly: in this as in so much else about her, Sophie had remained a woman of her word.

"Should we see what Connor put up for us to eat?" he asked, patting the bulging saddlebag. "A late supper?"

She shook her head. "Thank you, no, I'm not hungry," she said absently as she crouched down in the grass beside the water. "Look, Harry, lilies of the valley, the first I've seen this spring."

Carefully she picked a stem of the delicate flowers and held it up for him to see, the tiny white bells quivering from their arched stalks as she sniffed their fragrance.

"Ah, Harry, is there anything sweeter?" she marveled. "Each year, every year, they come with the spring. Some things never do change, do they?"

"Some things never do," he agreed softly, coming forward to take her hand with the flower. She held the lilies up to his nose, but it wasn't the lilies that interested him. "Some things remain exactly the same, no matter how many years pass."

"Others don't," she said wryly. "Look at you. You left for France a boy with a sunburned nose and a shy smile, and now—now you've become a black-clad highwayman, full of menace."

"That's only on the outside, and in a few of my darker corners," he said, even though he knew it wasn't true. He *had* changed—he'd only to think of George to realize how much—which was one of the reasons he wanted so desperately to recover a measure of those happier days with her.

He raised her up, and awkwardly she began to collapse back down, making him catch her around the waist to keep her from falling.

"My legs are jelly," she confessed sheepishly,

trying to push back and steady herself. "It must be from the riding, and that foolish lady-saddle."

"I'd rather think it was my effect upon you," he said, keeping his arm around her waist, enjoying how she'd let herself depend upon him, if only in this slight way. "And no one will see you here, lass, I promise."

Her mouth twitched up at the corners, seemingly against her will, yet just enough to make her dimples show.

"It's the lilies, Harry," she said, using the flowers to trace lightly along his jaw, "not you."

"Oh, it's never me." He looped the end of one bonnet ribbon around his finger and slowly pulled, drawing the strand outward until the bow beneath her chin gave way. Another tug of the ribbon, and the hat slipped from the back of her head and tumbled to the grass behind her, exactly as Harry had intended.

Too late she gasped, her hands clutching at her hair as she looked over her shoulder to where the bonnet now lay in the damp grass. "Harry Burton, that bonnet was new last week! I paid my own good money for it, to make a favorable impression upon Sir William!"

"I would buy you a score of new ones in its stead," he said, gently plucking the hairpins from her tightly coiled hair, "except that any hat that's as ugly as that one should not be replaced."

"That bonnet is eminently respectable," she declared, though she was making no move whatsoever to salvage the hairpins. "Not that you would understand such a notion."

"It was so eminently ugly, Sophie, that it frightened the horses." He worked the last pin free, and the thick coil of her hair pinwheeled free, slipping and sliding down her back with the old unbridled luxuriance. She'd always been too impatient as a girl to fuss with her hair, and the few times someone else had pinned it into a more ladylike knot for her instead of her usual haphazard plait, it was usually flopping undone within the hour, exactly as it was now.

She shook her hair over her shoulders and turned back to face him, tucking the lilies behind her ear with a jaunty defiance. All her primness seemed to have vanished, her eyes now full of the old challenge he remembered, and he felt his blood quicken and his body harden in response.

"So, tell me, Harry," she said, her voice husky and low. "Does mussing my hair like this make you happy, then? Now that I must look like some tumbled, tawdry hussy after haying, shall I no longer scare the horses?"

But before he could answer she reached up and grabbed his own broad-brimmed hat, sailing it away across the grass like a black, beaver-felt bat.

She didn't bother to keep the triumph from her voice. "Sauce for the goose, sauce for the gander."

He tightened his arm around her waist, drawing her closer. He could feel the warmth of her body through the rough wool of her clothes, the soft curve between her waist and hips. "The goose shall find herself cooked if she isn't more careful about taunting the gander."

"Oh, butter and beans," she scoffed, her expression becoming oddly solemn as she leaned back into the crook of his arm, her hands resting on his chest with her fingers fanned apart. "I suppose now you shall try to kiss me again, as you promised."

"I could," he said, lowering his mouth over hers, the familiar fragrance of her skin mingling with the scent of the flowers in her hair. "I can."

"No," she said, ducking her head away as she pushed harder against his chest. "No, Harry, please."

Disappointment and frustration welled up within him. "Hell, Sophie, if you're going to bring up all that damned nonsense again about you being a governess who can't—"

"No nonsense," she whispered, slipping her hands around his shoulders to draw his face down to hers. "I just wanted to kiss you before you kissed me."

Instinctively her mouth found his, turning the exact distance for their lips to meet and meld, and for

Harry to forget any idea whatsoever of protesting how, once again, she'd foxed him. He forgot, and remembered everything else he'd so loved about kissing her: how eagerly she'd sigh as her lips parted for him, how warm her mouth could be, how she seemed to melt against him, as if making her body touch his in as many ways as she could, how she tasted and smelled and felt and *loved*—yes, loved—him in return. They kissed, and it was as if his letters had never been returned unread. They kissed, and everything in life seemed once again possible, as long as she was there to share it with him.

He deepened the kiss, his hands sliding along her sides to pull her hips closer to his own and to let her feel the hard proof of how much he wanted her, how much he needed her. He'd sensed he'd somehow blundered when earlier she'd asked him about the other women in his life, and he didn't want to blunder again.

"Ah, Sophie, Sophie," he murmured, threading his fingers into her hair to hold her face before him. Lightly he feathered kisses over her cheeks, along the curve of her jaw and throat that he knew was most sensitive. "My own lass."

With a shuddering sigh, she gently twisted her face away from his lips, drawing far enough away from him to study his face. Her lips were wet and parted, her breathing rapid, leaving no doubt in his mind that she'd relished their kiss as much as he. Yet in the moonlight her eyes were enormous with uncertainty, their confusion punctuated by the spiky shadows of her lashes falling across her cheeks.

"I told you we weren't done, Sophie," he whispered, running his hand up and down her back, hoping the caress would comfort and reassure her, as well as remind her of the pleasure in what they *had* been doing before she'd pulled away. "I told you the moonlight would make—"

"No, no, no!" she cried plaintively as she pressed her fingers over his mouth to silence him. "That's not what I intended, Harry, not at all! I thought I could kiss you this once, for the last time—the farewell kiss we never had. I thought I was strong enough to do that, but instead I'm—"

But the crack of a gunshot at close range cut her off, the sound echoing sharply against the stone bridge as the acrid scent of the gunpowder filled the air. Automatically Harry pulled Sophie down, pushing her beneath the arch of the bridge and shielding her with his own body for extra measure. Now he heard horses on the road overhead, the jingle of harnesses and the scrape of the iron-bound wheels of a carriage or wagon, men's voices turned harsh and grim.

Damnation, why had he grown so blasted careless? Why had he dropped his guard so low that it might as well be lying across the toes of his boots?

"Who is it, Harry?" asked Sophie beside him, breathless now with excitement rather than desire. "Who would fire upon *us?*"

"Thieves, vagabonds, deserters," he said, pulling one of this pistols from his belt to check the powder. "There's a thousand possibilities. Damnation, Sophie, keep back in the shadows, where they can't see you!"

"Then let me have the other gun," she said, holding out her hand. "As you recall, I'm every bit as good a shot as you are."

"I don't care whether you are or not," he whispered sharply as another shot ricocheted off the stones. With two pistols, he would have two shots, while the others on the road would have—well, they'd have a great many more from the sounds of them, and he would rather not picture the outcome. "The pistols are our last resort. We'll have a far better chance hiding under here."

She made a *harrumph* of disdain, smoothing her hair back behind her ears. "I thought highwaymen always wished to make a brave stand before their enemies."

"Not always." He'd grandly told himself and his friends countless times that he didn't care whether he died or lived, but at present living seemed to be the vastly more appealing prospect. "And never with ladies in tow."

"Oh, yes, in tow, exactly like some aging coal

scow.'' She sniffed, and leaned around him to peer out into the darkness. ''And we're not exactly *hiding* from them, Harry. They already know we're here, else they wouldn't have bothered firing at us in the first place. Besides, even if they didn't see *us,* they would have seen the horses by now, there in your magical moonlight.''

''Why the devil can't you be a bit less rational?'' demanded Harry as he, too, looked at the horses, whinnying uneasily and tugging at their tethers. ''Why can't you make less sense and simply be frightened, like other women?''

''Because I'm not like other women, Harry,'' she said, unconsciously proving his point. ''Because that is how I am, and I cannot—''

''Come out, in the name of the sheriff of this county!'' roared a man from the road. ''Show your damned faces, you cowardly bastards, before we come in after you!''

''The blasted *sheriff,*'' muttered Harry crossly. ''Oh, hell. I suppose I must go.''

''Wait!'' Anxiously Sophie caught at his arm. ''How do you know he's the sheriff? How do you know he's not lying?''

''I don't,'' admitted Harry, tucking the pistol back into his belt. ''But I'd rather go out to him then have him come here and find you, too.''

''Then I'll come with you,'' she declared, taking his arm. ''I'll not let you go alone, Harry.''

"You'll stay here," he said firmly, slipping free of her arm. "I mean it, Sophie. Stay where you'll be safe. What would Sir William do without a governess for his boys?"

"Oh, bother Sir William," she said, reaching up to kiss him quickly on the cheek. Perhaps she was like other women after all; trust Sophie to find a way to be both practical and tender at once. "Settle things with them, then come back to me. But take care, Harry, please. Don't try to be a hero for my sake, mind?"

Don't try to be a hero for my sake: wasn't that precisely what he'd told George when he'd left with his regiment? And look at the sorrow that had come of that warning....

"I'll be quick, lass," he said, stopping just short of saying he loved her before he stepped out from beneath the arch and into the moonlight, his heart pounding and his mouth dry.

Ah, Sophie, Sophie, I do love you, even if I hadn't the courage to tell you.

He'd never be a hero. He hadn't been one to George, and he doubted he'd be one to Sophie, either. All he could be was his own sorry self.

And pray that, this time, that would be enough.

CHAPTER SIX

IF SOPHIE PRESSED her back against the underside of the bridge and leaned far to one side, she could watch Harry as he climbed up the bank, holding his hands out on either side to prove that he'd kept the pistols in his belt. Of course, this time he'd left off his highwayman's mask, and because she'd sailed his hat into the grass, his face was as unhidden as a man's could be. Surely that would be enough to show any sheriff—if in fact it was the sheriff waiting on the road—that Harry meant no harm, so they would hold their fire.

Please, please, please, Harry, keep both your temper and your wits about you!

He was either swaggering or sauntering, she couldn't say which for sure, except that his whole person seemed to announce that he hadn't a care in the world.

Oh, Harry, you great brave lordly daredevil, take care, take care!

"Good day to you, sheriff," he called in his best lordly drawl, even before he could see any of the men himself. "I am Harry Burton, earl of Atherwall. Is there some crisis in your county, sheriff, that you must waste your powder and balls shooting at me?"

Now, thanks to the moonlight, she could see a carriage, waiting on the road just beyond the bridge. On the box beside the liveried driver sat two rough-looking men with muskets, and another pair were on horseback behind the carriage, and every one of their guns were pointed directly at Harry's chest.

Don't you dare try to be a hero, Harry Burton, not on this night, not before I've told you how much I love you. Don't do it, Harry, else I shall never, ever forgive you.

"Atherwall!" A stout man in an expensively embroidered coat flung open the door to the coach and clambered down before the footman could help him. "Put aside your guns, men, this man's no thief. But damn my eyes, Atherwall, I'd no notion at all it was you, no notion at all!"

"Clearly," said Harry as the guards uncocked their muskets. "That isn't a carriage, Charleck, any more than you're a sheriff. That's a blasted man-o'-war, armed for battle with me as your enemy, just as you're a jumped-up country squire who only comes up to London for a fortnight in the Season."

"But I'd reasons, Atherwall," protested the other man, "good reasons, and—"

"There's not a single damned reason that I know

for trying to kill me, Charleck,'' said Harry sharply. ''What if I did the same to you, by way of an example?''

''Oh, Harry, don't,'' whispered Sophie unhappily. The good news was that this man wasn't the sheriff at all, but some gentleman that Harry had recognized by name. But the bad, bad news was that he'd made Harry angry, and an angry Harry was liable to do the reckless, impulsive things that a calm Harry would never consider.

''But my sister and I heard at the last inn there were thieves abroad on this road tonight,'' Charleck was saying, his face shiny with anxious sweat. ''The sheriff told us to hire these men as guards, to be safe.''

But Harry wasn't listening, his arms folded across his chest. ''Who the devil was supposed to keep me safe from you, then? Who would blame me if I'd fired first to protect the lady in my care?''

Not for me, Harry, not for my sake, and if this show is intended for my sake, I'm decidedly not impressed. I told you not to be a hero, I warned you not be gallant and foolhardy for me!

''You wouldn't do that, Atherwall,'' said Charleck uneasily. ''You'd stop as soon as you saw me, same as I did with you. You're a gentleman, and a peer.''

''But I'd do anything on a dare,'' declared Harry

with a slow, challenging smile. "You can try me, and see for yourself."

But Sophie wasn't about to let it come to that, and before he could make matters any worse, she clambered up the bank to join him.

"I know this highwayman you speak of, sir," she said breathlessly, not daring to look at Harry just yet. "This very night, he stopped my carriage and if his lordship hadn't come by when he did to rescue me, I do not know what ill might have happened."

Charleck frowned, doubt making him suspicious. "The earl of Atherwall saved you from a highwayman, ma'am? You were riding by yourself on this road?"

"I was travelling by coach," said Sophie quickly, wanting to stay as close to the truth as possible. "But the highwayman so frightened my driver that he abandoned me and drove away on his own."

"Miss Potts was very brave," said Harry beside her. "She didn't faint or wail the way most ladies would, but was confronting the scoundrel outright when I came to her assistance."

Sophie turned and smiled, relieved that the tension seemed to have slipped from his voice. With his dark hair tossing across his forehead and a conspiratorial glint in his eyes, his earlier antagonism now seemed so completely forgotten that she almost wondered if it had truly existed at all.

She liked being his conspirator again, almost as much as she'd liked kissing him. She liked it just fine and her smile widened.

And yet something still wasn't quite right. Harry was studying her with a curious mixture of disbelief and amusement, as if a parrot were roosting on the top of her head. Uneasily she patted at her hair, smoothing back the few stray wisps, and glanced down at her clothes. She was rumpled and mussed from travelling, true, but everything seemed as it should be, all buttons fastened, and she knew her face was as perfectly composed as a good governess's should be, the way she could do without even thinking of it. All that was missing was her bonnet, still in the grass beside the stream, but considering how Harry had lost his hat, too, that didn't seem worth his notice.

"So his lordship rescued you, eh?" said Charleck slowly, likewise looking her up and down with the peculiar, narrow-eyed intensity that men used when they wished they could see through a woman's clothing. "Doubtless you are most grateful to him."

"Yes, sir," answered Sophie warily. "I am indeed."

"And no doubt ready to demonstrate that gratitude, too," said Charleck slyly, and to Sophie's amazement, he winked. "I say, Atherwall, you always do find the beauties, don't you?"

Sophie drew aback with discouraging frostiness. The man must be addled to speak like that of *her*. "I beg your pardon, sir."

"Lord Charleck, might I introduce Miss Potts," drawled Harry, clearly enjoying himself more than Sophie thought he should. "Miss Potts, Lord Charleck."

"My lord," said Sophie, her voice still chilly. "I am sorry to disappoint you, but I am not one of his lordship's 'beauties.' I am a governess, on my way to my new position, when my carriage was stopped by the highwayman."

But Charleck was undeterred. "A *governess*," he said with relish. "I say, Atherwall, are you schooling her proper?"

There was that conspiratorial mischief in Harry's eyes again, meant for Sophie alone, as he shook his head and sighed. "Miss Potts is a very stern and proper governess. If there is any schooling to be done, she will be the one to do it, and I only her miserable pupil."

Before Sophie could answer, an older lady's face popped from the carriage window. "A *governess?*" exclaimed Charleck's sister indignantly. "The villain waylaid a governess? Oh, poor dear, come, let me look at you!"

Relieved to have an excuse to leave Harry and

Charleck, Sophie stepped closer to the carriage and gulped.

"I *know* you, miss," announced the older woman triumphantly, her oversized wig bobbing around her face. "You're Lady Wheeler's governess at Iron Hill. Potts, isn't it?"

"Mrs. Mallon, good day," said Sophie, misery growing as she dipped a curtsey. Mrs. Mallon had been an old acquaintance of Lady Wheeler's and a frequent visitor to Iron Hill. The older lady could be kind and generous to her friends, but she was also a notorious gossip, and Sophie's heart sank at the cruel coincidence of meeting her on this particular night. She and Harry should have stayed at the Peacock after all; they certainly couldn't have done any worse than coming here.

But if she kept herself properly meek the way she'd learned to be, her conversation deferential— and if she could forget again the outspoken, flirtatious banter that she'd been sharing with Harry— then perhaps she could talk her way free.

At least it would be worth trying.

"Yes, ma'am, I was governess to Lady Wheeler's boys," she explained demurely, keeping her head bowed. "But now that the youngest is finally going away to school with his brothers, I was no longer needed at Iron Hill, and thus have found another place with a family in Winchester."

Mrs. Mallon nodded. "Lady Wheeler has such

nice boys,'' she said fondly, ''and so very handsome they are, too. But they will grow, as all boys
do, no matter how attached they are to their governess, and then off you must go to another set of
children. That is your lot as a governess, isn't it?''

''Yes, ma'am,'' said Sophie. The worst part of
her lot was having to listen to ladies like Mrs. Mallon, speaking of her as if she weren't quite human,
but only a servant without any true emotions or
feelings. Mrs. Mallon would neither know nor care
that once Sophie had had the same dreams as other
well-bred girls, to have a home and husband and
children of her own. She'd become a governess
from necessity, not choice. But as for the only man
she'd ever loved—oh, that man would never want
the same, and without thinking she glanced over to
where Harry was still with Charleck.

''You might have done better to stay with the
highwayman,'' whispered Mrs. Mallon loudly, mis-
reading Sophie's thoughts. ''All the world knows
the earl of Atherwall is a dreadful rake. To be seen
alone in his company is quite sufficient to ruin a
lady's reputation, and as for a governess—why, you
should most likely never find a place in a decent
household again.''

''Yes, ma'am,'' said Sophie, the only acceptable
response as she swallowed back her protests. ''Yes,
ma'am.''

''Yes, indeed,'' said Mrs. Mallon severely. ''But

for Lady Wheeler's sake, I am willing to help you salvage this...this *indiscretion* of yours.''

"What indiscretion, Mrs. Mallon?'' asked Harry innocently—or his murky version of innocence, anyway—as he came to join their conversation near the coach, with Charleck following like a lonely puppy. "I rescued the lady with only moonlight to guide me, and surely there's nothing more discreet than moonlight.''

"Not whilst shared with you, my lord,'' said Mrs. Mallon with withering contempt.

"Ahh,'' he said dryly. "You wound me, ma'am. But if I defend Miss Potts, it is not because she cannot defend herself against you. She *could*, of course, but chooses not to, being too well-bred to descend to your depths.''

"She does not speak because she is a *governess*,'' said Mrs. Mallon scornfully. "She is not entitled to opinions. You, as a gentleman and a peer, must know that.''

Charleck shifted uneasily from one foot to the other. "Here, now, now, sister. You're painting it all a bit broad for his lordship, aren't you?''

Though Harry smiled still, the cheerfulness had abruptly left his face.

"I remember a great deal about Miss Potts,'' he said softly, and with unquestionable conviction. "And most of all, I remember that she is without doubt a lady.''

"Not at all," declared Mrs. Mallon imperiously, ignoring her brother's warning as she beckoned to Sophie. "She is a *governess,* my lord, and whatever memories you may have of her cannot be any older than this night."

"You are mistaken, ma'am," said Harry, and as Sophie recognized that familiar gleam of challenge in his eye, she wondered if Mrs. Mallon had any notion of what she'd started. "I've known Miss Potts since, oh, the sweet days of Eden."

Mrs. Mallon tipped her head back, the better to stare down her nose at Harry. "You are deluded, my lord."

He bowed low over his riding boot, adding a curling, courtly flourish of his hand. "No more so than you, ma'am. And while I may be so damned deluded, I do not bare my fangs and hiss like a gorgon to frighten others, as you appear to do."

Mrs. Mallon sucked in her breath, her mouth a wrinkled rosebud of disbelief. "You have the manners of a jackal, my lord," she said tartly, "and I'll not bear your company a moment longer. Come, Potts, here."

"Ma'am?" said Sophie, not trusting herself to venture more. But while she did not enjoy being called to heel like a naughty dog, she very much did like Harry saying everything she couldn't on her behalf. "Ma'am?"

"Don't stand there posturing like a chalkware

shepherdess on the mantelpiece, Potts,'' said Mrs. Mallon sharply. ''I shall see to it personally that you arrive in Winchester unharmed by this villain, or any of the others that are lying in wait along this road.''

''Sister, mind your tongue,'' warned Charleck urgently. ''Atherwall is an earl, not a villain.''

''Oh, hush,'' his sister snapped. ''I mean for Potts to ride in here with us, where no one shall think the worst of her.''

The footman unlatched the carriage door and flipped down the small folding step. But as the older woman beckoned for Sophie to join her, a tiny new spark of rebellion flared and glowed in Sophie's breast.

Perhaps it was Mrs. Mallon's condescending manner that was the tinder to that spark, or perhaps it had come from kissing Harry until she'd felt as if her feet had left the grass. Maybe it was simply the moonlight that was addling her wits, and making her wonder how she'd come to worry so much about other's opinions of her, whether good, bad or even the worst.

Twice tonight Harry had come to the defense of that old Sophie who'd been so bold and outspoken and cared not a fig for any opinions but her own. There must have been some merit to that other version of her for him to do that. For her sake, he'd first stepped into the face of gunfire, and now with

Mrs. Mallon he was confronting words that likewise
had the power to wound and scar.

For her, Sophie Potts. He'd done it for *her*.

She turned to look at him again, and flushed as
she realized he was already watching her. There
must have been a half-dozen other people scattered
around them—Mrs. Mallon, Lord Charleck, the
guards, the driver and the footmen—yet when
Harry looked at Sophie the way he was now, she
felt as if the two of them were once again completely, wonderfully alone.

Which, Sophie sternly reminded herself, of
course they weren't. Nothing in her life ever came
so easily, just as nothing like a carriage with a
cross-tempered old woman, her brother and a host
of others would be leaving her life with any ease,
either.

"Come, Potts," ordered Mrs. Mallon. "Stop
your dawdling, and come directly. I cannot bear the
draft from this open door upon my knees much
longer."

Yet still Sophie didn't move. She'd always believed she'd made her own choices in life, hadn't
she? It had been her decision to put her dying father's worries to rest by returning Harry's letters
unread, her decision to become a governess and
support herself. Now she could choose a place in
Mrs. Mallon's carriage, Sir William's children and

safely boring respectability or she could choose
Harry and…whatever it was Harry was offering.

These were her choices to make, weren't they?

A fire in the grate and a sturdy roof over her head
against the rain or stars and moonlight and dew wet
on the grass beneath her feet.

The rest of her days running in the same worn
path as these past ten years or one night of adventure and passion.

Predictability or ruin.

Security or Harry.

She raised her chin and drew back her shoulders
and gazed squarely into the other woman's eyes. "I
am very sorry, Mrs. Mallon," she said, her voice
steady with her decision, "but I regret that I cannot
accept your offer."

Mrs. Mallon's eyes narrowed beneath the stiffened curls of her wig. "Cannot, Potts, or will not?"

But it was Harry who answered for her. "Cannot,
should not, will not, shall not and forget-me-not,
too," he said. "I ask you, ma'am, how much more
clearly can the poor lass speak it?"

Slowly Sophie came to stand beside Harry. She
didn't stare soulfully into his eyes or take his hand
or otherwise make a foolish show. Standing beside
him was reassurance enough that he was there with
her: once again partners, conspirators, lovers.

And for at least this night, until the moonlight

faded with the dawn, she would not be alone, but with Harry.

"I thank you, Mrs. Mallon," she said, "and you, too, Lord Charleck, but I have decided. I shall continue to place my trust in his lordship's company, and travel with him."

"Then you will travel straight to the devil, with that man as your guide," predicted Mrs. Mallon with grim finality. "I am through with you, Potts, and so I shall tell Lady Wheeler. Come, brother, let us leave these two to their—their folly and wickedness."

Yet Sophie did not answer beyond what she'd already said. Instead she stood as proudly silent as she could, her arms folded squarely over her chest as she watched Lord Charleck hurriedly mutter goodbye and then hoist himself into the carriage beside his outraged sister. The driver cracked his whip over the horses' backs and the carriage lurched forward while the mounted guards followed, and in a matter of moments, the only sound once again came from the water running and dancing beneath the arched bridge and the sleepy birds in the branches overhead.

Her heart racing, Sophie finally turned toward Harry, only to find that, for the second time that night, he was already looking at her. His smile was so wide it was almost foolish, and so unguarded he seemed years younger.

"Damnation, Sophie, you stayed," he said incredulously. "You did that for me."

"Because of what you did for me, Harry." Her chest felt tight and knotted with not knowing what would happen next, yet she could not have looked away from him if her life had hung balanced on the edge of a sword—and maybe, in a way, it did. "That's why I stayed. For this night. For you."

"For you," he repeated softly, echoing her truth with his own truth. "For you."

Swiftly she looked away toward the grazing horses, unable to keep holding the intensity of his gaze. "But it wasn't wicked, the way Mrs. Mallon said, and it's not folly, any more than you shall lead me to the devil."

"I mean to try," he said. "Though you gave them every reason to believe I already had."

"I did not!" she exclaimed indignantly. "The only scandalous thing I did was to refuse to ride in their silly carriage!"

"You didn't have to say a word, pet." His voice dropped lower, deeper, with enough of a rasp to it to make Sophie shiver. "Charleck and his sister had only to look at you to learn the truth."

"What truth is that?" she scoffed skittishly. "Make sense, Harry."

"I am," he said, reaching out to touch her cheek. "You tried to play your governess role again, scraping your hair back and putting on that grim,

grim face, but this time it didn't work. This time you couldn't make yourself proper. It was too late. The truth was writ clear across your face, my dear Sophie."

He slipped his fingertips from her cheek to her mouth, rubbing his thumb across the swell of her lower lip, still sensitive from their kiss. "Here's the truth, here for all the world to see. This mouth doesn't belong to a respectable governess, but to a woman who's just been caught with her lover."

Her lover: no wonder her heart raced, because he was *right*. Why hadn't she realized it herself? It hadn't been a parrot on her head at all when Harry and Lord Charleck had looked at her so oddly. It had been Harry's kiss lingering on her lips, boldly there for the entire world to see.

Yet wasn't that what she'd chosen for this night, a lover's kiss to be treasured and remembered? She pressed her lips against his thumb, kissing his finger the way she'd kissed his lips. For now, she wouldn't be Miss Potts; she was only Sophie, Harry's Sophie, and he was hers.

"So what will come next for us, Harry?" she asked breathlessly. "Where shall we go?"

"A place where I won't have to share you with anyone else," he said, turning her hand so he could kiss her palm. "We'll go to Hartshall."

CHAPTER SEVEN

"HARTSHALL?" asked Sophie with a little frown of confusion as she drew her face away from his hand.

Ah, thought Harry, he'd no right making any suggestions when her thoughts were winding along other, more agreeable, paths. For that matter, he'd little wish to leave those paths himself, as much as he knew he must.

"Hartshall's a house of mine," he explained, "a little hunting lodge not far from here. I don't know why I didn't think to go there before this."

"Perhaps because it's not the hunting season," she said softly, following him now. "I do remember hearing of it, though. You would go there with your father and Georgie."

"Yes," he said, his mood clouding further at the mention of his brother. "We've always belonged to the nearby hunt, and when Father was still able to ride, he'd be sure to bring us along. A proper manly adventure, it was."

"And you would take me there now?" she asked wryly. "Am I part of the proper manly adventure?"

"The very centerpiece," he said, then sighed. The moment for such flirtation seemed oddly gone, as if the same moonlight that had charmed them earlier had changed from silver to dull brass. Now he sensed danger hiding in the shadows of every tree, and heard warnings in every owl's hoot and cracking twig, and he'd no desire to tempt fate by spending the rest of this night with her on the open road. "But I suggested Hartshall because you don't have a taste for inns."

She shook her head, curling a wisp of hair behind her ear. "You wish us to go to Hartshall instead of Winchester?"

"For this night, yes." He took her hand, threading his fingers into hers. "Perhaps it's having been shot at once this night or maybe because we've heard so much of highwaymen and roving thieves, but I'm finding it damned difficult to feel at ease here alone with you beneath the stars."

She grinned, but he didn't miss how her fingers tightened around his. Did she seek reassurance, he wondered, or did she mean to give it?

"You're afraid, Harry?" she asked, not expecting him to admit it. But why should she expect otherwise, given how he'd made a name for himself for cheating death however he could? "And here I'd always believed nothing could frighten you."

"Nothing did," he said, daring to hope that Sophie—being Sophie—would realize how rare this next confession was. "But that was when I'd only my own sorry neck to look after. Now I have you, as well, and I've turned skittish as an old hen."

"Ahh," she said, understanding even more than he'd intended, exactly because she *was* Sophie. "But that knife cuts both ways, you know. You have me to watch over, true, but I must also do the same for you."

He frowned, reminding himself that the same reasons that Sophie understood him made her speak this sort of nonsense as well. As independent as she could be, even Sophie must realize that men were here on this earth to protect women, not the other way around.

Or perhaps not.

"Here," she said briskly, releasing his hand so she could flip aside the front of his coat. "If you believe we shall be travelling in danger, then you should give me one of those pistols after all. If you wish to play the highwayman, then I can just as well be the highway-*woman*."

Deftly he dodged to one side, avoiding her hand while at the same time taking her arm by the elbow.

"A highway-woman, hah," he said as he steered her toward their horses. "Only if the full moon had stolen my wits."

"Please, Harry," she protested, making her steps stubbornly, willfully clumsy. "You know I'm perfectly capable with a pistol. Think of all the wagers you could win at that London club of yours if only you'd lay bets upon my marksmanship!''

Likely he could, but that wasn't the point. He helped her up into saddle and handed her the reins.

''What I know,'' he said firmly as he retrieved their hats from the grass, ''is that if I'd a shred of common sense, I should have put you into that carriage beside Mrs. Mallon myself, and let you find your way to Winchester with them.''

''Oh, butter and beans,'' she muttered darkly, jamming her bonnet down on her head. ''What you should hope and pray is that your final dying thought won't be that you should have given me the pistol.''

''What kind of governess has such murderous thoughts?'' he asked as he guided his horse alongside hers and back to the road. ''Or is that how you keep the peace among your little charges?''

''It works perfectly well with young boys,'' she said, still irritated enough that she kept her gaze on the road ahead and not on him. ''I am accomplished at the usual schoolroom studies, but I'm also skilled in such diverse areas as pitching cricket balls and tying flies for fishing—things that all young gentlemen must learn. And, of course, I can catch a frog or tadpole with nothing more than my hands.''

''Is that what you teach the daughters? How to catch a tadpole bare-handed?''

''What, instead of a husband?'' Finally she

laughed, a sound he'd missed so much. She hadn't bothered to straighten her bonnet, leaving it haphazardly askew with a dash that complemented that laugh.

"I suppose you could try the same techniques at Almack's," he suggested, "and see what kind of toad you can catch."

"Precisely," she said, laughing again. "Which is why I've never accepted a place with daughters. I couldn't, not in good conscience. I could teach girls their French and grammar well enough, but when it came to the skills a young lady needs—fine stitching on linen, playing the pianoforte, genteelly wielding a fan and pouring tea—I would utterly fail. I doubt I could so much as tie a decent bow for a hair ribbon."

"I'm sure you could," he answered loyally, "if you wished to."

"But how could I teach what I never learned myself?" she asked with her usual logic. "It's on account of being a motherless girl, I suppose, and spending too much time running about the manor with you and George."

"We always were to blame, weren't we?" It was reasonable that she'd speak of his brother so freely and with such affection, given that they'd shared so much of their childhood in each other's company. But each time she'd mentioned George's name this evening, it had been as if he still lived, even as if he were waiting for them at Hartshall.

Could she really not know otherwise? It was possible; the numbers of young men, even gentlemen, being killed in these wars with France were numbing, and the notice of George's death had been only one more among many.

"You're very quiet," she said, making him wonder how long he'd been riding in melancholy silence beside her. "More hobgoblins in the trees?"

"Their eyes are glowing on every branch." He forced himself to smile. No hobgoblins, he thought grimly, but ghosts, or at least one freckle-faced ghost in particular who'd died too young. He knew he should tell her of George's death now, that putting it off would only make the inevitable more awkward and painful, but he wasn't yet ready to reopen the raw wound of grief and guilt. Coward that he was, he couldn't do it, not even with Sophie.

"Then perhaps we might call upon those hobgoblins to show us the way," she said wryly. "We're lost, aren't we?"

"Not at all," he said, squinting purposefully up at the moon and all the stars around it. He might not be able to read the night sky with a sailor's finesse, but he did know enough to find north from south. Although they'd left the woods for open fields, rolling away on either side of the road behind low stone walls, ahead of them lay another copse of scrubby trees and bushes with an ancient oak twisting from the center. He'd recognize that oak anywhere, a gnarled signpost that was unmistakable to him.

"You see that old oak tree, there, with the branch blasted off by lightning," he said confidently. "Directly beneath that is the gate to Hartshall."

"You're certain we're not lost?" She looked to where he was pointing. "This is still the road to Winchester?"

"Tonight it is," he said, wishing she would forget Winchester altogether. Hell, he wished *he* could forget Winchester.

She sighed restlessly, twisting her hands around her reins. "I hope you're right, Harry. It's strange, but grand open spaces like these make me more uneasy than when we were in the woods."

"We'll be safe enough at Hartshall," said Harry. "You'll see. The lodge may not be large, but it was conceived like a veritable little castle. Even though King Charles was back on the throne when my ancestor built it, he still designed it as much as a fortress against Roundheads as for hunting."

Yet as they drew closer, the twisted old oak seemed hardly welcoming, with the narrow road to the lodge overgrown with last summer's brambles and moldy leaves.

"No gate?" asked Sophie warily as Harry's horse picked his way along the neglected road.

"No gate, nor walls, either," said Harry. "There never have been any. No clues for Cromwell's men, I suppose."

"No clues for anyone," she said, her uneasiness clearly growing. "You *are* certain this is Hartshall, Harry? I promise I will not think the worse of you if you must admit to being wrong."

He laughed. "For you, Sophie, I would admit it, if it were true. But it's not, so I won't, unless you wish me to lie, which I have never, ever done to you."

"Because you swore not to," she answered promptly. "I would not forget that. You swore that if you ever told me a falsehood, your tongue would turn black and your nose would fall off. At the time, I rather wished you would tell me a lie—just a small one—so I could see the effect."

He made a face at the prospect. "Forgive me if I don't oblige. There's the lodge now. I didn't lie about its being a fortress, either, did I?"

Squat and square, the lodge did look like a medieval fort, and even the wash of the moonlight couldn't soften the hard gray stone or diamond-paned leaded windows. Severe pointed arches ran along the lower floor, framing a narrow porch and the windows with gothic severity, and the flat slate roof had a small square tower on each corner that seemed better suited for sheltering long-ago archers than its true purpose of masking the chimneys.

Carved dragons disguised the rainspouts, and a web of ivy spread tightly over the walls, as if trying to pull the stones back into the ground.

How long had it been since he'd been back to Hartshall—four years? Five? No, he must be honest: he hadn't come back since George had died.

So why, then, had he brought Sophie here? Could he be honest enough to answer that?

"This lodge had better be manly, Harry, because no woman would be charmed by such a place," Sophie was saying now, not bothering to hide her misgivings. "Is there a caretaker or other servant?"

Harry shook his head, and swung down from the horse, then helped her dismount as well. "There's a man from the village who comes in with his wife every few weeks to make sure all things are as they should be, but no one lives here. No one ever has."

He stepped up onto the edge of the porch, balancing on the corner while he reached up into the dragon-downspout's mouth, ignoring the pointed stone teeth and curling tongue to grope inside the moss and old wet leaves.

"Here we are," he said, wiping the old-fashioned iron key to the front door on his sleeve before he held it out to Sophie. "You can go inside, while I see to the horses."

"I'll come with you," she said quickly, then flushed. "That is, if we tend to the horses together, than we'll be done that much sooner."

"Whatever you please." He grinned wickedly, his thoughts bounding back to other stables, other haylofts he'd shared with her. "Though I can't say whether you wish to be with me, or whether you're scared of the house."

"If I'm frightened," she said tartly as they led their horses to the small stable in the back, "it's because you've made me that way, with all your talk of thieves and hobgoblins and Cromwell's marauding zealots."

"Not you, pet," he said as he lit one of the lanterns hanging near the door, the practical yellow glow so different from the moonlight that had guided them this far. "You're the bravest creature in the entire universe, hands down."

"Oh, yes, quite the bravest," she said, bending to unbuckle her horse's saddle, the rounded curves of her hips and bottom pressing unwittingly against her skirts to tantalize him so badly he nearly groaned. Her bonnet had slipped off and her unpinned hair was a golden tangle down her back. He liked it that way, mussed and disheveled instead of smooth and prim, and he had a considerable need to muss it—and the rest of her—a great deal more. "As if any creature could be brave after you insisted on keeping your pistols to yourself, and making me helpless."

"Helpless, hell," he said, coming to stand behind

her. "You, Sophie Potts, have more weapons than any mortal man could survive."

"I do not," she answered promptly, and began to twist to face him.

"Don't turn," he ordered, spanning her waist with his hands, holding her steady before him. "Stay like this. Please. For me."

She shook her hair back over her shoulder, but as he'd asked, she didn't turn, still bending slightly with her hands resting on the mare's curving side. Gently he ran his hands along the sides of her body, tracing the differing outlines of her waist and hips, back up across her ribs. Even through the rough woolen fabric he could feel the warmth of her skin, the vitality of her flesh, full and ripe and waiting for him. His fingers grazed the undersides of her breasts, his touch making her shudder even through the layers of clothes.

"Harry," she whispered, her breathing ragged. "Oh, Harry, I—"

"Shhhhhh," he said, drawing her against his body, her back snugged against his chest. He guessed she was wearing some sort of stiffened linen corset or stays—he could trace the whalebone channels—but even so he could also feel how her nipples had tightened, hard little knots of desire jabbing at his palms. His touch grew bolder, his fingers spreading to caress her more intimately, and she rested her head back against his shoulder, her eyes fluttering shut with surrender.

"There you are, lass," he whispered, kissing the shell of her ear for good measure. "You know how good we are together."

Yet suddenly she frowned, her eyes opening. "What was that, Harry? Didn't you hear it? Footsteps, someone running, or—"

"Or no one," he whispered, striving to reassure her. "All I hear is the sound of your heart, Sophie. Listen to it, lass, how it's beating as fast as if you've run clear from that house at Iron Hill to be here, to be with me. Your heart doesn't lie, Sophie, and neither do I."

"Very well, then," she said, twisting around to face him. "My heart and my head, too, are both telling me not to stay out here with the stable door yawning open, but to go inside your little fortress to be safe."

He laughed, pulling her back against his chest. "There was a time when you liked stables and lofts filled with sweet hay."

She shrugged uneasily, slipping her hands over his shoulders and around the back of his neck. "Lofts filled with hay were well enough when we were stealing an hour here or there. But we have the rest of the night, Harry, as long as that moon outside shall last."

"That is all?" he asked, his voice turning moody

with his unhappiness. He didn't want her setting limits by the moon and the dawn, and he didn't want her to choose Winchester over him.

He didn't want to be left alone.

"Damnation, Sophie, that's not—"

"Now you hush," she said, a teasing scold, as she covered his mouth with her fingertips to silence him. "Once we're inside the lodge, Harry, I'll be able to think of nothing other than you, and you should recall that I have quite monstrous powers of concentration when I wish it. It will be vastly to your advantage to oblige me."

That made him smile, in spite of his melancholy. He couldn't help it. Even if she stayed only as long as the moonlight, a concentrating Sophie could make any man smile. One minute at a time, he told himself. Make every minute with her stretch and last, and perhaps the moonlight would, too.

He took her hand from his mouth and turned it gently so he could kiss the inside of her wrist, letting his teeth graze lightly across the veins showing through her pale skin.

"Then come inside, Miss Potts," he whispered hoarsely. "Inside, and I vow we'll put on the devil of a show for your hobgoblins."

CHAPTER EIGHT

WHENEVER SOPHIE had let herself imagine a reunion with Harry, she'd always pictured the scene as if she were still a lighthearted seventeen, with balmy sunshine and fields of wildflowers and fragrant waving grasses for her and Harry to lie upon, with a singing thrush or two and perhaps even butterflies dancing in the sky above.

Never, even on the grimmest, dreariest days, had she pictured such a joyful reunion taking place in a miniature stone fortress like Hartshall. By the light of the lantern in Harry's hand, she could just make out the furnishings in the large hall that seemed to be the entire lower floor: wooden shutters barricaded the windows, dark, heavy chairs and tables were studded with nailheads, battered old shields hung along the walls and a morose stuffed stag's head staring down from over the fireplace.

"So this is the famous Hartshall, Harry?" she whispered unconsciously, almost as if she feared the stag might overhear. "Perhaps you and George had manly adventures here, but I feel like some poor fairy-tale princess trapped inside the ogre's castle.''

Harry laughed, his arm around her waist hugging her closer. ''If you will be my princess, Sophie, then I promise I shall be only the most agreeable of ogres. Especially when I carry you up these stairs to my lair.''

''Ogre or not, you cannot carry me,'' she said, raising her chin in challenge. ''At least you couldn't when you were simply Harry instead of an ogre. I'm too tall.''

Harry held the lantern up beneath his chin so the light flared upward to distort his features into something quite ogre-ish indeed. ''Don't you cross me, Princess Sophie,'' he roared. ''You cannot escape!''

''I should like to see you try to stop me,'' she said, laughing, and before he could stop her she'd wriggled free of his arm and bolted up the narrow stairway in the corner. With Harry close behind her, she bunched her skirts high around her knees to keep from tripping and hurried up the narrow, twisting stairs, making her way by the jiggling light from Harry's lantern. By the time she reached the top, she was breathless from excitement and from laughter, and she hopped forward off the top step, determined to outrun Harry.

And then she gasped with shock, so stunned she nearly toppled backward down the stairs.

"There—there's someone in there!" she cried as Harry caught her in his arms. "At the top of the stairs!"

"Oh, sweetheart, I'm sorry," said Harry, cradling her to his chest, trying to calm her. "That's just old Nolly."

"Nolly?" Instantly suspicious even as her heart still pounded with surprise, she pushed back from his chest to study his face. "Who's Nolly?"

"Here, I'll make proper introductions." He drew her back up the stairs, holding the lantern high before them. "Miss Potts, this is Corporal Nolly. Nolly, Miss Potts."

Here the windows weren't shuttered, and by the moonlight that streamed through them Sophie now could see the foolishness that had so frightened her: a suit of mismatched armor, propped up to stand guard at the top of the stairs.

"Grandfather swore that helmet belonged to one of Cromwell's men that was killed on this very land," continued Harry, shifting his voice now to one of a campfire storyteller's hushed whisper. "His head with this helmet was sliced clear from his shoulders, and now poor Nolly's ghost is supposed to haunt Hartshall, looking for his lost head."

"Oh, butter and beans." Now disgusted with her earlier fear, Sophie slipped free of Harry's embrace and marched up to the armor and removed the helmet that served as the head and peered inside.

"This isn't nearly old enough for one of Cromwell's foot soldiers. See how this nosepiece has been patched on, here? It's a common fakery, pure and simple, no matter what your grandfather swore."

Harry sighed dramatically—which at least was better than having him laugh out loud—and went into the first bedchamber, using the flame from the lantern to light the wood piled waiting in the fireplace.

"Poor Nolly," he said sadly, pulling off his coat as he knelt at the hearth. "To be dismissed as mere common fakery!"

"What else do you expect from me, Harry?" she asked defensively, the helmet still tucked beneath her arm as she followed him. An enormous old-fashioned bed with bulbous carved posts and cut-velvet hangings nearly filled the bedchamber, but at least the rest of Nolly stayed behind them near the stairs. "A good governess recognizes true history from false, and as for ghosts—"

"Oh, I know, Sophie, I know it all," he said with the same resignation. He kept his back to her, the white linen of his shirt beneath his waistcoat pulling taut over his broad shoulders as he prodded the fire to life. "You don't believe in fate and you don't believe in ghosts and you—"

"I believe in you," she said softly, so softly she wasn't sure at first he heard her over the racket of his fire-making. "I believe in you, Harry, and always have."

"I suppose that's a good thing," he said, still concentrating on the fire, or at least pretending to be. "Especially since you won't find many others who share that opinion."

"You don't need them," she said loyally, hugging the helmet in lieu of him. "Or their opinions."

He stood, dusting the soot from his hands, and at last turned to face her. His expression was guarded, all teasing gone, and even in the moonlight she could see how closely his eyes were watching her, closely enough to make her blush. She could already feel the warmth rising from the new fire, or maybe it was simply the heat that came from Harry himself.

"Do you mean to say that you're all I should need?" he asked. "Are you willing to take that much responsibility for me, Sophie?"

"Perhaps." She swallowed her nervousness in a quick gulp. Answering a question like this one made her feel almost painfully vulnerable. But she'd always lived by the truth, hadn't she? Why should she hesitate now, with Harry, of all people in the world? "No, yes. That is, yes, Harry. I would. Yes."

"You're speaking the truth," he said, marveling, not doubting. "You'd never do otherwise, would you, Sophie?"

"Never." She swallowed again, as if the inexplicable lump in her throat were something tangible, real, instead of a single small word—love—that she couldn't make herself say. He was so handsome, so familiar, that it nearly made her eyes tear to look at him. Yet she would look, and she would remember, storing away this night's memory for always. "But if you knew I didn't believe in fate or ghosts, then you'd know I do believe in truth. No great mystery, that."

He nodded, and laughed, an odd, strangled sort of laugh that didn't sound like Harry's at all. "Damnation, I've forgotten our supper in the stable with the horses."

"What of it?" She took a step toward him, across the bare floor criss-crossed with diamond-shaped shadows, moonlight through the leaded windows. "I'd forgotten the supper, too."

He reached out to her, his fingers sliding down the tousled length of her hair. "You *make* me forget everything, Sophie."

She smiled, blinking back the tears in her lashes that she'd no reason to shed. "You make me forget, Harry, but you make me remember, too."

"Then I say we forget and remember together, Sophie," he said, his voice rough with longing and uncertainty. "But first you must surrender poor old Nolly's head."

She wanted to laugh, not only because what he'd

said was silly, but also to lighten the mood that had become so deadly serious between them. She wanted to laugh or think of something more amusing to say, but couldn't, not now. Instead she let him take the helmet from her, hoping he wouldn't notice the damp patches her nervous hands had left on the battered metal, and then she clasped those same nervous hands firmly before her, as if to keep them from mischief.

"Why, Miss Potts," he said as he gently settled his hands around her waist. "You feel as if you're carved from wood."

Her hands twisted, still clasped even as he drew her closer. "I know you believe I am the bravest woman you've ever known," she said, her voice trembling with emotion. "But oh, Harry, at this moment I feel like the most cowardly female in all Creation!"

He slipped his hand beneath her chin and turned her face up toward his, so she couldn't look away. She loved how she could see the little lines fanned from the corners of his eyes when his face was so close to hers, how she could still make out the boyish scatter of freckles across the bridge of his nose—fainter, but still there.

"Damnation, Sophie," he said gruffly, "Why should you ever be frightened of me, your old Harry? We've known one another forever."

"I know that." Finally she did force a smile,

albeit a wavery, quavery, sorry excuse for a smile that wasn't a fraction of what Harry deserved. "But that's likely why I am this way now. Because it *is* you, I want everything about this—this night to be right."

"Dear, sweet Sophie," he murmured. Carefully he prised apart her clasped hands and placed them on his chest. Instinctively her fingers spread apart, the better to feel the heat of his skin through the soft, fine linen, and the slight springiness of the dark hair that curled across his chest. "Here now, listen to how fast my own infernal heart is thumping. Doesn't that make you feel better, knowing we're in these sorry straits together?"

"What makes me feel better, Harry, is just you," she said, her voice husky and her hands still pressed against the hard wall of his chest as she arched up to kiss him. She was done with talking that only made her long for what she couldn't have; better, far better, to relish and cherish what was hers for tonight, and not waste another moment in regret.

Instantly he accepted what she offered, his mouth hungrily meeting hers, turning the exact degree to part her lips and sink deep within. His hands tightened around her waist, pulling her hips against his in a promise of more to come. But she'd never have enough of his touch or taste, of the way the heat of his mouth seared her own. The rough stubble of his beard against her skin reminded her of how much of the night had already passed, and with a new urgency, she slid her hands higher along his chest, searching blindly for the knot of his neckcloth.

Her fingers fumbled at first, then solved the puzzle, and with a flourish she slowly pulled it from around his throat, letting the linen slide across his skin like a caress. Next she unfastened the two buttons at his collar and eased it open, trailing her lips from his mouth along his beard-shadowed jaw to the salty hollow at the base of his throat. She remembered how sensitive a spot that was for him, and she purposefully made her kisses teasing and featherlight until he groaned, his hands moving restlessly up and down her back.

"Ah, Sophie, you haven't forgotten a thing, have you?" he said hoarsely. "But what in blazes has happened to saucing the goose as well as the gander?"

"Is the gander complaining?" She chuckled deep in her throat, her old confidence returning. She reached around his waist and slowly tugged his shirttails free of the back of his breeches, slipping her hands beneath the billowing linen to reach the man inside. "Doesn't he realize how much this goose has missed him?"

"Here now, enough," he said as he caught her wrists and brought her hands contritely forward. "What this old gander wants to know is why you've still so damned covered up."

"No reason," she said, tossing her hair back over her shoulders. She liked seeing him so disheveled, his shirt open over his chest and trailing out untucked beneath the hem of his silk waistcoat, and altogether looking less like a fine gentleman—or even a fine highwayman—and more like the old Harry.

"No reason not to change that, then." One by one by one, he began to unfasten the long row of worked buttons closing the front of her spencer, frowning a bit as he concentrated. Unable to wait, she began unbuttoning them from the bottom hem, until their hands met and bumped at the last button over her breasts.

He paused and cocked one brow suggestively. "Yours?" he asked. "Or mine?"

"Yours," she said, the word coming out in a breathy rush of anticipation, and with no mistake as to his other meaning, either. Swiftly she moved her hands aside, scarcely daring to breathe as he worked to free the last button. The button gave way, and with a little grunt of satisfaction, Harry peeled back the spencer from her shoulders and arms and let it drop to the floor behind her.

"A start," he said, deftly turning her around so her back faced him. He swept her hair aside over her shoulder, and began to undo the buttons along the back of her bodice and the tapes that tied the high waist beneath her breasts. He was more adept than he used to be, the buttonholes practically slipping open for him, and she didn't want to consider where he'd acquired such useful experience. He'd sworn the numbers of lovers attributed to him were exaggerated, but as he peeled her plain woolen gown back from her shoulders and kissed the now-bare nape of her neck, she couldn't help but feel the uneasy presence of those other women.

"Harry," she said, hugging the front of her gown close over her breasts as she turned back to face him. "Harry, please recall that I'm twenty-seven now, and—and that I'm not the same as I was before, and I—I wish you not to be disappointed."

"Hell, Sophie." He stared at her, incredulous. "Nearly the first damned words you said to me were that I'd changed. What kind of idiot would I be to expect otherwise with you?"

"You'll still be a handsome rascal when you're a hundred." She pulled the gown up a little higher, miserably wishing she could better explain. "But with women it's generally different, isn't it? Beauty and youth are always so bound together, and once a woman—"

"Sophie, look at me," he said, taking her by the shoulders, his hands heated on her bare skin. "Every other woman I have ever met has had to take her measure beside you, and not one—not *one*—has even come close to being as ridiculously beautiful as you are to me now."

"Then show me, Harry," she whispered, letting her gown drop and slipping her arms around his shoulders instead. "Just—just show me."

She did not have to ask him again, or, as she realized later, she likely hadn't had to ask him even that once. Now when he worked to free her from her gown, she helped him, yanking her arms free of the narrow sleeves and shoving the skirts down into a puddle around her ankles. Next came her corset, the laces snapping through the eyelets until she stood, breathless and ready, in only her shift and stockings.

Then it was his turn, kicking off his boots and tearing away at the buttons of his waistcoat and the fall on his trousers as she kissed him still, on each and every new place of him that was revealed. Finally he pulled his shirt over his head: surely, thought Sophie, not even the devil himself could stand before her in the moonlight any more proudly than Harry, her Harry, in his own glorious skin.

But before she could truly admire him he was kissing her again, kissing her hard and without any of his earlier gentlemanly finesse or teasing. She was glad of it, too, for now she wanted him with an urgency that was almost desperation, and a need that had had ten years to build to this fever pitch.

Now when they kissed, she felt light-headed with desire, her whole being focussed only on him. He backed her toward the bed and tumbled her onto the cut-velvet coverlet, and as she sank down deeply into the mattress she pulled him with her, the bed's old rope springs creaking beneath them. In one swift sweep of his hands, her shift was gone over her head and away, and at last there was nothing at all to keep them apart, the weight of his body settling familiarly onto hers.

No wonder she turned his name into a sigh of pure joy. She could not get enough of the feel of his heated skin against hers, and as their kisses grew more feverish still, her hands moved restlessly over his shoulders, the long curve of his back and the taut muscles of his buttocks, relearning this marvelous male body. His hand closed over the soft flesh of her breast, teasing the nipple into a tight crest of longing that radiated through her blood, making her want more, want *him.*

Her body felt heavy with desire, and when his hand slid lower, to stroke her gently between her legs, she knew he found her already wet and ready for him. Panting, she touched him, hard and velvety hot. She shuddered and shifted beneath him, parting her legs farther to welcome him within. One agonizing moment while her heart raced with anticipation, and then he was buried deep within her, the one place she knew in her heart he belonged.

She gasped as he began to move, arching to meet his thrusts and curling her legs over his back to guide him deeper. Earlier, by the bridge, he'd promised it wouldn't be the same, but better, and he'd been right. As the tension spiraled and the pleasure built within her, she cried out again, clinging to him as he took her with him to the bright flashing joy of release.

Neither spoke afterward, their limbs still intimately tangled and their bodies glazed with sweat. Now Sophie could feel the tears trickling down her cheek to puddle in her hair, but she didn't dry them, and neither did he. Gently she smoothed his damp hair back from his brow, relishing the tenderness she could show with so small a gesture. She didn't regret what they'd done, and she'd never wish it undone. But what, she wondered wistfully, what would happen when that devilish full moon finally set, and the cockerels crowed with a new day?

With a groan he finally pushed up from her, resting on his elbows to gaze down. "My sweet, beautiful Sophie," he said gruffly, tracing the trail of a tear with his finger. "Did I hurt you, sweetheart?"

She shook her head, and sniffed back her tears. "No, it was quite—quite the opposite of hurting, Harry. It was...perfection." She forced herself to smile, wanting to take the seriousness from his expression. "If you'd been a true highwayman, you know, you would have told me to stand and deliver, or rather, to lie and deliver."

But he didn't smile back, and the seriousness in

his eyes only seemed to grow more solemn and purposeful.

"No, Sophie," he said at last. "What I should have told you, being me, was that I love you, that I always have and I always will."

CHAPTER NINE

I LOVE YOU...

"Hush, Harry," said Sophie quickly, sadly, scarcely waiting for him to finish before she put her fingertips over his lips to stop the words. "Please. Don't spoil this by saying things you don't mean."

"But I do mean it, Sophie," he protested, gently moving her fingers aside. "Damnation, I've never meant anything more in my life."

Her eyes were enormous as she stared up at him, and as he watched another fat tear slipped from the corner of her eye down her cheek even as she smiled. "Ah, Harry," she whispered. "It's another of your dares, isn't it? You're daring me to say I love you back, aren't you?"

"*No.*" The word came out hard and brittle, and abruptly he rolled away from her onto his back, staring up at the canopy overhead. She wouldn't understand—how could she?—but he didn't want to explain. "I don't dare anyone to do anything, Sophie, not now."

She sniffed again and pulled the coverlet around

her as she sat up beside him, her tears forgotten now that she had a *problem* to solve.

"What kind of nonsense is this, Harry?" she asked softly. "You *live* for dares, for challenges, and you always have. What else has this entire night been but you daring me, and the other way around?"

"No," he said, so appalled that she'd interpret it that way that he couldn't meet her gaze. "I wouldn't do that to you."

"Of course you would," she said, ever reasonable. "Why, likely your first words to George were to dare him to climb from his cradle, and—"

"No more, Sophie," he said sharply. She might not believe in fate, but he certainly did. What other explanation could there be for how George's ghost was suddenly here between them, directly after he'd had the most earth-shaking sex of his life with the one woman he loved more than any other? "No more dares."

"Oh, butter and beans," she scoffed. "Since when?"

So this was to be his punishment, too. Before she could tell him she loved him in return—if, God help him, she did—he had to tell her the truth, and risk losing her altogether.

"Since George died, Sophie," he said, unable to soften this kind of news. "Seven years this June."

She gasped, shocked. "Oh, Harry, Harry, I didn't

know!'' she cried, her hair falling forward as she leaned over him. "Not little Georgie, not him! Oh, I am so sorry, but I did not *know!*"

"It was my fault, Sophie," he said, relentless with the truth now that he'd begun. "If I hadn't dared George that last time, then he'd be alive now."

"But how could that be possible, Harry?" she asked, drawing back from him. He could tell she was crying again, but this time for George. "How?"

"The usual way," he said, every detail of that night still hideously fresh even after nearly seven years. "We'd been drinking, and George was going off about what cowards the French soldiers were, how any good English gentleman worth his salt could thrash a score of Frenchmen before breakfast, and I said he, for one, couldn't."

"And that was *all?*" she asked, the horror in her voice so clear that he was surprised she didn't jump from the bed and leave him right then, the way he deserved.

"That was enough," he said grimly. "What more could you wish? Before my head had even cleared, my damned fool little brother had joined a regiment and was off across the Channel, and dead before the month was out."

"Poor, dear Georgie," she said sorrowfully. "Where was he killed?"

"He wasn't." The old bitterness and loss welled up in Harry's chest again. "That was the blasted irony of it. No hero's death for George, no glory, no slaughtering Frenchmen by the score. Instead he died in camp of cholera, dumped into the lime pits before he'd a chance to prove himself. And my fault for daring him, Sophie. My damned wicked hell-bent *dare*."

"Hush, Harry, hush," she ordered gently. "Isn't this tragic enough already?"

He turned away to sit on the edge of the bed, not wanting to see the reproach that surely must be in her eyes. "Now that you know the truth, Sophie, and understand," he said heavily, "you can leave again, and I won't think the worse of you for it."

"Oh, I understand, sure enough," she said, "but it's hardly enough to make me leave. What I understand is that for the last seven years, you've been blaming yourself for Georgie's death, as if you wouldn't have behaved in exactly the same pig-headed fashion if he'd dared you first."

"Hell, Sophie, it's not—"

"No, Harry, for once you shall listen to me," she said, slipping her arms around his waist and resting her cheek against his shoulder, her body warm and soft against his. "I am sorry about George, more sorry than I can ever say, for if you were meant to be my lover, then at the manor he was always my little brother, too."

"Georgie was the absolute best of little brothers," said Harry miserably, refusing to be consoled, even by Sophie. "His only fault was following too closely after his useless older brother."

"Now you *hush*," she said again, refusing to be put off by his gloom. "This is exactly what I mean, Harry. For you to squander your own life, risking it over and over in the foolish hope that someone shall make a dare, or wager, or challenge, that will make you lose your life, too, as punishment for George's death—why, you cannot do that to yourself, Harry. You simply cannot do that at all."

"Why in blazes not?" he said bleakly, recalling how even she had hushed him when he'd told her he loved her. "Who would care one way or the other?"

"*I* would care, Harry Burton," she said slowly. "Ten years is too long to wait to speak my feelings. Perhaps it's hearing what became of George, or maybe again it's that impossible moon. But I do care what becomes of you, you great foolish man, and no gloomy nonsense you try to toss in my way shall change my mind."

He grumbled, still unwilling to let himself trust, not even her—especially not her. "That sounds suspiciously like fate, Sophie, and I know you do not believe in fate."

"No," she answered promptly. "I don't. But I do believe in you, Harry. Neither of us has always made the best choices in the past, but I do think together we can make certain improvements in the future."

"You would share your future with me?" he asked, his heart racing as he stared down at his fingernails, as if he'd find her reply written there. If she gave the wrong answer, then he'd be done, finished, through. But if she gave the right one, an entire glorious world of possibility would open before him.

No, not for him. For *them*.

"I suppose I must," she said, rational, reasonable, even with something as irrational as this. "I don't really have a choice, do I? What else can I do when I love you beyond reason, Harry, and likely always will?"

"You do?" Stunned, he twisted around so their faces nearly touched. "Then why the devil didn't you say so before this?"

She wrinkled her nose and shrugged, smoothing her hair behind her ears as if that should be enough to smooth away his objections, too.

"Because I was still trying to convince myself of how *wrong* it was to love you," she said finally, beginning to sprinkle kisses across his forehead, cheeks and chin. "And it is wrong, too, not that my foolish heart seems to care."

"Not a foolish heart, but a wise one," he said, taking her into his arms to ease her back onto the bed. "Eminently wise, to see that we belong together. No wonder I love you so much, Miss Potts."

She laughed deep in her throat, managing somehow to sound joyfully seductive, or maybe it was seductively joyful. He didn't know, and he didn't care, though he was willing to be spend the rest of the night exploring the various nuances with her.

"I love you, my lord," she whispered. "I love you!"

And how, really, could he ever want more than that?

SOPHIE WOKE and languorously stretched her arms over her head. She wasn't sure how long she'd been asleep, though the silvery light in the room was still from the moon, not the sun, and the fire in the grate had burned down to a glowing embers. Could this really still be the same night? She smiled fondly at Harry asleep beside her, and once again curled herself around him and closed her eyes.

But then came the sound from downstairs, a thump and a small crash, and now Sophie was instantly, completely awake. She lay as still as she could, her ears straining to hear more over Harry's peaceful breathing. Harry had promised her that this little lodge was as safe as any fortress, yet though she could remember him unlocking the door with the key from the dragon's mouth, they'd both been too preoccupied with one another to bother locking that same door after them. Careless, careless, *careless!*

Now she was certain she heard voices, one man's raised in a cross-tempered oath, followed by another trying to quiet him. Whoever they were, she thought indignantly, they'd no business being here, coming to spoil her perfect night with Harry.

She eased herself from the bed, moving slowly so as not to wake Harry, and retrieved her shift on the floor. Harry's pistols were still on the chest at the end of the bed where he'd left them, and carefully she tipped one toward the moonlight, making sure it still was loaded.

"Sophie, love," said Harry drowsily, "what the devil are you doing with that gun?"

"Nothing," she whispered sweetly, quickly tucking the gun away in the folds of her shift. He'd already faced gunfire for her sake once tonight; now it was her turn to save him. "You go back to sleep, and I'll join you again in a moment."

"'Nothing', hell," he said, swinging his legs over the side of the bed and reaching for his trousers. "Your nothing is always something, and I— What in blazes was *that?*"

"Hush, now, or they'll hear you, whoever they are," she whispered briskly. The men sounded as if they'd been drinking, rumbling quarrelsome and swearing. "But I'll send them on their way."

"No, you won't," he said, deftly taking the pistol away from her. "This is my house, and I'll deal with them. You wait here, and for God's sake keep quiet."

She folded her arms over her chest with stubborn resignation. "This is just like under the bridge. Once again I'm allowed to do *nothing*."

"Except that now I can tell you I love you," he said, kissing her quickly.

"I love you, too," she said grudgingly. "And be careful, Harry. At least you'll have Nolly on your side."

He grinned, and headed down the stairs. At once Sophie scurried to gather what she needed: Harry's riding boots and black highwayman's cloak, as well as the battered old helmet from the armor. He could take back his old pistol. She'd just find another way to outwit the intruders, that was all.

Harry yawned, slowly walking down the stairs toward the voices. Likely the intruders were local boys, looking for a place for their drinking. Next time he'd be sure to bolt the door, so he could stay abed with Sophie, where they both belonged, and where he intended to return as soon as possible. He reached the last turning in the stairs, and paused just long enough to level the cocked pistol ready before him.

Two young men were crouching before a new fire in the fireplace, a bottle on the floor between them. They were unshaven and unwashed, their clothing the last tattered scraps of foot soldiers' uniforms with the buttons and braid long since cut off and sold: deserters, instantly recognizable, with little to lose.

"What the devil are you bastards doing in my house?" thundered Harry. Ever since his brother had died, he'd had a contemptuous hatred for deserters, and to find them here in Hartshall tonight struck him especially hard. "Get out now, before I send you to hell first."

At once the two scrambled to their feet, their mouths gaping and their empty eyes wide with fear.

"Go on, out with you," ordered Harry. "Leave now, and I won't tell the magistrate you've been here."

"Oh, aye, and who the hell are you, cap'n, givin' us orders?" asked a third man with red hair and a scar along his cheek, a man that Harry hadn't noticed, standing off to one side in the shadows. "We've as much a right t' be here as you."

"The hell you do." It was a shame that Harry hadn't noticed him first, for the red-haired man was aiming a Brown Bess musket straight at Harry's chest, and at this range, a musket would always beat a pistol. "I'm Harry Burton, earl of Atherwall, and you are trespassing on my property."

But the man only laughed, and so did the other two, following his cue. "Oh, aye, for certain you are, guv'ner. I'm His bloody Royal Highness th' Prince o' Wales.''

Outwardly Harry didn't flinch. Yesterday he wouldn't have given a tinker's dam for what happened to him next, but now, with Sophie upstairs and their life together stretching before him, he cared very much. Silently he willed her to stay hidden and safe; he did not want to imagine what would become of her if she fell in their hands.

"You will leave," he began again. "And you—"

But his words were drowned out by an unearthly moan echoing down the chimney and rising to a terrifying wail, the cry of a lost soul seeking solace.

"God—God preserve us," stammered one of the first men as they staggered back from the fireplace. "What demon is that?"

"It's the ghost of this place," said Harry with hushed awe, trying to look equally terrified instead of laughing out loud. He thought Sophie had been teasing when she said Nolly'd be with him, but bless her clever little soul, she hadn't. "One of Cromwell's men, looking for the head that the Royalists lopped off on this very spot."

"Ghosts don't be real," said the red-haired man faintly, just as the heavy footsteps began to drag slowly overhead. "They're only fancies."

"Fancies don't scream like that, Will," said the first man, crossing himself as he stared up at the ceiling. "Fancies don't come after th' living, t' steal their souls."

"Not this ghost," whispered Harry raggedly, backing down the stairs and away from the heavy footsteps above. "This one wants a new head, and he's not particular whose."

"Not if he don't be real," said the red-haired man, still striving to be brave even as he'd let the barrel of his musket dip. "He don't need a head then. He's not real, is he, guv'nor?"

But before Harry answered, the wailing moan came down the staircase instead of the chimney, making all three men jump and swear.

No wonder Sophie was such a success as a governess, thought Harry proudly. What boy wouldn't adore a governess who could do *this?*

"He tried to get my head last night," said Harry, repeating details of the stories his grandfather had used to terrify him and George as boys. "I felt him testing my throat with his very knife, but I woke and ran into the woods instead, where he can't follow."

Even the red-haired man had now begun backing away, inching toward the door. "You say he's bound to th' house?"

Harry nodded solemnly. "He cannot leave it, not for all eternity, until—"

"There he be!" bellowed the red-haired man, bolting for the door. "Retreat, lads, retreat!"

As the others crashed past him, Harry looked back toward the stairs. There at the top stood old Nolly himself, a long black cloak billowing around his headless shoulders and over the tops of his black boots, and as Harry watched he raised the empty helmet in his hands and let it drop down the stairs, bouncing and clattering so loudly that the three deserters running through the woods would likely hear the sound in nightmares for weeks to come.

"You can retrieve your head now, Nolly," called Harry, still watching at the open door to make sure the deserters did not return. "I don't think your audience is going to come back."

"It worked?" The front of Nolly's cloak parted, and Sophie peeked out, grinning gleefully. She dropped the cape over her shoulders, and began gallumping down the steps, hiking her shift up over Harry's riding boots so she wouldn't trip. "They believed in Nolly?"

"Even more than you did yourself, sweetheart," he said, slipping his hands inside the long black cloak to find her inside. "I owe you my life, you know. You and Nolly did what I couldn't."

"I wasn't about to lose you like that, Harry," she said, reaching up to kiss him. "Nolly wouldn't have it, either. And besides, you did your part, too, with all that nonsense about him looking for his head and being trapped in this house."

"It's not nonsense," protested Harry. "It's completely true."

She narrowed her eyes at him, ever skeptical. "Oh, yes, *completely* true. Look, it's almost dawn."

Through the open door, the once-glorious full moon had faded to a pale circle low on the brightening horizon.

"It's done," said Sophie wistfully, resting her head against his shoulder. "No more moon and no more strange mischief, either. Now instead I must think of Winchester."

"No, you won't." He dropped to one knee, gazing up at her with what he hoped was all the same love he felt in his heart. "Miss Potts, will you do me the honor of being my wife and my lady, never again mentioning Winchester in my hearing?"

She stared at him, too shocked at first to answer. Her once-neat hair was now a wild tangle, his cloak had slipped over one bare shoulder and her shift was twisted across the other, and she still wore his riding boots tall over her knees. Yet he'd never seen a woman more in her glory, and never known a woman he could love more.

"You would marry me, Harry?" she whispered, searching his face with disbelief. "I know you love me, yes, but you would marry me, too?"

"I wouldn't have it any other way, Sophie," he

said. "Can I take that *yes* as your acceptance, so I can rise up from my blasted knees?"

"Yes," she said, laughing with joy as she helped him up. "That is, yes, you may stand, and yes, I will!"

"That is good," he said, taking her into his arms the way he meant to for the remainder of his life. "And the rest, dear Sophie, I promise, will only be better. For you see, like poor Nolly, I've once again completely lost my head over you."

"Oh, butter and beans, Harry," she said as she kissed him. "Butter and beans."

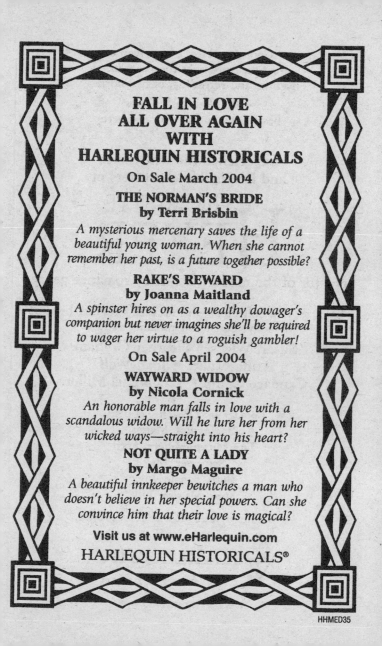

**FALL IN LOVE
ALL OVER AGAIN
WITH
HARLEQUIN HISTORICALS**

On Sale March 2004

**THE NORMAN'S BRIDE
by Terri Brisbin**

*A mysterious mercenary saves the life of a
beautiful young woman. When she cannot
remember her past, is a future together possible?*

**RAKE'S REWARD
by Joanna Maitland**

*A spinster hires on as a wealthy dowager's
companion but never imagines she'll be required
to wager her virtue to a roguish gambler!*

On Sale April 2004

**WAYWARD WIDOW
by Nicola Cornick**

*An honorable man falls in love with a
scandalous widow. Will he lure her from her
wicked ways—straight into his heart?*

**NOT QUITE A LADY
by Margo Maguire**

*A beautiful innkeeper bewitches a man who
doesn't believe in her special powers. Can she
convince him that their love is magical?*

Visit us at www.eHarlequin.com

HARLEQUIN HISTORICALS®

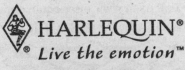